The
Traveler

(a jihadist's journey)

Books by Philippe Espinasse

Fiction:

Hard Underwriting (P&C Books, 2015)

Nonfiction:

IPO: A Global Guide (Hong Kong University Press, 2011; 2014)
IPO Banks: Pitch, Selection and Mandate (Palgrave Macmillan, 2014)

As Joint Author:
Study Manual for the IPO Sponsor Examinations in Hong Kong
(Hong Kong Securities and Investment Institute, 2013)

As Co-author:
The IPO Guide 2012 (LexisNexis, 2012)
The Hong Kong IPO Guide 2013 (LexisNexis, 2012)

THE TRAVELER

(a jihadist's journey)

by

PHILIPPE ESPINASSE

P&C BOOKS
The Traveler

ISBN 978-988-14272-2-9 (paperback)

Published by P&C Books, a division of P&C Ventures Limited
10/F Central Building, 1 Pedder Street, Central, Hong Kong

About the Author

Philippe Espinasse spent almost two decades working as a senior investment banker in the U.S., Europe and Asia. He lives in Hong Kong, where he now writes and works as an independent consultant.

He is also Honorary Lecturer in the Faculty of Law of the University of Hong Kong. He has published several nonfiction books and has contributed articles to a variety of newspapers and magazines, including *The Wall Street Journal*, *South China Morning Post*, *Nikkei Asian Review*, *China Economic Review* and the BBC News website. He also pens the "Clawback" column on Asian equity capital markets for Euromoney's *GlobalCapital*.

He published his first novel, *Hard Underwriting*, a thriller set in contemporary Hong Kong, in 2015.

Chapter 1

Mumbai, India, May 2016

IT WAS ALMOST MIDNIGHT on a weekday, late-spring evening, and the beach was now quiet. Most of those who had come there for a snack or postprandial walk had left, and their conversations and laughter no longer covered the endless rhythm of the waves. The loud music had died, and the food carts that sold *bhelpuri*, a popular snack made of puffed rice, potatoes and tamarind chutney, had long closed.

Soon, Ajay would retire for the night in the frail plywood shack he shared with two other boys, under a giant palm tree. In the distance, to the west, the lights of the upmarket district of Malabar Hill shimmered. They were barely a few hundred yards away, but might as well have been in another world. There, tycoons and Bollywood grandees lived in luxury villas he could not have imagined, even in his wildest dreams.

Behind him, the two and a half miles of the Marine Drive promenade, also known as the Queen's Necklace, formed a gracious arc lined with art déco buildings, all the way to Nariman Point. Bright streetlights dotted the road at regular intervals. To a casual observer on an elevated viewpoint, they looked like a string of pearls.

Ajay was only twelve and had lived on Chowpatty Beach for almost three years now. He had run away from his hometown in Bihar, at the opposite end of the subcontinent just below Nepal, after his parents had died in an all-too-common road accident. A distant relative had taken him in, but he had soon forced the boy, then only eight, to work the fields of their village. And so, one night, Ajay had left alone by foot on a dirt road to seek a better life elsewhere. Surviving on the generosity of strangers and the occasional petty theft, he had slowly made his way west, reaching Bombay after little over a year and settling in a makeshift hut facing the water.

The area was filled with tourists until late. He had soon learned some Marathi, the language people spoke in India's economic capital, in addition to his native Magahi, and even a few halting words of English. He made do with begging, as well as odd jobs for some of the local vendors. He was now a well-known fixture of the beach's colorful community. The previous September, Ganesh Chathurti, the Hindu festival for the elephant-headed God, had brought thousands of worshipers from all over the city—and beyond—over a ten-day period, to immerse clay idols in the Arabian Sea. People had been generous then, and he had amassed a few thousand rupees, for him a small fortune.

In truth, life was not much better than in Bihar but, like the hundreds of thousands who flocked to the city every year, he clung to the hope that, one day, he would make it big there. Bombay was not called the Maximum City for nothing.

Restless and wrapped in a filthy blanket, Ajay was

throwing betel nut shells at a passing crow when a shape on the shoreline caught his attention. It definitely hadn't been there before. Something had obviously washed up on the beach, perhaps a piece of driftwood or some other marine debris. The crow slowly hopped to reach it, repeatedly investigating the form with its beak. Soon, others joined it. This was odd. Maybe the sea had flushed out something that might be salvaged?

Ajay stood and slowly walked to the water line, his bare feet feeling the cold sand. It was almost pitch black, but his eyes by now were accustomed to the darkness and he soon reached his find. This was no piece of wood.

The body had obviously spent a lot of time in the water and had partially decomposed as a result. Half of it was still lying in the sea, the wavelets coming and going over the ankles and upper legs every few seconds. What was left of the clothing was in shreds and the skin was blistered all over, but the overall shape was unmistakably that of a human being.

Ajay lit a match and stared in shock at what was a dark, greenish face. Most of the lower jaw was missing. Even though he was still only a child, Ajay had already observed corpses. From time to time, a beggar or a sick vagrant passed away on a street corner and he had been able to peek at his leisure before they got taken away to the pyre. But what he was now facing was something different altogether.

The soft parts, including the eyes and lips, had been eaten away by mollusks and other marine animals, creating a ghoulish, discolored mask straight out of a horror movie. Two black, gaping holes in the face seemed to stare at him.

Small sharks and pelagic fish had fed on other areas, where the badly wrinkled skin had been ripped in many places. Most of the fingers had also gone.

Although Ajay could not have known this, the particularly cool temperature of the water that year had hindered bacterial growth after a few weeks, turning most of the tissues into a foul-smelling, slimy and soapy acidic mass.

Unable to move, he stared at the body until the match burned his fingers. It then dropped to the ground, half burying itself in the sand with a plume of smoke. As soon as darkness returned, terrified, he turned back and ran away from the beach as fast as he could.

Chapter 2

Mumbai, India, May 2016

THE DAY HAD not started well for Police Sub-inspector Deepak Sharma. A spilled cup of *masala chai* on his freshly pressed uniform shirt had already put him in a foul mood. The milky liquid had soon evaporated, but had left a rather visible dark ring on his left breast pocket. It now ruined the dignified aspect of the garment, which sported a blue and red ribbon at the outer end of the shoulder straps, as well as two shiny, five-pointed stars.

Chowpatty Beach was normally a fairly quiet beat. The routine consisted of dealing with petty crime and the occasional fight between drunken revelers. A dead body washing up on the beach was definitely a first—at least for Sharma.

The find had just been reported through an anonymous telephone call. As an SI, Sharma carried the lowest rank among officers who, under Indian police rules, can file a charge sheet in court. And as the most senior non-gazetted officer present that day, he was swiftly dispatched to investigate the matter. He adjusted his beige cap, grabbed his bamboo *lathi* and stepped out of the Gamdevi Police Station on Pandita Ramabai Marg, heading south, in the direction of Back Bay.

Sharma was rather overweight and, even though it wasn't particularly hot that day, his back was already covered in sweat by the time he reached Chowpatty, puffing heavily. In the distance, a crowd of perhaps twenty or twenty-five curious onlookers had assembled, eager to take a better look at the cadaver. He had little experience dealing with dead bodies, but he at least knew that preserving the scene of a find was vital to identifying any clues that might later shed light on a case. He stroked his imposing mustache and, fuming, walked faster in the direction of the crowd, waving his baton.

"Away, go away!" he shouted. "Don't touch anything or you'll have to answer for it at the station. *Tike*?" ("Understood?")

Unimpressed but still obedient, the group of bystanders slowly dispersed, allowing the SI to discover what the fuss was all about.

The badly damaged body was that of a male, perhaps in his mid-to-late forties. Even though the face was largely unrecognizable and the arms and legs had been half-eaten by marine animals, it looked as though he was Indian, or at the very least, from the subcontinent. Most of what was left of the clothing was ripped, but would have once consisted of what could perhaps best be described as a smart casual outfit. At first glance, it looked like he might have fallen at sea, perhaps from a sailing boat or some other type of pleasure craft. But that would have been weeks ago. Sharma made a mental note to check whether any disappearances had been signaled in the past few months.

He then grabbed his cell phone and called to request an

ambulance. From there, the body would most likely be taken to Sion Hospital, one of eight centers in Mumbai where a postmortem examination could be conducted, and the closest to Chowpatty.

Once he had made the call, Sharma squatted and, with great reluctance, searched the man's pockets for clues. The stench was revolting, and he turned his head away. The front pockets of the man's trousers were empty, except for what looked like a handkerchief, but he felt a small piece of plastic in one of the back pockets. He pulled it out carefully with two fingers. It was an OCI card, laminated and still perfectly legible.

The lifelong Overseas Citizen of India visa had been delivered in Madrid, Spain, in 2006, to one Vikas Gupta. For some reason, the name seemed to ring a bell, but he couldn't remember where and when he might already have heard it. It was of course impossible to match the face on the photograph, which was that of a bespectacled man in his prime, to that of the rotting body, but the odds were that it belonged to the deceased. If indeed that were the case, there would be records and Sharma's work would be considerably simplified. Maybe he was in luck after all.

Sharma walked a few yards away from the scene and bought some *chaat* from a vendor as he waited for the ambulance to arrive. It was still early in the morning, and there wasn't much else he could do until then. With Mumbai's chaotic traffic, it could take a while for the ambulance to turn up, he thought, as he took a bite from his *puri*. Once it did, he would look into that Gupta fellow and hopefully soon close the case.

Chapter 3

Singapore, February 2016
Four months earlier

ERWAN TANGUY STEPPED out of the terminal and was immediately engulfed in the hot, oppressive air. It was about 86 degrees Fahrenheit, and the humidity was at least ninety percent. There wasn't much in the way of seasons in Singapore—it either rained or it didn't—and the contrast with the near-freezing temperature inside the airport was striking. Already sweating, he took off his suit jacket as a uniformed attendant pointed out a taxi. He dropped his bag in the trunk before stepping, with relief, into the rear passenger compartment.

"Where to, Boss?" asked the driver.

"Ritz-Carlton, please."

"Ritz-Carlton, lah. No problem," repeated the taciturn driver in accented English. "First time in Singapore?"

"No. But it's been a while."

"Oh, you'll find many changes then, with the casinos at Marina Bay and whatnot. It's busy-busy now, but good for business. Cannot complain."

Outside, trees in bloom lined the east coast expressway as the Hyundai Sonata glided toward Marina Boulevard and the downtown area, the skyscrapers of the central business district gradually appearing in the distance. Soon, on the left, Tanguy saw a giant Ferris wheel and the three iconic towers of the Marina Bay Sands resort, linked by a seemingly floating infinity swimming pool at a height of five hundred feet. Singapore had changed indeed.

Although he had returned several times since, his first visit had been in 2001, on a backpacking tour in Asia before joining the École Navale, the French naval academy in Brittany. After three years, he had graduated as a lieutenant and joined one of the six units of marine commandos, specifically the Commando Hubert, based in Toulon in the south of France. Its specialties were counter-terrorism, hostage rescue and undersea offensive action by combat swimmers. The Commando Hubert was part of the Commandement des Opérations Spéciales (COS), the French Special Forces group, and he had seen plenty of action on all continents.

Every two or three years after graduating, the commandos were required to put their green berets back into play. At stake was each man's future with one of the units. One either passed the various trials or was asked to leave. It was the only way to weed out those who had become weak and keep France's sword arm in top fighting form. Some managed to stay only a few years, others twenty years or more.

Tanguy could have stayed but, more recently, he had transferred to the Service Action of the Direction Générale de la Sécurité Extérieure (DGSE), the covert action arm of France's external intelligence agency. Now in his mid-thirties, he had thus escaped the move to a desk job into which his career as a commissioned officer would ultimately have evolved.

He was of medium height, with black hair cut short. His friendly and sometimes laid-back demeanor could in a millisecond turn into cold ruthlessness, if dictated by circumstances. But, for now at least, everything seemed to be going according to plan, as far as his trip to the Lion City was concerned.

His instructions were to meet with the local chief of station at the hotel pool bar. Tanguy already knew Maurice Darret from his prior work in Southeast Asia. After paying off the cab, he made his way down to the bar. Darret, heavily tanned and dressed in beige trousers with a short-sleeved shirt, was already there, nursing a drink.

"*Mon Commandant*," he said cheerily, but without standing. "Good to see you again."

"And you," answered Tanguy, as he eased himself into a chair, dropping his bag on the floor.

"I was told your latest assignment had just ended in Abu Dhabi. Flying you over was faster than sending someone directly from headquarters. Plus, I know you already, which is an added bonus. You look in fine form, I must say. For someone who's just stepped off of a seven-and-a-half-hour flight, that is. Personally, I'm too old now for that shit. Every time those goons in Paris summon me back to La Piscine, I can't go to sleep for a week after I've returned. Anyway, let me order and then we can get straight down to business."

"La Piscine" was the nickname given to the DGSE's headquarters, on Boulevard Mortier in Paris' twentieth district, because of its location near a popular swimming pool.

Darret waived for the waitress and, even though it was only five-thirty in the afternoon, asked for a gin and tonic, as well as a Perrier for Tanguy. Having lived in Asia for much of his life, the chief of station had come to associate his drink with a form of preventive medicine against tropical disease. He could consume vast quantities of it without batting an eyelid. But, aside from his formidable drinking abilities, he ran a first-class operation out of Singapore that covered much of Southeast Asia. His contacts were extensive, and the intelligence his network gathered far-reaching. In other words, he was a longstanding, reliable operator, and headquarters had taken his request for assistance from the Service Action seriously. He took a long sip from his glass and started his briefing.

"So, here's the story, hotshot. As you know, we've been close to the Singaporeans for years. We sell them arms, and they also help us from time to time with tips on Muslim fundamentalists, especially intel from across the border, in Malaysia. No one knows much about this, but we actually managed to foil a number of terrorist attacks on French interests as a result of intelligence they had originated. I'll spare you the details, but the long and short of it is that when they've got something to say, we tend to listen."

"Right."

"Three days ago, I had a routine meeting with Colonel Tan from their Securities and Intelligence Division, at Bukit Gombak. We regularly share information with the SID, and I wasn't really expecting anything special, but he immediately mentioned something that grabbed my attention. As you may recall, Hocine Saadi, the twelfth terrorist involved in last November's shootings in Paris, slipped through the net. He was traced crossing into Belgium and was actually stopped three times and even briefly questioned at the border, but waived through before the full manhunt got underway. Some said it was bad timing but, if you ask me, fuck-ups don't come much bigger than that. Anyway, he was later rumored to have made it to Spain, but that could never be established, and then the trail went cold. Now, according to my friend Tan, Saadi's surfaced again and he'll be in Johor Bahru tomorrow."

"Do we know what for?"

"We believe he's to meet in the morning with a team from Abu Sayyaf, the Muslim independence movement in the Philippines, to arrange the delivery of arms and explosives into Europe. About two years ago, Hapilon, the leader of Abu Sayyaf, swore an oath of loyalty to Abu Bakr al-Baghdadi, so that figures. They have since grown much closer to ISIS, and it looks like our friend Saadi is now acting as some sort of go-between for the two organizations. For obvious reasons, the Singaporeans can't rock the boat much on the Malaysian side. Paris also fears that if we tip off the Malaysians directly, there's a high risk that the info will filter through to Saadi or his contacts and that they'll postpone the meeting. And don't even get me started on trying to get the Filipinos to intervene! God knows when we'll get an opportunity like this again. You're to cross into Malaysia tonight, to take out Saadi and as many of the others as possible. The exact instructions from above are to terminate them—with extreme prejudice."

Tanguy had absolutely no qualms about killing Saadi and his shady associates. That's what he was being paid for, and they were all linked to an organization that had killed more than 130 innocent people in Paris only a few months before. As far as he was concerned, he would gladly double-tap them any time, in the head or chest, and would not hesitate for a second in doing so.

"Smuggling arms from Asia makes sense," he said. "The shipping routes with Europe are now the world's busiest, so looking for them would be like searching for a needle in a haystack. And the borders across the Balkans are now much tighter than ever before, thanks to the migrant crisis. But all this is very short notice."

"We've been working twenty-four seven since I got the tip-off. True, there hasn't been a lot of time for preparations, but there's a high probability we can neutralize them if we move quickly and keep this tight and focused."

"How do I get there?" asked Erwan.

"We've got a car ready for you. Singapore plates. It was stolen earlier today, from a downtown parking lot. It won't be reported for a while—we've seen to that. You're to take the Bukit Timah expressway to the Woodlands checkpoint, on the Singapore side. Crossing at the second link at Tuas is faster, but it's best for you go the other way. Expect to be stuck in traffic for maybe two to three hours, but checks will be minimal, especially since today's Friday. It will be busy. Driving through the causeway will take you to the Malaysian side. Follow the inner ring road and then the Skudai highway. Check into the Thistle Hotel—more info and some gear will await you there. Your contact in Johor is called Lilly Ling. Here's your passport and the papers and keys for the car, and the parking receipt for the hotel valet. Everything matches. Your name's Marc Roberts, a French structural engineer. You visit often, generally for a couple of days at a time. They're still building a fair bit in Johor, and much of it is reclaimed from the sea, so your story will stand to scrutiny, no problem."

"And after it's done?"

"Change the plates to Malaysian ones. You'll get these in Johor. Drive north all the way to KL, which should take you just over three hours. Dump the car there, but not at the airport. You're booked on an eleven-forty flight for Charles de Gaulle, via Amsterdam, tomorrow night. If you miss it, you're on your own. You know the drill."

"Got it. Anything else I need to know?"

"We're done. Expectations are high. We have a lot riding on this, so failure's not an option. *Bonne chance!*"

Chapter 4

Johor Bahru, Malaysia, February 2016

AS DARRET HAD predicted, the traffic jams had been horrendous. Some sixty thousand vehicles made the crossing every day, but it was Friday night and commuters between Johor and Singapore were now returning home for the weekend while a younger crowd also crossed the border for a cheap night out. Driving an inconspicuous Toyota, Erwan Tanguy had plenty of time to observe them all as he approached the checkpoint. There were swarms of motorbikes and mopeds, as well as plenty of low-end sedans, many with extravagant spoilers and noisy exhaust kits, fitted in a vain attempt at converting them into fashionable sports cars.

Rednecks are the same all over the world, he thought as he left the Woodlands district.

Passport control on the Singapore side went without a hitch. He paid the toll with a NETS CashCard supplied by Darret. An overworked ICA officer, from Singapore's Immigration and Checkpoints Authority, briefly peeked into the back of the vehicle with a torch. Satisfied, he waved him through and Tanguy navigated the series of roadblocks that led to the causeway. The narrow six-hundred-yard crossing, built under British rule, spanned the Straits of Johor.

Underneath, pipes exported valuable water from Malaysia into Singapore. Checks at the Malaysian end were even more cursory and, after paying another toll, he was soon in Johor Bahru.

The capital of the Sultanate of Johor, the southernmost city in peninsular Malaysia and home to five hundred thousand people, didn't make a great impression. Arriving from Singapore, the contrast between the island nation and this sleepy provincial town—even if it was part of Malaysia's second-largest metropolitan area—was marked. There were almost no tall buildings, and the city seemed stuck in a time warp, back in the late 1960s or 1970s.

It also had a bad reputation. Drug-related violence and muggings happened with alarming frequency, with snatch thieves sometimes operating in broad daylight. The streets were much darker than in neighboring Singapore, even though the two cities faced each other over just a narrow stretch of water. But everything was considerably cheaper in Johor, from petrol to food and, especially, real estate.

Tanguy left the ring road and followed the Skudai highway. Soon, the Thistle, the only modern hotel in town, appeared by its side. It was a poor relation to the Ritz-Carlton he had left just a few hours before, but he wasn't too concerned: he wasn't there on holiday. He left his Toyota in the parking lot just on nine in the evening. The receptionist saluted him with one hand on his heart, handing him the magnetic key pass to his room with the other. Tanguy had only settled in for a few minutes when the telephone rang on the nightstand.

"Mister Roberts?"

"Yes?"

"I'm Lilly Ling. I believe a mutual friend in Singapore mentioned I'd be in touch." Her English was flawless, with barely a hint of an accent. "Please be outside the reception area at ten. I'll pick you up there. I'm driving a black VW Polo," she added, before hanging up.

At the appointed time, he made his way downstairs. As he stepped outside, a car stopped just in front of him. The front window on his side opened. The driver was a woman. He climbed into the front passenger seat to join her, and she immediately accelerated away.

Lilly Ling was in her mid-twenties and strikingly beautiful, with long black hair and unforgettable dark eyes. As her name hinted, she had unmistakable Chinese features, but she was most likely of mixed race, Tanguy decided.

"Welcome to Johor," she said. "I'm afraid there's not much to see. Let me drive for a few minutes to somewhere quiet, and then we'll talk about tomorrow."

Tanguy nodded. She soon made her way into an open parking lot behind a double bend and stopped the car.

"Here should be fine. And if anyone comes, we're sure to see them before they can see us."

Lilly Ling got out of the car, retrieved an unusually thick manila folder from the trunk and gave it to Tanguy. It was rather heavy.

"Here's your plane ticket for tomorrow night. Economy, I'm afraid. Here are the Malaysian license plates for your car, and a weapon."

Tanguy opened the folder, examining its contents. There were several file photographs of Hocine Saadi, taken from various angles, as well as other people he did not recognize.

The gun was a P226 TacOps. It was a black handgun with a polymer grip, a stainless-steel slide and cocking serrations. It fired 9-millimeter Parabellum cartridges and was a favorite of Special Forces operatives. Many, however, had now replaced it with the more recent Glock 19, which was cheaper than the SIG and also very durable, with a simple operating system and few moving parts. All the serial numbers and marks had either been erased with acid or filed off. He pointed the gun down and briefly aligned the tritium fiber-optic front sight with the rear combat night sights, slowly easing his index finger down on the double-action/single-action trigger.

In the envelope he also found two super-capacity, twenty-round magazines, both fully loaded, as well as a Surefire Weapon Light that could be mounted on the Picatinny rail below the barrel. The light would illuminate whatever direction the weapon faced and would also temporarily blind anyone in its path with its high-intensity LED beam. He briefly flicked on the ambidextrous switch, covering the lens with his other hand to hide the six hundred lumens of stunning white light. Everything looked brand new and in perfect working condition. Satisfied, he returned the weapon, plates and documents to the folder, except for the photographs.

"What's the plan tomorrow, Lilly?" he asked.

"Saadi's already arrived. We know that much, but we don't know where he's staying tonight. He was spotted attending prayers this afternoon, but we lost him after that."

"Is there a chance he might know we're after him?"

"That's very unlikely. He never saw my contact before today."

"Right. And what about the meet-up tomorrow?"

"We've been monitoring communications and believe it's set for ten a.m., on the first floor of a house in the old quarter. We'll drive past it later. I'll show you. There's only one door to the building, two windows on the front side and two at the back. It's a low rise—only two floors. It's been empty for the last few days and should also be so tonight. I doubt we'll be spotted going near it. The immediate vicinity is usually quiet. He's likely to meet with at least two people from Abu Sayyaf," she added.

Erwan was now looking at the pictures that had been included in the package.

"The first one's Jainal Saleh. He's known to be in charge of supplies and logistics. The Filipinos and the Malaysians have been after him for years, to no avail. The other man is Abubakar Andang, one of Hapilon's closest associates. The gathering must be important since they've sent people from his inner circle."

The pictures were of two men in military fatigues, with tactical vests over their chests. Their gazes were hard and determined. One wore a beard, but the other was barefaced. They were both probably not much older than thirty-five, but their appearance betrayed the weariness that comes with years of living and fighting in the jungle. Tanguy instantly filed their faces in his photographic memory.

"There may be a handful of bodyguards, but they have no reason to believe we're after them. Any security ar-rangements should be pretty light," said Lilly. "Any questions?" she asked.

"Nope. All clear," replied Tanguy, after replacing the photographs in the folder. "Shall we go drive past the house, then?"

"Right."

Lilly started the engine and drove in the direction of the old quarter. As they approached, they saw that many of the streets along the way were busy. Johor was almost on the equator, and people enjoyed being outside at night to relax in the cooler air, especially when the weekend had only just started. They passed rows of run-down and dimly lit Chinese shop houses, outside of which noisy diners enjoyed a late meal. There were also a number of karaoke places. Inebriated young men queued for the chance to massacre local tunes and squeeze teen prostitutes, often spending the rest of the evening in a cheap hotel that rented rooms by the hour.

"We're almost there. It'll be on the next block, the house with the street sign," said Lilly, now driving more slowly.

They were now in a quieter area. In the daytime, there was a high probability that it would be largely deserted. The building was unremarkable. Right now, it looked uninhabited.

The perfect place for a clandestine meeting—or a deadly shootout, thought Tanguy.

Lilly passed the house and turned right, so he could see what the back street looked like. It was equally deserted. She then shifted into higher gear and drove back in the direction of the Thistle to drop him off.

"How did you become involved in all this?" he asked, along the way.

"Have you ever heard of the May thirteenth incident?"

He confessed that he had not.

"Well, here's the story. After Malaysia gained independence from Britain in 1957, there was an uneasy period of cohabitation between the Chinese and Malay communities. Outbursts of ethnic violence occurred after *Merdeka,* or independence, starting in Penang. As you may recall, the same also happened in Singapore, in 1964, which led to its expulsion from Malaysia the following year. Then came 1969. It was an election year. The governing coalition had managed to keep a majority of seats in parliament but new political parties, essentially Chinese, scored significant wins. On May thirteenth, a victory parade in Kuala Lumpur was soon marred by major incidents. It started with fistfights and stones and bottles being thrown between opponents, but things quickly took a turn for the worse as cars were set alight. Many shops were looted. Soon, ethnic Malays were chasing the Chinese with *kris* and swords. The Chinese retaliated with gang members and fighters from some of their secret societies and triads. As the streets descended into chaos, the army was deployed to put an end to the riots, but the killing continued over several days. Officially two hundred people died, most of them Chinese, but some said more than four times that number succumbed to the violence."

"That must have been a really painful episode."

"My grandparents were both killed that day. My father was barely four and was left to fend for himself on the streets of KL, eventually finding his way into the Merdeka Stadium, alongside thousands of other Chinese refugees. Ultimately, a

French couple working at the embassy took him in. They never left the country and raised him as their own son. So you see, we never forgot. My family's gratitude to your country never wavered, from one generation to the next."

After a long pause, she added, "You just make sure you kill those bastards tomorrow."

The car stopped in front of the hotel. To his surprise, she kissed him softly on the cheek as she squeezed his hand, and then she was gone.

Chapter 5

Johor Bahru, Malaysia, February 2016

ERWAN TANGUY WOKE UP at dawn on account of the jet lag and checked out of the hotel after a light breakfast. He first drove to the parking lot where Lilly Ling had begun briefing him. It was still deserted, which allowed him to discreetly change the plates of his car to the Malaysian ones. There was, of course, always a risk that he might be stopped by the police for a casual check of the vehicle's license and registration, but the possibility was remote and he would decide what to do there and then, if and when it happened.

He next drove back to the area where the meeting was due to take place and parked in a back street, not far from the house. He had already checked the route from there to the highway that would later take him to Kuala Lumpur. He did not want to get lost or have to drive several times in the same streets during his getaway.

Lilly had said the meeting was scheduled for ten in the morning, and he had a good three hours to spare. He decided to position himself in a discreet location, in the shade, some two hundred yards away from the house. The spot afforded him a good view of all comings and goings from the building—a typical shop house with some sort of covered terrace on the front. His observation post was partially hidden, and he sat down on a low, wraparound wall for what would likely be a long wait. He did not want to take any chances, and arriving early would enable him to know exactly how many adversaries he had to face before he moved in for the kill. His P226 was lodged in the back of his trousers, hidden under his untucked shirt. He knew he would soon need to fight and had dressed accordingly, choosing to wear comfortable jeans and tennis shoes.

Even though it was still early in the morning, it was already hot, and he regularly hydrated himself with a large bottle of mineral water he had bought on the way at a roadside stand. Nothing of note happened until nine-fifteen, when an aging brown Mercedes drove past the house, from his left, and then stopped after some thirty yards. The Malaysian license plate started with a "B," which indicated it was registered in Selangor. He mentally noted the registration mark. There were three passengers.

The driver remained at the wheel after the car had parked. He was obviously some sort of bodyguard. Tanguy would need to neutralize him first. The two other men alighted and slowly made their way toward the house. He recognized them instantly from the photographs supplied by Lilly. Jainal Saleh still sported a beard and wore a white *salwar kameez*—a long, loose shirt over baggy cotton trousers—and leather sandals.

The other man had a more youthful appearance and was casually dressed in western clothes, sporting an outfit of blue jeans, a yellow T-shirt and trainers. Tanguy immediately identified him as Abubakar Andang, one of the other leaders of Abu Sayyaf. Saleh was carrying a small document case that might perhaps contain a weapon, but they did not appear otherwise armed. They must have thought the house was secure since they did not even send in the bodyguard as an advance party to check the premises. However, it was also possible that weapons had previously been deposited there, to allow for a more discreet arrival.

Tanguy stood and moved closer to the corner of the house, to make sure he could not be spotted.

For half an hour, nothing more happened. The two Filipinos were still in the building, likely on the first floor, as Lilly had suggested, with the bodyguard chain-smoking cigarettes in the driver's seat of the Mercedes.

Then Tanguy spotted a third man in the distance, slowly walking in the direction of the house, facing the front of the Mercedes. The bodyguard did not stop him and, as he passed the vehicle, Tanguy recognized him as Hocine Saadi. The trio was now complete. Saadi wore baggy trousers with an ample military-style beige smock jacket. Both his hands were buried in its side pockets. It was impossible to tell if he was carrying, but the odds were probably that he was. He was a hardened man, unlikely to turn up at a meeting to discuss a major arms shipment without first making sure he had the firepower to defend himself and escape, if things ever turned sour.

Tanguy waited for Saadi to enter the building and prepared to move, after allowing him time to reach the first floor. He would then disappear behind the house that served as his observation post and walk back in the direction of the Mercedes through a side street. He would face the vehicle at a ninety-degree angle and neutralize the driver. He would then run to the house and, with the element of surprise, shoot its occupants before returning to his own car.

He did not want to risk alerting the terrorists by shooting the bodyguard. The gun had no suppressor, and he would need to kill him barehanded.

Tanguy was just about to leave when he noticed a powerful black motorcycle heading fast for the Mercedes. There were two riders: a man with a woman riding pillion, both dressed in leather racing overalls with full-face helmets. The bike overtook the Mercedes on its right side and sharply braked as it came level with the driver. The female passenger bent and appeared to hit him sharply through the open window, before dismounting and running back toward the house as the other biker made a sharp U-turn. The whole thing had happened in an instant, and Tanguy was taken completely by surprise.

The woman was now inside the house, and the rider had positioned the motorbike just outside its front door, obviously waiting for her to return. Tanguy could no longer afford to use the back street as he had first planned—it would take too much time, and he now also needed to firmly keep his eyes fixed on the house. The distance between him and the rider of the motorcycle was also too great for him to walk in the open in his direction, or even to take a reasonably accurate shot at him with the pistol.

Who were they? CIA? MI6? He doubted that they were Malaysian, or even Filipino. It was even more unlikely that they were Singaporean, given the briefing the SID had made to Darret. The Chinese had their own issues with Muslim fundamentalists, but Johor was way off their own turf, and they were not known for violent covert action overseas.

Not knowing whom he was facing, there was the risk of injuring or even killing a friendly party. Whoever the riders were, they were obviously no friends of the terrorists. His brief was to make sure Saadi and his accomplices did not leave the scene alive. It did not extend to terminating possible allies.

He was still weighing his options when the woman ran out of the house and vaulted behind her companion on the motorbike. The driver revved the engine loudly twice before roaring off in the direction from which they had come. Tanguy noticed that the woman had lifted the visor of her helmet. As the bike came level with him, she looked at him intensely before the driver accelerated and disappeared in the distance.

She was Asian, that much was sure, but her gaze had lasted only a fraction of a second and it was impossible to be more precise. But he was sure he could recognize her if he ever got the chance. The license plate had been masked with dark tape, so there was no way the bike could be traced that way. It was an MV Agusta Brutale RR, a high-end Italian motorcycle, and a fairly recent model to boot. Production for that make was limited, so there couldn't be too many in Malaysia, or even in Southeast Asia. That might be a lead to pursue.

No shot had been fired, at least none that he had heard. He first ran to the Mercedes, still keeping his eyes on the door of the house. As he reached the car, he immediately saw blood on the cream leather seat. One of the man's carotid arteries had been neatly slit, and there was a clean but deep cut from one side of his throat to the other. From where Tanguy had been positioned, he had thought the man had only been punched unconscious.

It was now entirely obvious what had happened. Blood had gushed out and spurted all over the dashboard, as well as the windscreen. He had not noticed any weapon as the woman had entered the house, but everything had happened so fast. Hers would likely have been a small blade, perhaps a *karambit*—a small, curved knife commonly used in Indonesia and Malaysia. It resembled a claw and was a favorite of practitioners of *silat*, a local form of martial art. It usually had a round finger guard at the edge of the hilt, which made its user difficult to disarm in close-combat situations. It also allowed the blade to be maneuvered without the user losing his—or, in this case, her—grip.

The driver no longer presented a threat. Tanguy rushed to the house and walked up the small staircase. He had drawn his gun, holding it with both hands, his palms overlapping the grip, his thumbs parallel to the barrel along the left slide. The staircase was unlit, but he had switched on the Surefire light, sweeping it to all angles as he climbed up. He reached the first floor within a few seconds. The door was ajar.

He slowly pushed the door with his foot and entered the room, slightly bent, the P226 still pointed ahead of him. Blood had sprayed everywhere, on the walls and windows, like a macabre version of an abstract work by Pollock. Bright red tears were still dropping, sliding down in slow motion toward the bottom of the window frames. The three terrorists were strewn about in odd positions. Furniture had been knocked over, testimony to the violent and hasty fight that had just taken place. The men had been executed in the same fashion as the driver of the Mercedes. The killing would have been extremely fast, and they would hardly have had a chance to defend themselves. Whoever that woman was, she was lethal.

After checking that the adjacent room was empty, Tanguy moved from one body to the next, to confirm that the men were indeed dead. The document case Saleh had carried was on the floor, open and empty. The killer would likely have recovered its contents. It looked like Saadi had made an attempt to grab a Smith & Wesson M&P9 pistol from his right jacket pocket, but he'd clearly had no time to use it. The woman would have moved from one man to the other, twisting and turning as she slit them, like a demented ballerina. Surprisingly, the Filipinos had not been armed, perhaps relying on the illusory protection offered by their bodyguard in the street below.

Careful not to leave any fingerprints, and walking around and over the bloodstains that splattered the floor, Tanguy ascertained that the M&P bore no marks that could provide clues as to its provenance. With his cell phone, he then took several pictures of the scene, as well as each of the men, and swiftly uploaded them to a DGSE safe box using an encrypted connection before erasing them from the device. He would write a detailed report later—that could wait. He then walked back to his car, making sure no one in the street saw him. Someone would soon notice the crime scene in the Mercedes, and he could not afford to stay put.

There was nothing else he could do. His mission had been to kill Saadi and the Filipinos, and they were now all dead. It wasn't yet clear who had executed them, but that would eventually come to light.

He drove to Kuala Lumpur on the north-south expressway, passing endless palm-oil plantations en route. No one stopped him on the way. Once in the capital, he left the car in an underground parking lot, away from the surveillance cameras, and thoroughly wiped it clean. He then got rid of the P226 after having disassembled it, dropping the various components into several street bins in the central business district.

He finally bought a train ticket to Kuala Lumpur International Airport at KL Sentral station and boarded his flight to Europe with plenty of time to spare.

Chapter 6

Mumbai, India, May 2016

IN MUMBAI, THE AMBULANCE had arrived to pick up the dead body, as requested. Sub-inspector Deepak Sharma had supervised the macabre work and then returned to the Gamdevi police station, where he was based. A young police constable brought him a cup of tepid *masala chai*, of which he made a prodigal consumption as he started working on the case in the privacy of his small office.

He first logged onto a database of the Immigration, Visa and Foreigners Registration and Tracking (IVFRT) service. He navigated to the section with records of Indian Permanent Residence Programmes and quickly found information pertaining to a Vikas Gupta, carrier of a French passport, to whom an OCI card had indeed been granted in Madrid in 2006.

So far, so good, he thought.

Gupta was some sort of scientist, whose specialty was virology. Sharma wasn't too familiar with the term, but a search on the Rediff information portal soon informed him it was the study of viruses and virus-like agents. It sounded high profile, and Gupta had previously worked for the likes of the Institut Pasteur in France as well as, most recently, in what was called a BSL-4 laboratory facility, just outside the Spanish capital. He had also done work at the Microbial Containment Complex in Pune, about ninety-five miles from Mumbai, which was apparently another so-called BSL-4 lab.

Another Internet search confirmed to a decidedly curious Sharma that "BSL" stood for "biosafety level." A BSL-4 laboratory basically conducted research into viruses for which there were no known preventions, antidotes or treatments. BSL-4 was the highest level of safety, and there were only fifty-eight such facilities around the world, including fifteen in the United States. There were four in India—in Bhopal, Hyderabad, and New Delhi as well as the one in Pune, where Gupta had at one point been based. By contrast, there were thousands of lower-level, BSL-3 laboratories worldwide, whose focus was instead on viruses that could cause serious or lethal diseases, but that did not ordinarily spread between people, and for which a cure or preventives readily existed.

He now stared, mesmerized, at a photograph on his computer screen. It showed people wearing what were essentially space suits with powered respirators. The article said they worked in isolated facilities with dedicated exhaust and vacuum systems. There were very strict protocols for entering and working in these places. Personnel also had to pass a security risk assessment, and the number of those with access to the freezers in which the most dangerous viruses were stored was strictly limited. There were detailed records of all individuals who could work on the most lethal pathogens.

The sub-inspector had heard of some of the virus names—Ebola, SARS, H5N1—and had even recently seen a Bollywood movie in which a muscular hero thwarts an evil plan to spread such diseases in a bid to topple India's government. It was the stuff of nightmares, and it also sounded way above his pay grade.

He felt a chill down his spine. Could Gupta have been murdered for what he knew? Now nervous, he gobbled a *Bikaneri bhuja*, a crispy fried snack, his heel frantically tapping the leg of his chair as he accessed another database on his computer.

The National Crime Records Bureau of the Ministry of Home Affairs tracked people known to be missing or kidnapped. Maybe there was a record of Gupta's disappearance? He clicked on the link for missing persons and scrolled down the list of names. Faces on a series of mostly low-quality photographs stared at him. Many of these people were most likely dead, and most would never be found. It was probably a long shot, but Sharma was trained to follow procedure.

Much to his relief, Gupta was the third one on the list. He was in luck! Satisfied, he stroked his mustache between his thumb and forefinger as his face split into a wide smile. There was a reasonably clear picture of a man in his mid-forties that matched the one on the OCI card. The age, height, build, complexion, shape of the face and even part of the dress appeared to correspond with those of the body he had seen on the beach. The date of the disappearance was stated as just a few weeks before. There was also a contact name for the officer assigned to the case, in Colaba, only a few miles away.

Deepak Sharma immediately looked up and dialed the number of Assistant Inspector of Police Ajay Mishra, to inform him of the day's discovery.

"API Mishra," a voice answered.

"Respects, Sir! SI Sharma speaking. Gamdevi Police Station. I believe we found one of your missing persons, one Vikas Gupta."

"Is that right? Well done, you! Where did you find him?"

"He washed up on Chowpatty Beach this morning, sadly dead as a dodo. The body had spent a considerable amount of time in the water."

"Well, that figures. He was reported missing a few weeks ago. Some people from Europe were looking for him. Between you and me, that's all I know, really. Secret stuff. High priority. I'm just coordinating enquiries and was told to refer any leads to the RAW."

What Mishra was referring to was the Research and Analysis Wing, India's primary foreign intelligence agency.

"The RAW! I see. Well, case closed then."

"As far as you and I are concerned, it certainly looks that way, Sub-inspector. I'll notify those involved immediately."

"And please let me know about arrangements regarding Babaji Gupta's body. It's in a pretty bad state."

"I'll email you the details shortly. Thank you for *doing the needful*."

Chapter 7

Urumqi, China, May 1989
Twenty-seven years earlier

THE CROWD HAD ASSEMBLED just outside the *bazaar* on South Jiefang Road. It had spread out to the nearby maze of narrow alleyways that surrounded it, and soon cars were being wrecked and set ablaze as stones and other projectiles were hurled at the windows of the government headquarters. It was the first time since 1949 that the Xinjiang province of the People's Republic of China had seen such unrest, and the protesters had chosen Urumqi, the provincial capital, to make their voices heard.

Previously a major hub on the Silk Road, the city was now the largest metropolis in China's western interior and home to almost two million people. In truth, it had never really been a peaceful place. Oirat Dzungar tribes united under the authority of a *Khan* had originally controlled the city before the Qing Dynasty wiped them out in a genocide that killed eight hundred thousand people. The Qianlong emperor renamed it Dihua, and it would later be fought over by Turkic and Hui Muslims, as well as Nationalists and Communists. But the violent events that were now unfolding were a first since its name had finally changed to Urumqi, after the founding of the PRC.

It wasn't exactly clear what had caused the commotion. Some said it was a peaceful march against a recently published book, which purported to describe the sexual life of Muslims, that had suddenly turned sour. Others argued it was a thirst for freedom and rebellion against central Communist power, as would later also be unleashed on June 4 of that same year in Tiananmen Square.

Indeed, in both cases, the incidents appeared to involve a large contingent of students. But what would unfold in Beijing less than a month later would principally involve Han Chinese, whereas the events in China's faraway Xinjiang province pitted the latter against the Uyghurs, the largest Muslim minority there. In 1989, no one spoke of a clash of civilizations just yet, but what was happening seemed to lend credence to the idea that cultural and religious identities would dominate conflict in the post-Cold War world.

Whatever the reason for them, the troubles were spreading fast. They had now reached Hongshan Park and People's Square. The protesters had even received reinforcements from some of the faithful praying at the nearby Tartar Mosque, prompting the authorities to send in the police, in full riot gear, to try to contain the flow. They soon fired tear-gas grenades and blocked access to some of the city's major streets.

Running to escape what was fast turning into uncontrollable mayhem, Ehmet and Temur soon found themselves trapped between an angry mob and rows of uniformed policemen, waving truncheons and taking a stand behind heavy-duty man-size shields.

Temur was a boy of only nine, with a round face framed by long, dark hair and intelligent eyes that were pale gray in color, as they often were with people of Turkic origin. His mother had died from ill health shortly after his birth, while his father had never made it back from a trip to Kashgar, then a twenty-four-hour drive by bus. The vehicle was later found buried under a landslide on the Karakoram Highway. For the last three years, Temur had lived with his uncle Ehmet, himself a widower who worked in the bazaar.

Temur never ceased to marvel at the endless rows of shops that lined its passages. They unfolded into a giant oriental maze, offering all kinds of foods, spices and household goods, at all hours of the day or night, and he always enjoyed the excitement offered by the indoor market's sounds, smells and colors.

The boy would normally have been at school at that time, but it was a Friday and he and his uncle had attended prayers together before returning to the bazaar for a pastry treat. That's when it had all started. They had been unable to escape the crowd that converged toward Jiefang Road, and were left with no option but to unwillingly join the unrelenting flow of students.

The protesters' cries grew louder and angrier and, after several attempts to contain them had lasted the best part of an hour, the troops were given the order to disperse the crowd and regain control of the area. Without warning, the officers started to advance, slowly at first, banging their batons against their shields with a frightening noise, like warriors from another era, before breaking into a full charge.

Ehmet immediately understood they were in deep trouble and pushed Temur into a small side alley that provided access to a private courtyard.

"Whatever happens, stay there and do not move until I return to pick you up," he said.

"But, Uncle, what will happen to you?" asked the boy, now frightened.

"Temur, find a hiding place, quick! This is no time to argue!" was the reply.

He did as was ordered. In the courtyard was an empty fountain. It was perhaps three feet deep, and he swiftly climbed over the parapet. To any onlooker who didn't come too close, he would be invisible and could safely await the end of the troubles, crouched on the bottom.

The last thing he saw, before lowering himself onto the cold blue tiles, was his uncle being caught in the middle of a battle between the riot police and protesters. It was a violent clash and, for most of an hour, Temur lay there, all curled up, trying to imagine what was happening just a few feet away, beyond the relative safety of the small courtyard.

Officially, more than a hundred and fifty people were wounded that day. But the riots would soon pave the way for more violence. The following year, things would escalate into a fully armed uprising in the town of Baren, southwest of Kashgar. It would leave fifty dead, after more than a thousand soldiers from the People's Liberation Army had been sent in to restore order. That time, the protesters' motivations were unmistakably ethnic separatism, fueled by calls to *jihad* against the Chinese occupants. More violent incidents would follow, in Lop Nor in the south, in Yining to the north and then in Urumqi again, in 2009, when some two hundred people would be killed, leading to an unknown number of arrests, convictions and executions. Today was only the beginning.

Temur finally found the strength to leave his hiding place. Silence had taken over. His uncle had told him not to move, but he had never returned. It would soon be dark, and he could not wait indefinitely.

He peeked slowly above the parapet and, seeing nothing alarming, climbed over it and ventured toward the passage that led back to the main street. There he was greeted with a scene from a battlefield. He saw several broken carts that would have belonged to street vendors, their wares now scattered everywhere. It seemed like people had dropped whatever they were carrying, there and then, in a bid to escape. Bags of rice and pulses had burst open; he even saw shoes, abandoned amid the commotion. But his uncle was nowhere to be found.

Temur was wandering, dazed, toward the bazaar when a tall man approached him with a kind voice. He wore a gray *salwar kameez* and a skullcap. A full black beard framed his angular face. A black and white *shemagh* was on his shoulders, and one of his huge, muscular hands was nonchalantly playing with a *mishaba*, a string of ninety-nine prayer beads, each corresponding to one of the names of Allah. He looked like he was in his early thirties, and appeared to genuinely take pity on the boy.

"Who are you? You seem lost. Are you looking for someone, Little Brother?" he gently asked.

"My name's Temur," answered the boy, dead serious. "I'm looking for my uncle, Ehmet Beg. He's the only family I've got. We were separated when the police attacked. I haven't seen him since."

"That's a fine name you've got. A warrior's name," said the man gravely. "Maybe he was arrested? Many people were. But why don't we first try to see if he's at home? He probably went there, to wait for things to quiet down, *Inch'Allah*," he offered.

Temur was not in the habit of following strangers, but the man sounded kind enough, and also religious. Above all, he needed to find out what had happened to Ehmet.

"And who would you be?" he finally asked, perhaps to reassure himself.

The bearded man bowed slightly, his palm over his heart.

"My name is Ismail Khan. You're not to fear me, Little Brother. Now, where does your uncle live?"

"Just off Helongjiang Lu, not far from the bus terminal."

"Let's go, then," said Khan jovially. "What are we waiting for?"

Chapter 8

Urumqi, China, May 1989

TEMUR HAD DIFFICULTY keeping up with the man's pace. Khan was clearly accustomed to walking a lot, and he never seemed to tire. The bus terminal was only a few miles away to the east, not far from the Yashan Forest Park. They talked along the way, and Temur learned that Khan was originally from Pakistan. He seemed to travel a lot throughout Central Asia and even beyond, to the Middle East, although it wasn't exactly clear what he did for a living.

He's probably a trader of some sort, thought Temur.

There were many like him, who sourced goods at one end of today's Silk Road to sell them at the other, moving from Turkey to Western China, passing through Iraq, Iran and Afghanistan, as well as other countries in the region. He had seen and even talked to many of them, in the bazaar.

Temur explained to the stranger how he and his uncle had first left the mosque and then how the crowd had pushed them into the street. He told him how they had been unable to go any further and had separated just as the police had started to charge.

Most of Urumqi was now deserted. Clearly, something very unusual had happened, and people had returned to the safety of their own homes. They now followed Helongjiang Lu. As they approached the bus terminal, Temur signaled for them to turn left.

In contrast to the rest of the city, the street where he and his uncle lived was remarkably busy. As they rounded the corner, they immediately saw the three police cars parked outside the house, their blue lights on, the markings on their doors unmistakable. A swarm of uniformed officers had deployed around them. Their manners were aggressive, and they appeared to be looking for something—or someone.

"Stay here. Let me find out what the matter is. I won't be long," commanded Khan, gently but firmly, before walking toward the small crowd of onlookers.

Temur saw him speak to several people, away from the police cars. He could not hear what they were saying, but Khan shook his head gravely a few times and, as he returned, Temur already knew it would be bad news.

"We can't stay here, Little Brother. You have to be brave now. Your uncle's dead, may Allah have mercy upon his soul! He was killed by those infidels," he said, his face now tensed, as he spat on the macadam.

"It happened just after they charged. They ganged up on him and he succumbed to their beating," he added.

Temur's face had suddenly turned pale. He had guessed something serious had happened, but the realization that he would never see his uncle alive again still came as a complete shock.

"Can I see him?" he asked, the only thing he could say.

"That would be unwise, Little Brother. The police are here to round up people he would have known and lived with. They believe him to be one of the ringleaders, you see, and they're searching for accomplices."

"But that's completely untrue!" protested Temur.

"You and I know this, but they'll never believe us," said Khan.

"What are we to do, then?"

"We have to leave this place and put ourselves out of their reach, Inch'Allah. And we have to do it quick."

"But where shall we go?"

"Don't worry, Little Brother, I'll take care of you from now on," he said, patting Temur's shoulder with one of his big-knuckled hands. "Everything will be all right."

Suddenly, Khan's voice hardened, as he appeared to look up to the heavens above.

"In the Name of Allah, the Most Beneficent, the Most Merciful, I swear to you that the death of your uncle will not remain unpunished! One day, those Chinese dogs will pay dearly for what they have done," he added.

Then they left and walked in the direction of the bus terminal.

Chapter 9

Kashgar, China, May 1989

THEY HAD CAUGHT the first bus to Kashgar, the westernmost major city in China's interior, more than nine hundred miles away from Urumqi. The road was now marginally better—Chinese engineers had seen to that—than the one on which Temur's father had met his untimely death, but it still took the best part of nineteen hours to complete the journey.

There were several stops along the way, at Bayingol, Aksu and Kizilsu, and most of the trip was across deserted, windy steppes and perilous mountain roads bordered by steep precipices. To the north was Kyrgyzstan; to the west, Tajikistan and to the south, Pakistan. They were now in the bosom of the famous "stans" of Central Asia.

Urumqi was one of the most polluted cities in China, if not the world but, as a new day began, the sky turned from darkness to a crisp blue palette of the kind Temur had almost never seen. It was the first time he had traveled this far, and grief and sadness soon turned into curiosity as he discovered new landscapes and horizons.

The people on the bus were mostly traders who carried their wares from one city to the next, selling or bartering goods as their ancestors had done for more than a thousand years, except that they now traveled in a motorized vehicle instead of on the camels or horses that would once have assembled into caravans on the Silk Road.

Almost all the Asian races and nationalities were present, often recognizable by the types of skullcap and other headdress they wore: Chinese, Kyrgyz, Tajik, Afghani, Uzbeki and Pakistani. They spoke different languages and had a wide array of customs and religions, like the inhabitants of a modern Tower of Babel. Temur was fascinated, his eyes open wide, taking in all the novelty.

"So, where are we going, then?" he asked Ismail Khan.

"First, we'll stop in Kashgar. I have friends there, in the bazaar. Good Muslims. They'll help us, Inch'Allah. It's a long journey, so we'll need to rest. We'll also get you new papers, to leave China and cross into friendlier lands. How about 'Temur Khan' for a name? Then I can be your new uncle."

Temur pondered for a few seconds.

A new name for a new life, he thought. "Why not?" he said. "Temur Khan," he repeated. "I like it."

"Good. Do you know, Little Brother, that there are more than twenty bazaars in Kashgar? But the one near the east gate of the city is the biggest of them all. It dates back more than two thousand years, and there are more than four thousand booths. That's where we're going."

"And how long will we stay there?"

"Not more than a few days, just enough time to sort things out for the both of us. Then we'll cross into Kyrgyzstan and, finally, we'll reach Osh, in the Ferghana Valley, next to Uzbekistan. It's our final destination."

"Osh," repeated Temur.

He'd never heard of it. But the idea of Uzbekistan nearby was exciting: he knew it was there that Tamerlane, the legendary conqueror from the fifteenth century, after whom he was named, was buried in the Gur-e-Amir mausoleum in Samarkand.

However, what Temur did not know was that Osh—and the rest of the Ferghana Valley—would soon become a hotspot for violence of all kinds.

The roots of the problem lay in the division by Stalin of what was a vast expanse of fertile agricultural land into national republics, namely Uzbekistan, Kyrgyzstan and Tajikistan. As often happens, this demarcation had been decided arbitrarily, largely ignoring the mosaic of ethnicities that had existed for centuries. The then U.S.S.R. began to dominate Uzbekistan's economy as the country became a powerhouse centered on the cotton trade. Russian immigrants flooded into the valley to work on collective farms.

The ancient feuds started to surface after the invasion of Afghanistan in 1979. As the war ended in early 1989 and the Soviet Union began to crumble, ethnic tensions became increasingly commonplace. The Kyrgyz, traditionally nomads and farmers, started competing for resources and moved into the cities to seek work. There, the Uzbeks, who for centuries had been merchants and traders, often had the upper hand.

Economic pressure soon turned into violent inter-ethnic clashes and riots, which became widespread. On their side, the Tajiks generally washed their hands of the whole situation, since the Ferghana Valley was isolated from the rest of the country by a high mountain range and the government's influence hardly ever extended beyond the capital, Dushanbe. Meanwhile, the tinderbox that was the Ferghana Valley would soon evolve into a hotbed for Muslim fundamentalism.

Ismail Khan and Temur arrived in Kashgar just in time for the *Maghrib* prayer, at sunset. They first went to the mosque to offer thanks for their safe passage. They then walked to the East Gate Bazaar. Khan navigated with ease through its maze-like alleys until they reached a small shop that belonged to an Uzbek merchant.

His name was Farruck Durdona, and he traded in colorful *ikat* silk fabrics. Underneath a black skullcap with white paisley embroideries he had a jovial face and a happy demeanor. His eyes were slanted, but strangely of a clear blue, reminiscent of the shimmering domes for which his home country was famous.

Durdona welcomed them warmly with a strong, dark and very sweet tea and pastries, before showing them to a room decorated with thick nomadic carpets on one of the two upper floors. After Temur had retired for the night, Durdona and Khan spent a long time talking in the shop downstairs, planning the rest of the journey.

Very early on the morning of the third day, Khan presented Temur with a well-worn Pakistani identity document bearing his new name.

"It's a fake, of course," he said, smiling. "But it will stand up to scrutiny—don't worry. It says you entered China two weeks ago, at the same time I did. The guards at the border will stamp it when we leave later today, and that will be the end of it. But keep it safe, as we'll need it again before we arrive in Osh."

Before they left, Durdona presented Temur with an ikat fabric belt, something to remember him by. They thanked their host profusely and hired a battered taxi to complete the rest of the trip. It took a full and exhausting day, but the road was spectacular, twisting and turning through a grandiose landscape. They stopped at the Irkeshtam pass, one of the world's most remote border crossings. They cleared immigration, first at the Chinese checkpoint (where the guards strangely worked on Beijing, rather than Xinjiang, time) and then at the Kyrgyz one.

Finally, once in Osh, they arrived at Khan's house—which, unbeknown to him at the time, Temur would call home for the next seven years.

The neighbors had nicknamed it "the blue house" because of the color it was painted. Although fairly ordinary in appearance, its walls hid a roomy and welcoming interior with particularly high ceilings. It was simply decorated, but it clearly belonged to a well-traveled and cultured man, and also to one who took the teachings of the Quran very seriously. There were no images or paintings throughout the house, and the walls were bare.

The influence Khan would subsequently have on Temur's education was to be considerable. But for the moment, he showed the boy to a large room that was comfortably furnished with a bed, a writing table with a chair and a chest of drawers. On the table was a copy of the Quran.

"This will be your room, Little Brother," said Khan.

It was certainly much bigger and more luxurious than any Temur had known previously. *Ismail Khan must be a really rich man,* he thought.

"You can clean up in there," Khan added, showing the boy to a tiled room nearby that was meant for ablutions. "Later, you and I will have much to talk about, while we eat dinner."

Chapter 10

Osh, Kyrgyzstan, May 1989

FOR TEMUR, LIFE in Osh soon turned into a familiar routine. No one ever questioned why he had suddenly turned up at the blue house. He was simply Khan's nephew. The Pakistani man had taken him in, after his parents had passed away. It was pretty much the truth, in any event.

He would rise with the first call to prayers and then go to school, to continue his formal education. He soon showed impressive abilities in class and also made a few friends there, but much of what he really learned came from talking to Ismail Khan. Khan was often away but, when in town, he never failed to tell Temur about the countries and cities he had visited, as well as the customs and manners of the people who lived in them.

Khan also made a point of teaching him foreign languages. Within a few years, Temur became reasonably fluent in several: Arabic, of course, the language of the Quran, as well as Urdu and Pashto, in addition to English and his native Uyghur.

Many visitors came to the house, and Temur always learned something from them as well. They came from all over the region and beyond, but they all had several things in common: they were all Sunni, and all rejected many of the developments subsequent to the first generations of Islam. Their beliefs were austere and conservative, and they scorned anything that had to do with Western values and the American way of life in particular, which they saw as degenerate. They believed their faith to be the true Islam and, over the last seven years, many had also been part of the thirty-five thousand or so Muslim volunteers who had fought in Afghanistan against the Soviets and their regime.

More than half of these volunteers had come from Saudi Arabia. Others had not been fighters in their own right, but came from conservative monarchies in the Gulf and had bankrolled the *mujahideen*—jihad fighters—showering them with greenbacks to buy light weapons and RPGs.

All spoke openly in the presence of Temur. After all, he was still a child and had become family to Khan, so he could therefore be trusted implicitly. His knowledge of the *Hadith*, records of the traditions and sayings of the Prophet Muhammad, also never failed to impress those who came to the blue house either as messengers or guests. How could such a religious boy mean any harm?

Khan was a man with connections, who acted as a go-between, linking believers in jihad from the Middle East to Central Asia and beyond. His international background and reliable credentials made him indispensable, as well as a key figure in the events that would subsequently change the world forever.

After two years, in 1991, a group of Muslims seized the headquarters of the Communist Party in the city of Namangan, in the Ferghana Valley. Their leaders, Tohir

Yuldeshev and Juma Namangani, were both close friends of Khan. He had helped them plan and execute this spectacular action, which signaled the start of what would become a longstanding armed struggle. He also helped them to disappear, after a prize had been put on their heads. As Temur grew into a confident teenager, he looked up to them and longed to join their fight.

In 1996, he turned sixteen. Now almost a man, he finally got the chance to accompany them and Khan as they crossed into Afghanistan to evade arrest. There, Yuldeshev and Namangani created what would later be known as the Islamic Movement of Uzbekistan, or IMU. Its objective was to overthrow Uzbekistan's first president, Islam Karimov, and establish an Islamic state under *Sharia'h* law there.

As the Taliban seized power, they welcomed these volunteer fighters with open arms. The IMU rallied a number of disaffected Uzbeks and Uyghurs and established training camps, operating on the porous borders between Tajikistan, Afghanistan and Pakistan, waging a guerilla war and abducting foreigners, including geologists and mountain climbers, to help finance the movement. Much of the initial funding came from Pakistan's Inter-Services Intelligence (ISI) agency. Recruits ballooned to about two thousand.

Soon thereafter, the IMU rallied to the cause of a man called Osama bin Laden, leader of a nebulous terrorist organization called al Qaeda. Some six hundred of its combatants were incorporated into bin Laden's elite 055 Brigade and joined the fight against Ahmad Shah Massoud, the military and political leader of the United Islamic Front for the Salvation of Afghanistan, better known in the West as the Northern Alliance. Temur Khan was among them.

Chapter 11

Afghanistan, June 1996

THE 055 BRIGADE was largely made up of Arab mercenaries and other *mujahideen* fighters from the Middle East, Central Asia and Southeast Asia. Almost all of them had previously seen action in Afghanistan against the Soviets prior to joining this new fundamentalist foreign legion.

They were well armed and equipped, with gear that had been taken from the enemy or supplied by the Taliban as well as the Sudanese government, often financed through a circuitous route by some of the regimes in the Gulf. Some of it—such as communications equipment, sniper rifles and even night vision goggles—was sophisticated, and the brigade usefully complemented the more basic forces deployed by the Taliban themselves.

The brigade's fighters were also well trained and disciplined, and all fully believed in the cause they fought for. They were willing to give their lives to achieve the tactical objectives decided by bin Laden and the leadership of al Qaeda, which made them particularly dangerous and feared.

They did not have any heavy weapons, such as artillery (although they could count on the support of a handful of

aircraft), but instead fought as part of small, mobile units—
not unlike Special Forces in the West—to back up the
regular troops on the frontlines of Afghanistan's civil war.
But what really set them apart was their ideological
indoctrination and motivation.

At first, Temur helped with menial tasks, such as tending
the wounded or dying, carrying messages and taking care of
supply logistics for the combatants. He next became familiar
with disassembling and cleaning all sorts of weaponry and
devising improvised explosive devices (IEDs), learning the
differences between those that were triggered by wire, radio,
cellular phones or infrared beams, or even operated by
suicide bombers. There was little time to waste in a war
zone, and he soon got to know much of the brigade's
equipment. But still, he wasn't deployed to directly face the
enemy on account of his age and youthful appearance, and
he also had yet to kill an infidel.

One day, he was chosen to accompany a group of fighters to ambush a convoy of the Northern Alliance that
carried arms and reinforcements on the road to Taloqan, in
the northeast of the country. At some point, the road
narrowed as it reached a small pass, which was where the
mujahideen had decided to position themselves. They only
expected a couple of four-by-fours, as well as a few trucks,
and thought the whole episode would be over within several
minutes. But, as a scout spotted the column of dust in the
distance, it became clear that the convoy was larger than
they had been led to believe. At its head was also a T-62
Russian-made tank that must have been seized from the
Soviets after their retreat from Afghanistan.

With a crew of four, it was covered in steel armor, with a depth of 8.4 inches on the front of the turret, and armed with a 115-mm smoothbore gun. It also carried a 7.62-mm coaxial, general-purpose machine gun and a 12.7-mm anti-aircraft heavy machine gun as secondary armament. Its thirty-seven tons and effective speed of up to thirty-one miles per hour presented a formidable challenge to the fighters.

Everything that occurred next happened very fast. Through a light well mounted on the cupola, the tank's commander spotted a bright flash ahead, as the sun briefly reflected on the aluminum pole of a radio antenna, giving away the assailants' position. He immediately alerted the gunner, who quickly unleashed a shell, and then another, after fifteen seconds or so. The tank typically carried forty rounds for the main gun, although, unlike later Russian tanks (none of which would ever be sent to Afghanistan), they needed to be loaded manually rather than through an automated carousel.

Through a pair of binoculars, Temur saw the casing-removal mechanism eject the shell cases through an opening port at the back of the turret. Depending on the skill of the loader, the T-62 had a rate of fire of four to five rounds per minute, and it could also aim and fire while moving, thanks to a two-axis stabilizer. Even though the men of the 055 Brigade were fanatics, there was little they could do against a monster such as this, which had appeared out of nowhere and without warning.

The first shell did little damage, as it hit well wide of the mark, but the second and third caused a number of casualties among the mujahideen, who started to scatter away from their positions and retreat. The tank was now perhaps just five hundred feet from the pass, and it was only a question of time before its machine guns started to cut down anyone who strayed within range.

Next to Temur, a fighter had collapsed, his body pitted with fragments of red-hot shrapnel. Still hidden behind a rock, Temur decided to take a chance and seized the man's RPG-7 anti-tank rocket-propelled grenade launcher that now lay unattended. It was a rugged weapon, almost three feet in length, and only weighed fifteen pounds. While it was in theory reloadable, he doubted he would have time to fire a second grenade.

The launcher was essentially a steel tube that was wrapped in wood to protect the user from heat. Its end was flared, to shield the blast and reduce recoil. Temur ignored the telescopic sight and focused instead on the back-up iron sight to aim at the turret of the tank. He stood there, a *pakol* Afghan flat cap on his head, a chest rig with magazine and grenade pouches tightly secured above a long beige *salwar kameez* that flapped into the wind. He now distinctly heard the metallic sound of the tracks and instinctively pressed the trigger.

The gunpowder booster charge launched the five-pound grenade at a speed of 375 feet per second, unleashing a cloud of blue smoke. After three feet, the rocket motor ignited and the velocity increased to 970 feet per second as two sets of fins deployed in flight.

It normally took more than ten or even a dozen RPGs to destroy an armored vehicle, as the hunter-killer team first focused on destroying the tracks to immobilize the tank and then attempted to pierce its armor once it could no longer move. Shooting at the turret, where the armor was also the thickest, was therefore a massive gamble, but it was the first time Temur had actually used an RPG and he didn't know any better.

But to his and everyone's surprise, the 85-mm-high explosive anti-tank (HEAT) grenade smoothly glided inside of the 115-mm smoothbore tube of the tank's main gun before exploding, instantly killing the entire tank crew in a ball of fire. The top hatch popped open under the pressure of the blast, unleashing a cloud of dark smoke. It was an impossible shot, but he had done it! He had destroyed the beast!

Dazed, he stood there, mesmerized. As in a dream, the realization of what he had just done finally kicked in. He dropped the RPG and turned to his fighting companions, as the clamor of the *Takbir*, the call of Muslims to remember and cry out the name of Allah, rose around him.

"*Allahu Akbar!* God is great!"

Suddenly invigorated by what had just happened, the men quickly regrouped. Now no longer fearing the danger posed by the tank, they launched a final assault on the convoy to obliterate or capture its vehicles and slaughter their occupants in an orgy of violence. The attack would yield a major haul of weapons and ammunition. They celebrated by shooting salvos of bullets in the air from their Kalashnikov automatic rifles.

Temur joined them with relish. Hesitant at first, but soon encouraged by his companions, he even slashed the throats of several men from the enemy convoy with a combat knife. Some pleaded for their lives, but he sacrificed them all, like animals, all for the greater good of the cause he passionately believed in. By nightfall, his hands and even some of his face were covered in blood. It had been a day he would not forget in a hurry. At long last, he had truly joined the ranks of the mujahideen. His metamorphosis into a fighter for Islam was complete, and he had finally been bloodied in battle. He had now been to the dark side, and there was no turning back.

After the battle, Khan spoke to Temur.

"You did very well today, Little Brother. Without your destroying that tank there and then, we would have suffered many more casualties. You are now a hero to the men. I give thanks to Allah for putting you in my path, and you are for sure destined for something great in this world, Inch'Allah."

"I just did what I thought was right. I was also very lucky," he answered.

"That may well be, but, for my own part, I'd rather believe God must have guided your hand to serve our purpose. I also saw how you fearlessly killed those bastard dogs afterward. I and all those in the brigade are in awe of you."

A few days later, Khan went to see Temur with more news.

"You and I will leave in the morning," he said. "The *sheikh* himself has just heard of your exploits, and he would like to meet you."

Chapter 12

Peshawar, Pakistan, July 1996

THE MEETING WITH bin Laden left a lasting impression on Temur. It took place in Peshawar, the capital of Kybher Pakhtunkhwa province in northeastern Pakistan, near the border with Afghanistan. It was a journey of more than 375 miles, but the sheikh had asked to see the boy and no one dared question the complex logistics associated with arranging such an encounter. It took them three days, resting in safe houses as they stopped, slowly making their way south.

They did not get to see much of Peshawar—neither the smugglers' bazaar, where guns (among them, locally made submachine guns) and drugs (including cannabis and opiates) were openly on sale, nor the famed Kahabat Khan Mosque. Immediately after arriving, late at night, Khan and Temur were taken to a small, badly lit house not far from the Balar Hissar Fort. The stronghold had been built in the fifth century by Babur, the first Moghul ruler, and defended the approach from Rawalpindi and the Khyber Pass, thanks to walls that were twenty feet high and twelve feet thick. The location was discreet, and there was nothing to betray the fact that the house accommodated the leader of al Qaeda.

As they entered, they were taken to a small room toward the back of the home. It was sparsely furnished, with only carpets, cushions and a few trays with tea and pastries that had been placed on the floor.

Seated in a corner was none other than bin Laden himself, dressed in a traditional Afghan tunic, with a pakol cap and an old British-issue camouflaged smock jacket. His personal weapon, a shiny AK-74, was leaning against a wall.

Next to bin Laden was another man with a dark beard. He was perhaps fifty. Like bin Laden, he was also very tall—almost six foot six—and strongly built, and wore a *pagri* turban. His face bore what looked like shrapnel scars, one of which straddled a blind eye.

Ismail Khan bowed slightly upon entering, introducing Temur.

"This is the boy Temur I've already told you about. Without a doubt, he's one of the finest warriors we've got. In only a short space of time, he's built quite a reputation for himself, and the men love him dearly."

Temur was taken aback at how he had just been introduced. He had immediately recognized bin Laden from pictures that widely circulated among the jihadi fighters. His dreamy eyes with dark patches underneath, and his long beard, were unmistakable. However, he did not yet know who the other man was.

"I've heard a lot about you," said bin Laden, now taking Temur's hands in his. "I wish I had more men like you, who disregard safety for their own life for the greater glory of our sacred cause. Men who can single-handedly face up to a tank and bring it down as if they were the sword arm of

Allah Himself, may His Blessed Name remain forever in our hearts! Please sit down and tell me more about it. But first, let me introduce you to Amir al-Mu'minim, Mohammed Omar."

The title bin Laden had just given the other man was Commander of the Faithful. It had been bestowed on him after he had retrieved what was said to have been the cloak of Prophet Muhammad himself, held inside a series of chests in a mosque in Kandahar. According to legend, whoever seized the cloak would become the leader of the Muslims.

He was, however, better known in the West simply as Mullah Omar. Like bin Laden, he was a veteran rebel fighter and mujahideen of the anti-Soviet era. He had now taken Kabul with his followers and was just about to become the leader of the Islamic Emirate of Afghanistan.

Mullah Omar normally resided in Kandahar, a city he almost never left. The two men had not yet joined forces in hiding—that would only happen after 9/11—but they already shared the same ideals, as well as a common hatred of America and the Western world in general.

After bin Laden had let go of his hands, Temur bowed respectfully and sat, as he had just been invited to do. He then recalled for their benefit how he had brought the tank down, much to his surprise, with a grenade launched by an RPG-7. He didn't boast and told the tale exactly as it had happened.

"A most talented young man," finally observed Mullah Omar, after Temur had finished his story. "And also one who carries so much promise. I've brought down a few of these armored monsters myself in my time, and it sure is no easy task. Doing it single-handedly would be near impossible. You are to be commended, Temur, and Allah for sure watches over you."

"Indeed," added bin Laden. "Such a feat was certainly remarkable. But you must surely be destined for things greater than fighting skirmishes in the tribal areas. Kabul has just fallen, and it would be a shame to lose you in the pitch battles that will ensue, for there is still so much left to accomplish."

"But, Amir, my greatest wish is to die fighting for jihad," protested Temur.

"Of that, I have no doubt," replied bin Laden. "But someone of your talents should surely take the battle to the infidels instead. You speak several languages, Ismail tells me. That is a great asset. And you are still young, which is a blessed opportunity. We have great plans for you, Temur. But they will require you to live away from here and also to sit and wait for a long time, probably for years. But when the time comes—and, believe me, when it finally does, it will be glorious—you'll destroy those rabid dogs such that your name as a martyr will be remembered on this earth for centuries to come!"

"Allahu Akbar!" chanted Khan, seconded by Mullah Omar.

"I will of course do as you order," acknowledged Temur.

"Then listen carefully," continued bin Laden, in a soft and fatherly tone, his palm now resting on Temur's shoulder, "for this is probably the last time we'll meet."

Chapter 13

Paris, France, February 2016

"GODDAMMIT, TANGUY, I just can't believe you fucked that one up!" said Colonel Le Pan, who headed the DGSE's Service Action and to whom Erwan reported.

"The intel was first rate, and all you had to do was turn up and shoot the bastards, but you allowed God knows who to be there ahead of us and also made us look like a bunch of hicks," he added, banging his fist on the table in the soundproof meeting room.

Le Pan was a brash former paratrooper, with a matching haircut, who had seen plenty of action in Africa as well as in the Gulf and Afghanistan. He was made for wearing battledress and Tanguy thought that civilian clothing did not suit him at all.

Le Pan's short temper was legendary within the service, where he was better known to all simply as "The Bear." But he also knew that Tanguy was one of his best and most experienced men. All the swearing and gesticulating were there more to make a point rather than out of genuine anger. The buck stopped with him, and he had to sound the part, which he certainly did.

"With all due respect, *mon Colonel*," answered Tanguy,

"my orders were to terminate Saadi and his associates, and that's exactly what happened back there, in Johor. I turned up at the crack of dawn, with plenty of time to spare, but those who killed them arrived and left so quickly, I didn't get a chance to act, especially with zero backup. Moreover, it was immediately obvious they were after the same targets, and I didn't think it wise to engage them. They could have been allies, after all. Eliminating terrorists is one thing, but bumping off friendlies in the process wasn't part of the brief."

"I know, I know," answered an irritated Le Pan, waiving a dismissive hand. "Did you at least find out who they might have been?"

"According to Darret, it's unlikely to be a settling of accounts by local criminal gangs. There are triads and secret societies operating in Malaysia, of course, but none of them is bold enough to dare take on a major terrorist organization like Abu Sayyaf. That would invite a war they might well end up losing. Plus, they seem to actually be on friendly terms, as far as drug-related activities are concerned."

"So it was a covert job," said Le Pan, thinking on his feet. "Is that what you're inferring?"

"Most likely it was. They were not Singaporean; that much we know. And the SID there is also adamant that they were not Malaysian. Darret has their intel in high regard, so we've no reason to think otherwise. The Yanks and the Brits have also denied all involvement, and I don't see why they would have kept us in the dark on that one, anyway. They knew we wanted Saadi badly, so mounting a covert op without telling us first would have been plain stupid."

"I agree. Saadi was ours; nothing to do with them. It's not like when they took on bin Laden in Pakistan."

"I also doubt the killers would have been from NICA, the Philippines' National Intelligence Coordinating Agency. In the past, they've arrested members of Abu Sayyaf, including Edis, who was linked to al Qaeda, but covert action in a neighboring country would be a tall order for them. It's not their style, and the Americans would most certainly have known, too. They seemed to be completely in the dark on that one."

"So who, in that case?"

"It only leaves the Chinese. The woman on the motorbike was Asian, and they obviously have their own issues with Muslim fundamentalists."

"That figures. Last July, ISIS issued a call to Muslim Uyghurs to join its caliphate. Some of them could have been in contact with Saleh and Andang. If Saadi was buying arms from them, a bunch of *muj* in China might have done so as well. If that's the case, a kill by the Chinese would make a lot of sense."

"Indeed. And, remember, last November, ISIS also executed a Chinese hostage. So things are certainly taking a turn for the worse, as far as China's concerned. It's not surprising they would up the ante and try to nip this in the bud before the situation in Xinjiang gets out of control."

"Right. Are there any leads on the bike—the Agusta? You mentioned it was pretty high-end gear."

"It is, and we've looked into it already. We managed to track one down in Malaysia that was imported by a Chinese business. It was paid for and the bike was duly delivered, but we could not find any further trace of the company that bought it."

"That screams 'MSS' from a mile away," said Le Pan.

"MSS" referred to the Ministry of State Security, the Chinese intelligence and security agency.

"Right. You mentioned that the female operator looked at you as they were leaving the scene?" he added, casting an eye on the report Erwan had filed after the mission.

"Only for a split second, but I'm sure I could recognize her if I saw her again."

"I'm more worried that *she* might have been the one who recognized *you* in the first place, back there. It would mean they already knew what you were up to, and also that our op might have been compromised from the word 'go.' In other words, the Chinese might have a mole within our ranks. This could end up proving very serious indeed."

"We've no reason to believe that. It was just a glance. She may simply have noticed me as they were riding away. After all, the area was pretty quiet and there was hardly anyone around. The whole thing was put together at very short notice, too, and Darret is surely beyond reproach. He's the one who volunteered the intel in the first place."

"I don't want to take any chances. I'll hook you up with the SL right now. See if you can identify that woman first. If we can find out who she is, we might be able to trace her whereabouts and who she might potentially have been in contact with at our end."

"SL" was short for the Service des Liaisons, formerly known as SEREX or Service des Relations Extérieures, which was in charge of liaising with foreign intelligence services. They would have records of people the DGSE knew of and was in contact with at the MSS. As a starting point, it made sense. If she could be identified, Le Pan would then make a decision as to the next steps.

"*A vos ordres*, mon Colonel," said Tanguy, now standing to attention, even though he was wearing civilian clothes.

"Find that bitch, Tanguy! You're dismissed," concluded Le Pan stiffly, pushing his chair away from the table. The meeting was over.

Chapter 14

Paris, France, February 2016

ERWAN TANGUY MADE his way to the area within the confines of La Piscine that housed the SL. A few calls by Le Pan had ensured he was given access, and he was greeted on arrival after clearing security. Like all five directorates of the DGSE (administration, operations, intelligence, strategy and technical matters), the SL was under the direct authority of the agency's Directeur Général.

Tanguy followed a man who introduced himself as Pascal Boissard to an anonymous meeting room at the end of a damp basement. It was a far cry from the high-tech digital world portrayed in the movies, but it was certainly much more secure. There was nothing that could be hacked there.

"I was just told you're interested in the MSS; is that right?" asked Boissard.

"Correct. I had a recent encounter with a woman in Southeast Asia. The Bear suggested you might have a file on her. I only saw her face for a split second, but I should be able to recognize her from a photograph. We've reason to believe she's an operator from the Guoanbu."

"Guoanbu" was the Chinese name of the MSS.

"Ah, Asian women!" sighed Boissard, rolling his eyes

and dreaming of exotic locations beyond the dreary basement in which he worked. "Can you tell me more about her?"

"I'd say early to mid-thirties, max. About five foot six. Slim, but athletic. She was wearing a motorcycle helmet, so I didn't get to see her hair, but I'm pretty certain she had clear eyes, maybe gray or green. That should be unusual enough. She's very dangerous: she killed several men with a small knife. She probably would have had some sort of Special Forces training, I suspect."

"My, my, quite a character! Please wait for me for a few moments. I'll show you some photographs when I return. If we have a record of her, then we can access her file next."

After about twenty minutes, Boissard returned with a laptop. It was unusual in that it didn't have a hard drive. Security was paramount, and downloading information was subject to very strict protocols and controls. He didn't plug it in, inserting a flash drive in the sole USB port and clicking on the icon that appeared on the screen.

"I've uploaded photographs that might be relevant on the thumb drive," he said.

A photograph of a young woman soon appeared. Tanguy took a look, but it was not the one he sought.

"Not her."

Boissard kept flicking through a series of faces, as Tanguy dismissed one option after the other.

"We're almost done," Boissard finally said, after about twenty minutes. "There are just a few left for you to look at. If she's not there, then we're at a loss."

The face that next flashed on the screen, however,

caught the officer's attention.

"Wait a minute," he said, "can you blow that one up slightly?"

"Not a problem."

The photograph was that of a young woman in uniform. She was barefaced, with sharp, well-chiseled features and unusually clear eyes that looked straight at the camera. She was perhaps thirty-five. It was certainly a face one could not forget, and one that conveyed great strength of character and assurance. There were three red stripes over a gold background and one star on her collar insignia, so her rank was that of a field officer—a major, to be precise. On her arm was the insignia of the People's Liberation Army Special Operations Forces, a white thunderbolt over a dagger on a red background, with blue and black vertical stripes at the edges of the crest.

"That's her," said Tanguy. "Can you get me her file?"

Boissard noted down the number at the bottom of the photograph. He then ejected the flash drive and took the laptop with him.

"I'll be back shortly," he said, before leaving the room.

After about ten minutes, he returned. Without a word, he handed a printed document to Tanguy.

"Just knock on the door when you're done," he said. "No notes—you know the drill."

There was no paper to jot anything down, and Tanguy knew he was expected to memorize any information that might be relevant. No copy would be made, nor given, of the document, which itself would later be shredded. The original never left a highly secure digital archive.

Her surname was Xie and her first name Wei.

"Xie Wei," said Erwan aloud, as he started reading. She was a major in the Special Forces Unit of the Shenyang military region, in Liaoning province in northeast China. Shenyang was formerly known by its Manchu name, Mukden.

"She's probably locally born. That would explain her high cheekbones and the clear eyes," he thought.

Her unit was also known by the name of Siberian Tiger, and its members trained in ground, air and water operations, with a particular emphasis on survival skills, either in small groups or alone. Its operators were forced to spend several months at a time in the wilderness, including forests, deserts, mountains and even the country's steppes of Inner Mongolia, and were expected to live off the land without any man-made shelter. They also all had extensive parachute and scuba diving training.

China's Special Forces totaled perhaps twelve thousand or even as many as fifteen thousand, compared to France's three thousand operators, but Xie Wei clearly was one of the very best. She'd had a stellar career so far and had scored highly in several military competitions, which is how she had come to the attention of international intelligence agencies.

She had won second place in the 2012 Sniper World Cup. She was also part of the Chinese team that had won first place at the 2013 Fifth International Warrior Competition, organized by the Jordan Armed Forces, at the King Abdullah II Special Operations Training Centre. In 2015, she had led the Chinese commandos who had won the coveted Golden Owl in Kazakhstan, a competition for

Special Forces units from around the world—renowned for high levels of risk-taking and cruel ordeals—beating both the Russian and American participants as well as teams from Belarus and the host country. The contributors had endured a grueling sixteen exercises over five days to test their accuracy in shooting as well as endurance, strength, concentration and ability to apply camouflage and orientate themselves in unfamiliar terrain, amid treacherous weather and without any modern navigational technology.

The terrorists from Abu Sayyaf were used to living and fighting in the jungle, but they clearly had met their match in Xie Wei.

There was little else of interest in the file. She was believed to have conducted a number of covert operations for the MSS and was last seen in Hong Kong, where she had trained the local Special Operations Company of China's People's Liberation Army (PLA), also known as the Five-Minute Response Unit, based near Stanley in the south of Hong Kong Island. Her current whereabouts, however, were unknown.

Erwan Tanguy memorized what he had just read. He then knocked on the door and handed the document back to Boissard. He now knew who had beaten him to his target in Johor.

Chapter 15

Xinjiang, China, February 2016

"CAPTAIN CHAN, what happened was completely unacceptable!"

Xie Wei had arrived a few hours before in Xinjiang, in western China. She had traveled by helicopter from Urumqi to a small, isolated outpost that was under the watch of a single company—about a hundred men. Its mission was to guard a sizeable depot of weapons and ammunition that supplied part of the Lanzhou military region. The camp was heavily fortified and defended, surrounded by several fences, one of which was electrified. At each of its four corners were watchtowers, with automatic machine guns and searchlights.

Xie Wei was in a foul mood and had immediately ranked the capabilities of the man she now faced as mediocrity squared, at best.

"Take me through the whole thing again and, this time, you'd be well advised not to omit any detail. I'm not in the mood for pleasantries," she continued harshly.

"Well, as I've already mentioned, we had a visit yesterday from a major, just like you. It was toward the end of the day, around nightfall. It would have been around seven-thirty or so. We can check the exact time with the guard post—it would have been logged. He said he was from the 6th Motorized Infantry Division in Kashgar, which both his uniform and credentials also stated. He arrived in a Mengshi with a driver and was accompanied by a Jiefang truck. Everything looked in order, so we let them in."

"Go on."

"He had a mission order from headquarters to move some gear to Kuqa: specifically, cases of QBZ assault rifles and assorted ammunition, QJY machine guns, automatic grenade launchers, grenades and several 82-mm mortars. They also requested twenty charges of Semtex-1C plastic explosives. It was all stated on the list, marked 'urgent.' I made a copy for you, with all the serial numbers, of course. I had no reason to doubt the request. We regularly receive similar orders and never had any issues."

"But I take it you generally know of such visits ahead of time? Didn't it occur to you to check with Lanzhou? A simple call would have sufficed."

"But I did call!" protested the captain. "I know my job, Major! Again, everything checked out. It's only when I mentioned the shipment again to Lanzhou early this morning, after they'd called me, that I realized we'd been taken for a ride."

"And may I ask what number you dialed last night?"

"The major himself dialed it for me."

"To save you the effort of looking it up yourself, I presume? How fucking stupid can you be? You're a disgrace to the entire officer corps, and I'm being polite! You thought Xinjiang was a shitty posting? I'll make sure you'll end up in some godforsaken backwater in Tibet, counting prayer beads atop Mount Everest! That'll teach you! What did the man look like?"

"He was quite tall. Muscular. Square jaw. Seemed like the genuine article. Impeccable uniform. Although, now that you've asked, come to think of it, he was perhaps not Han Chinese."

"And what makes you think that?"

"Hmm...his eyes. They looked like those of the locals around here. Quite clear. Actually not unlike yours, if I may say so. Although, of course, you're clearly one of us, Major. Forgive me, I was just trying to make a point."

"So, after you made the call, they just took everything and left?"

"Well, we helped them load the truck. There were only three of them, you see, the officer and the two drivers. It would have taken all night otherwise."

"I just can't fucking believe what I'm hearing," said Xie with a sigh.

"But what else could we have done? After all, he was a senior officer."

"So this would have taken a few hours, at least?"

"About two hours. It was quite a long and detailed list of equipment. After that, they left just as they had arrived, maybe around ten."

"You didn't find it strange that there was no armed escort protection for such a sensitive convoy, traveling late at night?"

"Well, not at the time. But of course, now that you've mentioned it, it actually does seem a bit unusual."

"With Uyghur terrorists at large in the region, it should

have rung alarm bells, Captain. Of course, if they did come across some of these Muslim dogs later, and a little bird tells me that they did, they were probably greeted with open arms as they laughed all the way to Kashgar! Did you at least keep a record of the registration marks of the two vehicles?"

"Of course, it's all here," he said, handing over a small file that contained his report. "And I've also taken the liberty of printing pictures of these men from the security video. The film was very grainy—unfortunately, there were some issues with maintenance of the cameras, it appears."

"Issues with maintenance? Does anything ever fucking work in this joint?"

"But the footage might perhaps still help, Major. We can then issue orders for these men to be intercepted."

"At least you're finally starting to talk some sense," said Xie, looking into the distance from a window in the captain's office.

"Why, thank you, Major...Say, you're quite young for such a senior rank," he added in a sultry voice. "You really must have great *guanxi*. Is your father a general? And, allow me to be quite daring here, you're quite a looker, too. You'll go far, I can tell."

Xie Wei spun around and forcefully punched the captain, just once. She heard a loud crack as her fist met his elbow. He lost his balance and tripped, banging his head against the wall. He cried out in pain, his left hand grasping his forearm.

"Ahhh! You've just broken my arm!"

"Just be grateful I didn't break both! Good day to you, Captain."

Chapter 16

Muscat, Oman, September 2001

IT WAS 8:46 A.M. in New York when American Airlines Flight 11, a Boeing 767 with ninety-two passengers and crew members, crashed into floors 93 to 99 of the North Tower of the World Trade Center, instantly killing everyone onboard as well as hundreds of people within the building itself. The plane had taken off less than an hour before from Boston Logan airport and was en route to Los Angeles when Egyptian national Mohammed Atta, as well as other hijackers, put an abrupt end to its journey.

The time in Oman was nine hours ahead of New York's and there, as around the world, television programs were interrupted to broadcast the news. Temur did not pay much attention to the newscast at first, which he caught on a wall-mounted television in the hospital, as he wrapped up his duties for the day. But, as United Airlines Flight 175 also smashed into the South Tower at 9:03 a.m., he immediately understood what was happening. A faint smile lit his face.

"*Allahu Akbar!*" he whispered to himself.

The news then kept coming, fast. The Federal Aviation Authority banned all flights to New York and closed the surrounding airspace. Next, the Port Authority shut down all bridges and tunnels providing access to the city. At 9:31 a.m., President Bush spoke from Sarasota, Florida, where he was visiting an elementary school, citing an "apparent terrorist attack against the U.S." Only minutes later, other hijackers on American Airlines Flight 77 crashed a plane into the western façade of the Pentagon in Washington, D.C., killing the 59 people on board as well as 125 within the building.

A news anchor announced that all flights bound for, or over the continental United States were being diverted to other destinations and that the White House and the Capitol Building, among others, were being evacuated. Soon, the South Tower of the World Trade Center—one of New York's most iconic buildings, where an earlier bombing attempt had been foiled in 1993—collapsed.

"Oh my God, it's falling down! It's falling down! It's horrible!" said the journalist, engulfed by emotion, as she provided live commentary on the event.

Around Temur, a small group of workers from the hospital—doctors, nurses and janitors—had assembled. All were now focused on the small television screen. The news kept coming relentlessly. Nothing like this had ever happened before to the world's most powerful nation, at least not since Pearl Harbor, some sixty years earlier.

"Temur, what's up?" asked Gamal, a medical orderly in a white coat, who had just arrived on the scene. "What's happening?"

"America's under attack," he answered. "Planes have crashed into buildings in New York. Apparently, hundreds of people are dead. Maybe even thousands."

Soon, the news anchor announced that another plane, United Airlines Flight 93, had just crashed in Somerset County, Pennsylvania, after an attempt by some passengers at regaining control from yet another group of hijackers. As the story unfolded, the North Tower of the World Trade Center also crumbled to the ground, white smoke and debris now engulfing south Manhattan.

The scale and sophistication of the attack were unprecedented. Temur knew of only one man who could have planned and ordered its execution: Osama bin Laden.

Deep down, he resented not being part of the plan. How exhilarating it would have been to hold the stick of an aircraft, steering it toward a high-rise building, bringing jihad to a hated country!

But he had his own mission to accomplish. He needed to be patient, bin Laden had said, and wait for the signal that would ultimately put him on a collision course with infidel nations. Meanwhile, the unbelievers in the U.S. and their allies would now no doubt come down with great force on the mujahideen, in a war that would define the new century.

It had been more than five years since he had met the leader of al Qaeda in Peshawar, and Temur had just turned twenty-one. He had followed the instructions given to him that night in northeastern Pakistan, soon thereafter making his way to the Persian Gulf and arriving by boat in Muscat, the capital of the Sultanate of Oman.

As the wooden *dhow* that had ferried him from Karachi alongside a disparate cargo of goods, including textiles, food and electronics, had anchored, a man in his fifties called Aziz Mohammad had been waiting for him on the dock.

Aziz was a chubby, bespectacled fellow with a fondness for pistachios, but he was also a longstanding member of the Muslim Brotherhood who had spent time in Afghanistan alongside bin Laden and a fellow Egyptian, Ayman al-Zawahiri. The latter had been involved in the earlier bombings of the U.S. embassies in Dar es Salaam in Tanzania and Nairobi in Kenya, as well as that of the USS Cole in the Yemeni port of Aden. Like Zawahiri, Aziz was a doctor by profession and worked at a clinic in Oman.

Cautiously, Aziz had first established Temur's identity by asking him to respond to a coded phrase, one of the Hadith of the Holy Quran. Temur had provided the correct answer, and they had then gone together toward the bazaar, which extended beyond the *corniche*, the promenade on the waterfront, in a small maze of alleyways. They had exited at the other end, where a car was waiting to take them to Aziz's house at the other end of town, near the airport, close to where the Chedi Hotel would open a couple of years later. Aziz had taken him in at his house with no questions asked.

In Oman, thanks to Aziz, Temur completed his second-ary education and enrolled with the first intake of the Oman Medical College in 2001. Ironically, it was a U.S.-style private institution, affiliated with West Virginia University. Temur had just started a four-and-a-half-year program that led to a bachelor of pharmacy degree. Theoretical lectures in biology, chemistry, pharmacology and, of course, pharmacy, among other topics, alternated with practical training. Temur was helping as a volunteer at the hospital pharmacy the day the hijacked airplanes had rammed the twin towers.

It was humbling to have to return to school while some

of his fellow mujahideen continued jihad, but Temur knew that his day would come and, meanwhile, pursued his studies assiduously. He left the hospital and returned home but, that night, he was unable to focus on his homework. He turned on the television and watched, fascinated by the commentary on the events that were unfolding on the eastern American seaboard. At four in the morning, he collapsed on the sofa. When he awoke a few hours later, the television was still on. On the screen, President George W. Bush was now addressing the nation:

"These attacks are evil, despicable acts of terror," he said.

"America, its friends and its allies will stand together to win the war against terrorism," he added.

Temur switched off the TV set, gobbled down a quick breakfast and left for the Bousher Campus, to attend his first class of the day.

A couple months later, Temur saw President Bush again address a news conference along with French president Jacques Chirac.

"A coalition partner must do more than just express sympathy; a coalition partner must perform," the American leader said.

"That means different things for different nations. Some nations don't want to contribute troops, and we understand that. Other nations can contribute intelligence sharing. But all nations, if they want to fight terror, must do something," he continued.

"Over time, it's going to be important for nations to

know they will be held accountable for inactivity," he finally said.

"You're either with us or against us in the fight against terror."

Temur smiled. He knew exactly which side he was on.

Chapter 17

ERWAN TANGUY HAD returned to see The Bear to convey what he had discovered about Xie Wei. The colonel was yet again in a bad mood, but that was nothing special. In truth, the contrary would have been worrying.

"So, she was Chinese all right," he said, as a faint smile illuminated his rugged face. "Just as we both thought."

"Indeed. And she looks like a pretty tough cookie, too. Of course, we already knew that, given the carnage she left behind back in Johor."

"Special Forces, eh? Siberian Tiger unit, you said? She's right up your alley, Tanguy, a cold-blooded killer. Any idea where she might be now?"

"We're working on it, but she's most certainly back in China. She'd have had no reason to stay put down south. Just like me."

"Makes sense. Well, thanks to you, I now have my work cut out to find out whether the Chinese have infiltrated one or even more of our stations in Asia. It was bound to happen sooner rather than later, I guess. Darret has a clean record, but he's been there for too long and may have gone soft. The Chinese are becoming increasingly assertive, too. It seems their level of testosterone increases in sync with their GDP, these days. Who's that girl again, the one you met the evening before?"

"Her name's Lilly Ling. On our payroll from time to time, but not formally employed by the service. Malaysian Chinese, as it happens. Grandparents killed by Muslim fanatics at the time of independence, or so she said. Darret would know the full background to the story. She claimed a longstanding loyalty to France but, thinking of it further now, maybe I'm not so sure."

"She's going straight to the top of my list of possible moles."

"Do you want me to return to Singapore, to take care of things, so to speak, just in case?"

"Absolutely not! To start with, she knows what you look like, and seeing you again so soon after what happened would ring alarm bells. Let's not assume she's anything other than smart. I'm ordering you to stand down the case. I don't want another fuck-up. You've done enough already. Do I make myself clear, Tanguy?"

"Crystal clear, Sir."

"Good."

"We seemed to get along well, though," he added. "I don't think she'd have cause for suspicion, really."

Tanguy recalled Lilly Ling's sweet kiss in the car that evening in Johor, as she had squeezed his hand before leaving him to accomplish his mission. Another meeting would clearly not qualify as a hardship.

"Don't go rogue on me, Tanguy! You're staying put. And don't make me say it again! Meanwhile, try to locate that Xie Wei bitch. If she steps outside of China, we might even get an opportunity for an unfriendly chat, if you see what I mean! Unless she beats the crap out of you beforehand, as she did with those Abu Sayyaf fellows."

Tanguy didn't pick up on Le Pan's insult. Deep inside, he knew that any encounter with Xie would be brutal, perhaps even deadly.

"I'll see if I can track her down."

"Good. Now, go execute. Over," said The Bear, effectively dismissing him with another wave of one of his impossibly thick hands.

Erwan Tanguy stood to attention and left the room.

He thought the SL could fairly easily trace Xie Wei. Monitoring the movements of the Special Forces unit in Shenyang would probably soon point to her whereabouts, one way or the other. From there on, the DGSE could get a fix on her. The opportunity to intercept her communications or even abduct her would come next. He made a request for Boissard to see if he could find anything and alert him through his inbox. There wasn't all that much he could do in the meantime.

His mind was still focused on the possibility of seeing Lilly Ling again. If she indeed was a mole, the trail would lead to Xie in any event, and he could kill two birds with one stone. Of course, Le Pan's instructions had been unambiguous, but it wouldn't be the first time Tanguy had cut a few corners.

He left La Piscine and walked for about twenty minutes in adjacent streets. Through a series of abrupt U-turns, stops in front of bow windows and trips through a couple of underground passages, he ascertained no one was following him.

Next, he entered a building that rented self-storage units to both individuals and corporate clients. The business catered to people who were moving or renovating houses, or who were posted abroad for a substantial period of time. Larger boxes were used to deposit equipment, archival documents or even non-perishable goods.

Tanguy had long kept several storage boxes at various places dotted around the French capital. They were in anonymous locations, and all that was needed to rent one was an ID with a photograph, the authenticity of which no one ever bothered to check. Access to the premises was through a personal electronic code, which only allowed access to the floor on which the rented unit was located. It was possible to gain access seven days a week between the hours of six in the morning and ten at night, which suited his purpose perfectly.

In his personal box were several passports of various nationalities, all bearing his photograph, but all slightly different and in different names. They were perfect fakes and would enable him to travel discreetly, below the radar of even the DGSE. He selected a Belgian passport in the name of Jean-Claude van der Welde and pocketed rolls of assorted currency—U.S. dollars, Euros and Singapore dollars—but left the couple of firearms and assorted ammunition the storage unit also contained behind.

He then went to a nearby travel agency and booked himself an economy-class ticket to Changi Airport, Singapore. Traveling cattle class sucked, especially for such a long journey, but it would be more discreet and he could also pay for the ticket in cash. The cost of a business-class ticket would be above the threshold, and payment by credit card would be required under new anti-money-laundering rules that had just come into force. It wasn't a direct flight. There was a short connection in Abu Dhabi, which would muddy the waters further, should anyone take interest in the travels of M. van der Welde.

It was a Thursday. The following Monday was a bank holiday of the kind France is famous for, and he reckoned he had a few full days ahead of him to investigate what Lilly Ling was up to before The Bear managed to find out what he was doing and all hell broke loose in the service. The flight left later that same afternoon. He still had a couple of hours to pack and make his way to Charles de Gaulle Airport.

As he left the shop, he saw the street was jam-packed with taxi drivers protesting against unfair competition by mini cabs and drivers that hailed business through mobile applications. They kept blowing their horns and were visibly outraged.

"This country's beyond salvation," he sighed, as he descended the stairs to a metro station, blending in with dozens of other anonymous travelers.

Chapter 18

Xinjiang, China, February 2016

AFTER CAPTAIN CHAN had left to have his broken arm attended to, Xie Wei sat at his desk in his office and grabbed the documents he had gathered for her to look over. The room was functional, with hardly any personal touch in sight. Clearly, the captain hated his posting in Xinjiang. The climate was harsh, the food didn't agree with him and the population was hostile, especially toward anyone in uniform. He was probably not expecting to be stationed there for long. How wrong he was. She would see to that.

Xie Wei sipped a tepid tea from a canteen cup, adjusted the desk lamp and focused her attention on the dossier that lay open on the bare wooden, standard army-issue table.

She started with the registration marks of the two vehicles. The EQ2050 was, in effect, the Chinese equivalent of the American Humvee and, as such, a relatively recent model. It was built by Dongfeng Motors and was better known by the name of Mengshi, meaning "fierce warrior." By contrast, the Jiefang CA-390 was an all-purpose sixty-ton dump truck, widely used across all units of the PLA and largely copied from the Russian ZIL models. It was much older, by at least three decades, and a much more common vehicle. It would probably be very difficult to track that one down.

As she had expected, a few telephone calls confirmed that both registration marks were fakes. No surprises there. In addition, while many Jiefang trucks would have been sold or reconditioned over the years, no military EQs had been reported missing and all could be accounted for.

However, she knew there was also a civilian version of the Mengshi, known as the Hanma. It was not inconceivable that one could have been painted and disguised as a military vehicle. It was the perfect car to show off one's wealth, and a number of newly rich would have acquired it for that very purpose, especially those living in China's more remote regions, where its four-by-four transmission could come in handy. While not an old model *per se*, it had still been in production for seven or eight years, so any enquiries down that route would likely take time, especially if the car had come from outside Xinjiang. And time was not something she really could spare right now, if she wanted to catch the perpetrators.

The photographs, stills from the footage of the security videos, were also close to useless. As Chan had said, they were very grainy. The uniforms worn by the men were still fairly recognizable, though—all *bona fide* PLA issue—but the film had been shot from too far away for their faces to be readily identified. Maybe the footage could be enhanced, but she doubted it.

Acquiring uniforms would be child's play. Soldiers who had previously served, or who were even currently in service within the PLA, would have access to all manner of equipment. And they numbered several million. Faking rank tabs, badges and patches also wouldn't be too difficult, nor would faking identity documents. China wasn't known as the world's factory for nothing, and some of these might even be authentic, for all she knew!

The list of equipment that had been stolen was chilling. The terrorists had staged an impressive heist, only stopping short of acquiring heavy artillery—but that would be another kettle of fish altogether. There was enough hardware to mount sizeable attacks on several PLA outposts. If these were successful, then the assailants would lay their hands on yet more arms. Before long, Xinjiang could become even more of a tinderbox than it already was. She had to track down and destroy those responsible. Fast.

That left only one avenue to pursue—the telephone number dialed by the man who had impersonated the major from Kashgar. After another couple of calls summoning the data and a twenty-minute wait, she had the information. It was a mobile telephone number of the pre-paid variety. No doubt its user had pretended to be someone in a position of authority at the headquarters barracks in Lanzhou and was for sure pretty good at it; she had to give him that. Chan was a dumbhead, no question about it, but he dealt with Lanzhou on an almost daily basis and even he had been fooled.

Maybe the impersonator had served there at some point in time, and therefore knew the drill and routine. Perhaps she could dig in that direction, too, but again, finding out would most certainly take time. Meanwhile, things might get worse before they got better.

The SIM card would have been paid for in cash, so the user would, in theory, be untraceable. However, that number may well have been used before, and perhaps several times. If a pattern could be established, she might uncover something. And then…

Xie Wei dialed yet another number. The beauty of China was that everything was centralized, and also that everyone had a mortal fear of State security, which suited her just fine.

More than twenty thousand geeks worked in the third directorate of the general headquarters of the PLA, also known as the *san bu*. Their responsibility was the interception of communications, through dozens of listening stations dotted around the country. The largest was based in Beijing, in the district of Xibeiwang. There were also several in Xinjiang itself: one in Dinyuanchen, which primarily targeted communications emitted by Russia, and another in Changli, near Urumqi, which focused, among other things, on satellite communications.

The request she made to Beijing was in turn relayed to Changli, stressing a national security matter of extreme urgency. After forty minutes, she had a list of all the calls made and received on the mobile telephone number since the SIM card had first been activated. There were only a handful, fewer than she had hoped.

The GPS locations were also stated, all in busy areas within some of the larger cities in Xinjiang. The user was no fool. Finding him or her would be like trying to locate a needle in a haystack.

However, two of the calls received were from the same

number. That sounded perhaps more promising. It certainly wasn't a random event. If in turn that number were more active, there would be patterns, because people have routines. Its owner might therefore have unwittingly created a geoprofile of where he or she might be based. And then Xie would strike, relentlessly, until all of those Muslim bastards were terminated.

She next called Beijing again, with another request for big data analysis. She had to shrink that haystack.

Chapter 19

Abbottabad, Pakistan, May 2011

THE FIRST UH-60 Black Hawk helicopter shook violently as it experienced a hazardous airflow that caused a sudden loss of lift. The pilot tried his best to control the vortex ring state but, by then, the sixteen-foot-high concrete walls of the house's compound had stopped the rotor downwash from diffusing. The raid had previously been rehearsed a number of times, but always on a mock target enclosed by a loose wire mesh fence, rather than the brick and mortar wall that actually surrounded the house, making for unforeseen landing conditions at the time of the assault.

The chopper's tail rotor hit one of the walls, sending the aircraft into a soft crash landing as it rolled onto its side. The pilot chose to bury its nose into the ground to stop it from tipping over, as it finally came to rest against the wall at a forty-five-degree angle, unable to ever fly again. The helicopter had been heavily modified as an experimental stealth aircraft to make it fly more quietly, therefore also making it harder to detect by radar, but its actual landing was anything but discreet. Soon enough, dogs started to bark in the distance.

Seeing this, the pilot of the second helicopter chose to

land safely outside of the compound to avoid a repeat of the incident. Its cargo of U.S. Navy SEALs from the Red Squadron of the Joint Special Operations Command's U.S. Naval Special Warfare Development Group (DEVGRU, more commonly known as SEAL Team Six, the name of its predecessor) quickly disembarked and scaled the walls that were only summarily protected by barbed wire, entering the grounds.

A dog handler with a Belgian Malinois named Cairo, along with four of the commandos armed with Heckler & Koch H416 military assault rifles, as well as an interpreter, stood guard outside to alert the assault team to any approaching party. The dog would later also be used to find any hidden rooms, once the SEALs were safely in the house.

The assailants blew up the doors to the main building to gain access. The time was now close to one in the morning, and the operation that had been code-named Neptune Spear had entered its most delicate phase. The mission's name had been chosen after the trident featured on the Navy SEALs' insignia, the three prongs of the Sea God's spear representing the Special Forces' operating capabilities on sea, in the air and on land. To those in the know, the insignia was otherwise also known as "The Budweiser," because of its resemblance to the Anheuser-Busch eagle logo.

The night was dark, as the raid had been purposefully scheduled at a time of little moonlight, and there was also no light inside the house, as CIA operatives had previously cut the power to the surrounding area. The SEALs, however, were each equipped with L-3 GPVNG-18 ground panoramic night vision goggles, with four image-intensifier tubes and four separate objective lenses arrayed in a panoramic orientation. The two center lenses of each unit pointed forward, giving their user more depth perception, while two other tubes pointed slightly outward from the center to increase peripheral view. Any target that came within their field of vision would stand out almost as if in full daylight, even in complete darkness.

The main building was three floors high and would be cleared from the ground up. As the first team of SEALs entered the house, they were immediately fired upon with an AK-47 from behind the door of the adjacent guesthouse. A short firefight ensued, ending with the death of Abu Ahmed al-Kuwaiti, the man later revealed to have been Osama bin Laden's courier. It was he who had unwittingly led the CIA to their target at the end of this narrow dirt road, two and a half miles from the city center of Abbottabad, on the far-eastern Pakistani frontier with India.

The SEALs then moved forward into the house, meeting minimal resistance, wounding al-Kuwaiti's wife and killing his brother, Abrar, as well as the latter's wife, Bushra. The building was also home to a number of other women and children, located throughout. Some were even found later on the balcony of the house's third floor, behind a privacy wall that stood more than six-and-a-half-feet tall and whose sole purpose was to hide from view bin Laden himself, whose considerable height was six foot three. They were all rounded up and restrained with plastic handcuffs as bin Laden's adult son, Khalid, was shot dead after confronting the assailants.

As the SEALs reached the third floor, they finally encountered bin Laden himself, dressed in *kurta* pajamas, and took a first shot at him as he swiftly retreated to the safety of his own bedroom. One of his wives had inadvertently called him by name, helping the commandos to home in on their target.

The mission was unambiguously a kill operation; it was never the SEALs' intention to capture the leader of al Qaeda alive. They punched through the room's door, as another of bin Laden's wives screamed in Arabic. She was shot in the foot as 5.56-mm NATO 77-grain open-tip match rounds were unleashed on her husband, ending a hunt that had lasted for almost ten years.

"For God and country—Geronimo, Geronimo, Geronimo," radioed in the SEAL team leader.

"Team leader, please repeat. Over," asked Vice Admiral McRaven, the commander of the Joint Special Operations Command, by way of confirmation.

"Geronimo. EKIA," replied the SEAL, signaling "enemy killed in action." "Over."

Positive identification of bin Laden's body was conducted through facial identification, using a photograph taken at the attack's site and run through software operated by the CIA in Langley, Virginia. The body was also roughly measured, as a SEAL operator of known height lay down alongside bin Laden's corpse, prompting President Obama to cynically remark in the White House's Situation Room that "we donated a US$60 million helicopter to this operation. Could we not afford to buy a measuring tape?"

The remainder of the thirty-eight-minute raid was spent

recovering weapons, computer hard drives, thumb drives and cell phones as well as a variety of documents, for subsequent deciphering by CIA analysts.

The grounded helicopter was finally blown up to safeguard its classified technical features, just as bin Laden's body was taken away in a body bag in a back-up Chinook helicopter, together with the first team of SEALs.

After safely landing at Bagram Airfield, the largest U.S. military base in Afghanistan, the body was then flown to the aircraft carrier Carl Vinson in a V-22 Osprey tilt-rotor aircraft, escorted by two Navy fighter jets. There, after further DNA testing, the body was washed, wrapped in a white sheet and placed in a weighted plastic bag, before being lowered into the North Arabian Sea, after Muslim religious rites had been performed.

Such were the events that were reported across the globe, after a press conference by President Obama early on the morning of May 2, 2011. What was never told, however, were bin Laden's last words, spoken in a halting whisper, as he coughed up blood, succumbing to multiple shots fired by a H416 automatic rifle. Had the Arabic spoken by the operator who had squeezed the trigger extended beyond colloquial terms, he would perhaps have understood these words as follows:

"Temur...unleash the wrath of God!"

Chapter 20

Muscat, Oman, May 2011

LIKE MILLIONS AROUND the world, Temur Khan learned of bin Laden's demise through the media. Over the following days, he attempted to find out as much as he could about the circumstances that ultimately led to his one-time mentor's untimely death.

Even though an AKS-74U carbine and a Makarov pistol were found on a shelf near the door of his bedroom after he had been shot, bin Laden himself was seemingly unarmed at the time and had allegedly not presented a direct threat to the SEAL team. But they had received clear instructions to kill, rather than take him alive. While this had, unsurprisingly, not bothered the vast majority of the American public, opinion in Pakistan as well as across the Muslim world in general had been much more divided and, in many cases, openly critical of the far-reaching power of America's sword arm.

Among the many details of the operation, Temur even learned why the American flag patch on the SEALs' right shoulders was reversed, so the stars would never be shown facing backward.

It also transpired that the members of the military involved had been temporarily transferred to the CIA prior to executing the assault, so that there wouldn't be any legal issues with the mission. The United States was not at war with Pakistan, so its armed forces could not be seen as having waged what could amount to open hostilities in a foreign country and, even worse, one that was often viewed as an ally. *How twisted is that?* Temur thought.

Temur's mind switched from grief to anger but, for many years, he had known that such a day would ultimately come and had prepared accordingly.

"One day, eventually, the Americans and their allies will find me and perhaps even kill me. One cannot escape one's fate. But, when it finally happens, this is the day when you, Temur, must take over and pick up the torch to show the way to the world's True Believers. It may take years, but this will be the spark that ignites a wave of destruction such as the world has never known," the leader of al Qaeda had said, that evening in 1996, in Peshawar.

It had now been five years since Temur had graduated from the Oman Medical College, and he had worked in Oman's only JCI-accredited hospital ever since, where he was now responsible for the institution's pharmacy. It was a good position, even though the work was not particularly challenging.

Temur had been a gifted student and had even graduated with honors. Studying had not been too demanding of him. His studies had covered many topics, from biology to chemistry to pharmacology and, of course, pharmacy. But of particular interest to him had been pathophysiology and epidemiology.

In his spare time, Temur had delved with relish into the investigation of outbreaks of infectious diseases, going much deeper than what was outlined in the curriculum. He now had to actively start preparing for what would become his purpose in life. He embarked on the task meticulously. Temur was anything if not patient. No stone would be left unturned as he carefully planned when, how and where he would strike.

Almost four years after bin Laden's death, Temur was finally ready. In addition to planning his mission with the utmost care, he had relentlessly trained his body. He was now in peak physical condition. He could run marathons, something he never would have dreamed of before, and in a competitive time to boot. He had also become ruthlessly proficient at hand-to-hand combat and self-defense, either barehanded or with a bladed weapon. He spent some time at a shooting range to further hone the skills he had learned as a teenager in Central Asia's tribal areas. He might still look like a mature student but, unbeknown to everyone, he had become a very dangerous man.

Temur abruptly resigned and moved to Europe. Over the years, he had amassed few personal possessions. He sold some of these, and gave most of the proceeds to Muslim charities, before breaking the lease of the small apartment he rented downtown.

He first flew to Doha, in Qatar, and then onward to Madrid, in Spain, where he based himself in a small apartment not far from Plaza de España, at the western end of the Gran Via. It was a busy, popular area, bordered by some of the city's highest skyscrapers, including the Edificio España, a boxed building built in the 1950s in Franco's era. The adjacent streets were flush with tourists and immigrants alike, many from Latin America, Africa and the Maghreb, and also housed many shops, cinemas and fast-food outlets. He would be anonymous there.

It wasn't Art Nouveau or Modernist architecture, or even shopping opportunities on account of a much-weakened Euro, that had attracted Temur to Madrid. Of much more interest to him was the presence in the outskirts of the city of one of the world's fifty-eight biosafety level 4 (BSL-4) laboratories. The facility conducted research into viruses for which there was neither a cure nor measures for disease prevention. Most of the pathogens studied there were life-threatening.

For several years, Temur had patiently tracked a number of executives who worked at such sites, and he had amassed a great deal of information on them. Their activities were discreet by their very nature, but there were always symposiums held in one part of the globe or another in which he took particular interest, either through his studies, work at the hospital or even simple searches on the Internet. Finding lists of attendees at such events had been child's play.

Unearthing their profiles through social networks had followed. Vanity often prompted people to post more than they reasonably should. It was just human nature. Many of their professional credentials were openly available, sometimes with a variety of details, on LinkedIn or other open-access databases, while much of their private lives was similarly revealed for all to see on Facebook, Instagram, Twitter or Google Plus.

After scouting many names, Temur Khan finally set his sights on Vikas Gupta. A French national of Indian origin, Gupta had arrived in the Spanish capital in 2006, after working at the Microbial Containment Complex in Pune, near Mumbai, as well as at the Institut Pasteur in Paris, France. He was now based in Spain's only BSL-4 facility, in Alcobendas, close to Madrid's Adolfo Suárez international airport in Barajas.

Gupta lived on Calle Antonio Maura, one of Madrid's best addresses, in the district of Salamanca. The street's classical facades stretched from the western entrance of the Retiro Park to the Plaza de la Lealtad, which was fronted by the Ritz Hotel on one side and the Madrid Stock Exchange on the other.

Gupta was now in his mid-forties, of medium height and build, with prematurely gray hair and round metal glasses that framed a somewhat tired face. He enjoyed the life of a reasonably wealthy and no doubt well-qualified expatriate, with his wife, Deepika, and thirteen-year-old daughter, Parvati. Although the parents still struggled somewhat with Spanish, even after several years, their daughter had settled in well and made a number of friends of her age. For her part, Deepika enjoyed the leisurely existence of an expatriate housewife, which revolved around lunch with female friends, yoga classes and shopping expeditions on the Calle Serrano.

For weeks, Temur shadowed the three members of the family, becoming increasingly familiar with their respective routines.

Chapter 21

Madrid, Spain, March 2016

A FEW DAYS before the start of the Semana Santa, or Holy Week, celebrations, Vikas Gupta left home early for his office in Alcobendas in his BMW sedan, as he did every weekday.

Temur watched him drive away as he casually sat on a bench on the opposite side of Calle Antonio Maura from where the scientist lived. Gupta emerged from the underground parking lot and drove down the street in the direction of the Plaza de la Lealtad, then turned right in a northerly direction on the Paseo del Prado.

Temur knew that Gupta's wife and child were set to catch a flight at Barajas airport later that morning. They would first land at Paris Charles de Gaulle Airport and then connect with an Air France flight bound for Mumbai, where they planned to spend a couple of weeks, taking advantage of the week-long holidays in Spain. Gupta would remain in Madrid for the duration of their trip, catching up on work. No one there would question his wife's absence over the next few weeks, and the international school was generally understanding of the peripatetic lives many expat families lived.

Temur had previously parked a vehicle just in front of the building that housed the Guptas' apartment. It was an old SEAT Inca panel minivan. It had seen better days, and its white paint was scratched all over, but it was fully functional and, above all, anonymous. After a couple of minutes, it was clear that Gupta had not forgotten anything at home and would not return in a hurry, so Temur walked slowly back to the SEAT, in which he continued to wait, silent but alert, in the driver's seat.

He had already checked that there were no CCTV cameras in the street. There were two news kiosks at opposite ends of Calle Antonio Maura, but they were located far away from the building, as were a couple of café terraces, which, in any event, were usually empty. This was a residential area, with only a handful of shops, and there was almost no chance of a casual observer paying attention to what would ensue.

At about nine-thirty, Deepika and Parvati Gupta emerged from the front door at street level, pulling heavy wheeled suitcases behind them. They were already late for their first flight of the day, and they quickly crossed the wide pavement to hail a taxi on the street. Cabs were normally plentiful in Madrid, but it was already rush hour and none was in sight as they came level with the SEAT van.

Temur had seen them both approach in the rearview mirror and had already stepped outside of the vehicle. He went to the mother, quickly restraining her from behind as he pressed a thick white cloth to her nose and mouth.

He had previously soaked the cloth with desflurane, a highly fluorinated methyl ethyl ether, commonly used as an inhalational anesthetic. Procuring it had been child's play for a registered pharmacist. The agent was in liquid form at room temperature and had the most rapid onset of the volatile drugs used for general anesthesia, due to its low solubility in blood. Conversely, one of its drawbacks was a rapid offset, although by the time Deepika Gupta had recovered her senses, she would already be far from the swanky streets of Madrid's Salamanca district.

She immediately collapsed in his arms. Panicking, Parvati was about to scream at the sight of Temur, who was wearing a surgical mask for protection. He swiftly silenced her with a slap and sent her to sleep, just as he had done with her mother. He opened the van's wing doors and dropped both the woman and child on the floor of the rear compartment, along with their luggage. He climbed inside and secured their arms and legs with thick cable ties, after having gagged them with duct tape.

He waited for a few seconds to make sure no one had seen him, got into the driver's seat, started the engine and drove in the direction of the Carretera de Fuencarral, not far from where Vikas Gupta worked deep inside the Alcobendas biosafety lab.

After about twenty-five minutes, Temur arrived in the nearby municipality of San Sebastián de los Reyes. He turned onto a quiet street and stopped in front of a large metal garage door. He stepped outside of the van to unlock it and slowly drove the vehicle inside.

The place was unusually large, although there was nothing to betray its true size from outside. At the far end was an enclosed room, solidly built of concrete blocks, with a thick, sealed door and a heavy, triple-glazed window with a one-way mirror tint that would allow him to check on the room's occupants unobserved. All of the room's walls had been soundproofed. There was also a small basin for ablutions and a portable chemical toilet. Once in the garage, he locked the door to the street.

Deepika had by now fully awoken, although her daughter was still asleep. She had received the same dose as her mother, but it would take longer for the agent to dissipate in her case.

Leaving the luggage inside the van, Temur supported the mother as he brought her to the room before carrying Parvati to it. He cut their plastic restraints after having securely fastened two thick chains around them, each securely embedded in the back wall. The chains were long enough for the women to move freely in the room, but prevented them from reaching as far as the door or window. In a corner was enough water and food to last several weeks.

As he removed the duct tape, Deepika questioned him, haltingly:

"What do you want? And why are we here?"

"Mommy, I'm scared," called out her daughter in a plaintive voice, as her drowsiness also wore off.

Temur ignored them both and simply recorded a short video of them with a cheap digital camera. They looked very frightened, which was the effect he was trying to convey. He confiscated their mobile telephones and anything they might use to engineer an escape, such as keys or a metal nail file. He finally locked the door to the cell as they continued in vain to call out to him.

He searched their luggage for any other electronic devices that might give away their location if prompted, but found none.

Next to the SEAT van was another car, a small, inconspicuous Nissan. He opened the doors of the garage, started its engine and left, after securely locking the access doors again.

Within less than thirty minutes, he was back in the Salamanca district of the capital, where he left the Nissan in a public lot. He walked to the building where the Guptas lived and climbed the stairs to their apartment. After putting on disposable plastic gloves, he opened the front door with the set of keys he had taken from the mother. He already knew there was no alarm, and also that the family did not employ a domestic helper.

Once inside, he sat in the comfortable living room and patiently waited for the father to return.

Chapter 22

Xinjiang, China, March 2016

IT HAD TAKEN Xie Wei almost twenty-four hours, but she finally had a good lead. The terrorists had been careful with their use of telecommunications, making calls from what they thought were random locations, well away from arms caches, safe houses or even their own houses.

But, thanks to software that analyzed patterns, as well as GPS data provided unwittingly by the insurgents, she had been able to make significant headway. The hunt was now on in earnest, and she would soon go in for the kill.

The breakthrough had come as a result of the identifiers attached to all mobile communications.

The first one was the number of the SIM card, known as an IMSI (International Mobile Subscriber Identity). The other identifier was the unique number of the handset itself, or IMEI (International Mobile Station Equipment Identity). Its fifteen decimal digits included information on the origin, model and serial number of each device. Even the Iridium and Thuraya satellite phone networks used IMEI numbers on their transceiver units, as well as SIM cards, making their communications traceable.

The geeks at the MSS in Changli had previously identified within the Xinjiang region a number of calls for which there had been frequent changes between the IMSI and the IMEI. In other words, the owners of these handsets changed SIM cards often, in a bid to avoid detection. By comparing these communications with mobile numbers linked to the one dialed from Captain Chan's office at the time of the weapons heist, Xie Wei had found a match and finally zeroed in on a particular user.

Key to identifying the phone's location had been a GPS geocode. It had revealed precisely where a propaganda image posted online from the cellphone—a photograph of a black flag, embroidered with a call to jihad written in Arabic—had been taken. Even though Xie didn't yet know the name of the terrorist, she had a clear geographic profile that was just as actionable.

She was now on her way to the city of Hutubi, in a convoy of Mengshi four-wheel-drive vehicles, together with a number of fellow operatives from China's Special Forces. Hutubi was a sensitive location and home to an important underground gas storage facility, the largest of its kind in China and also the first large-scale auxiliary system to the west-east gas pipeline network. Hutubi had been brought to the media's attention following an explosion that had killed twenty-one coal miners in a well-publicized accident a few years before.

The Mengshis abruptly stopped in front of an anonymous house, two floors high, built of concrete and seemingly unfinished. Bags of cement and a sand pile framed an already well-worn door. The commandos, all clad in camouflaged uniforms, were armed with CS/LS5 submachine guns. They had red-dot scopes and foldable stocks for close-range combat, and each was capable of firing thirty 9x19-mm Parabellum cartridges.

The team kicked the door open and cleared the premises with alarming efficiency, rounding up the occupants, two Uyghurs in their mid-thirties. The men, who both wore skullcaps typical of their ethnic group, were clearly not expecting members of the military to break into the premises. Stunned, they handed over their ID cards to the soldiers as requested.

Xie Wei took a good look at them. She went to the first one and slapped him, hard, making him lose his balance.

"Where are the weapons that were stolen two days ago?" she asked loudly, her hard, piercing eyes totally focused on the task at hand. "Don't make me ask twice, *chan tou*," she warned him, using a derogatory term that meant something like "rag head."

"What…what weapons? I don't know what you're talking about," replied the Uyghur, defiantly, although his palm rested on the cheek that had received Xie's painful backhand strike.

"I said not to make me ask twice," countered Xie, as she shot a single round from her gun into the man's knee, shattering the kneecap and severing the cruciate ligaments. The man dropped to the floor, screaming in pain and flailing wildly, like a stunned fly that had hit a window panel.

Xie now turned her attention to the other man.

"I'd tell you if I knew anything, but I haven't stolen any weapons!" he screamed in a full-blown panic.

Xie unsheathed a push dagger. It was a short knife with

a T-shaped handle. The blade was now protruding between the second and third fingers of her clenched fist, less than an inch away from one of the man's eyes.

"Where are they?" she asked again.

The man was shaking, almost crying. A growing dark stain soon appeared across his thigh as he wet his loose cotton trousers.

"Don't tell them!" yelled the one who was lying on the floor, his hands locked around his knee, blood oozing through his clenched fingers.

Xie kicked him there with her combat boots. She heard a loud crack, and the pain made him lose consciousness.

"I will find out eventually. If you don't talk, you'll die. But, before that, we'll round up all the members of your family and execute them, one by one. I'll even enjoy doing it. Now, one last time, where are they?"

The man anxiously looked for clues from the other Uyghur who was lying motionless on the floor, but received no answer.

"Just...just outside Fu...Fukang," he finally said, between gasps.

"Chin, make sure he tells you where exactly," she next said to an impossibly tall non-commissioned officer, whose bulging muscles made his combat uniform appear several sizes too small.

"And I'll want a list of all those involved as soon as possible. I'm done here," she added.

Next, out of hearing range from the Uyghur, she added, for the benefit of the mountain of muscles: "Once you've recovered the gear, get these two to headquarters in

Lanzhou for enhanced questioning. We've wasted enough time."

The sergeant stood to attention and flashed a cruel smile.

As she was about to leave in one of the Mengshis, her cell phone rang. It was her commanding officer.

"It looks like we located the weapons. The men are heading there now and will soon round up all those responsible," she reported.

"Good work, Major. As usual! Now, I need you to travel to the Horn of Africa in a week's time, to represent the motherland. Military exercise. Hosted by the Republic of Djibouti. Desert theme. The Americans and the French will be there, as will the Brits and the Germans. As you may recall, that's where we recently established our first-ever foreign military outpost. While it's logistics only for now, the location's strategic and also key to our anti-piracy mission. The nation's One Belt, One Road initiative very much depends on it. Make us proud and compete with all your might!"

"Smash the Gang of Four!" Xie replied cheerfully, echoing the party slogan that had been in vogue just after Mao's death.

Chapter 23

Singapore, March 2016

ERWAN TANGUY WAS back in the Lion City. The shops there advertised winter clothes that looked suspiciously like beach wear, as a hot, oppressive humidity continued to engulf the former British colony. There were no seasons on the equator.

The flight had been uneventful, save for the relentless vocalizations of a couple of babies and, after a quick shower at a nondescript guest house on Joo Chiat Road, he was on his way to see Maurice Darret.

Darret's cover was as head of the French chamber of commerce. He was genuinely taken by surprise by Tanguy's visit when the latter turned up uninvited at his office.

"Mon Commandant," said Darret, "I wasn't aware you were back in town. What is the matter?"

"I'm here unofficially. The Bear doesn't know."

"I see. Eunice," said the chief of station, to his secretary, "I'll pop out for a while. Will you please take any messages?"

They walked together to a nearby mall and ordered drinks at a small coffee shop. There, they would blend in among office workers on a short break and expat housewives on shopping expeditions with toddlers in tow. The place was noisy but the tables well spaced. They would not run the risk of someone overhearing their conversation.

"So. What's the score?" asked Darret.

"You obviously recall what happened in Johor. We've now identified who killed Saadi and the Filipinos before I had a chance to get to them. Chinese. MSS. I'd like to meet that contact of yours, Lilly Ling, again. Something's not quite right about her."

"Erwan, old boy, as much as I'd like to help, I can't allow it. I won't let you compromise the integrity of my networks in Southeast Asia, and especially for the sake of a personal vendetta."

"Maurice, please hear me. It very much looks like that integrity's been compromised already! The Bear's concerned we may have a Chinese mole and, for once, I'm minded to agree with him. Where can I find her? And the sooner the better."

"So, what you're really saying is that the shit's going to hit the fan come what may. What's your plan?"

"I just want to talk to her. She had Saadi under surveillance, so it's likely either she or someone she was in contact with spilled the beans to the Guoanbu. Either way, we need to find out. Fast."

"Goddammit, Tanguy, you're not leaving me much of a choice! Okay, let me set up a meeting tonight."

"Where?"

"Let me think. There's a wine bar, upstairs from a Spanish restaurant called Qué Pasa, on Emerald Hill. It's off Orchard Road, near the Chatsworth international school. Be there at ten. I'll bring her to you."

"Thank you. And please don't tell Le Pan you've seen me. It's probably best if we can nip this in the bud before he finds out and sends in the cavalry all guns blazing."

"Tanguy?"

"Yes?"

"Please *do* stay put until tonight, will you? Catch up on your beauty sleep, have a swim, enjoy the sights, do a bit of shopping, but don't go stirring any more shit in the meantime."

"Roger that."

That evening, Tanguy left his hotel early. After grabbing a bite of surprisingly tasty chicken rice at a hawker center, he arrived well before the appointed time. He easily found the bar but decided to let Lilly Ling and Darret arrive first, and spent a good thirty minutes walking around the area to make sure he was familiar with all possible exit routes, should the events take a turn for the worse.

He then waited opposite Qué Pasa, seated on a bench. At ten on the dot, Maurice Darret arrived on foot from Hullet Road. He was alone. He spotted Tanguy right away and went straight to him.

"I'm afraid you were right."

"What do you mean?"

"Lilly's dead. I found her as I came to pick her up. She lived in Malaysia but also rented a small shop house in Singapore, off Club Street."

"What happened? And what did you do with the body?"

"Her throat was slit, not long before I got there. I carried her to my car and put the body in the trunk. There wasn't much time for anything else. Don't worry, no one saw me. I'll send a team to clean things up at her place, first thing in the morning. Do you want to see her?"

"Where are you parked?"

"In a side street, over there," he said, waving his hand in the distance. "Just one minute away."

"Sure. Lead on."

Tanguy followed Darret, who was wearing a large un-tucked batik shirt over a pair of jeans. It was early in the week and, even though Emerald Hill was a lively evening spot, the streets nearby were quiet.

"There, the blue Nissan," said Darret.

They scanned the area for any onlookers, but no one was around. Darret then unlocked the trunk. In it was the body of Lilly Ling, wrapped in a small tarp. There was a wide cut from one side of her throat to the other. Blood had spurted all over her clothes. It made for a gruesome sight, but at least she would have died quickly. Tanguy bent over, halfway inside the trunk, to take a closer look as Darret kept watch.

Suddenly, a sixth sense honed by years of covert work alerted him. For a split second, a flash of metal reflected light from a nearby street lamp and he spun around to face the danger. Darret was about to hit him with a *kukri*, a heavy Nepalese knife with a curved blade, similar to those used by the Gurkhas in the British army. The cutting edge was almost twelve inches long, and it was designed primarily for chopping. Darret would have hidden it under his colorful shirt, the back of which reached halfway down his thighs. No doubt he had also used it to kill Lilly Ling earlier.

Tanguy sprung back like a jack-in-the-box and grabbed Darret's wrist with his left hand, blocking the attack. He hit him on the base of the nose with the palm of his right hand, pushing upward. Cartilage broke on impact with a thudding sound. Blood oozed over Darret's face as broken pieces of bone were driven by Tanguy's strike into his brain. He collapsed to the ground, the knife falling on to the road with a sharp ping.

Tanguy finished him off with a kick. There was a sharp crack as Darret's head jerked back, before it finally rested at an odd angle.

Tanguy ascertained he was dead and placed the body in the trunk of the Nissan, atop that of Lilly Ling. He tore a piece of cloth from Darret's shirt and used it to pick up the kukri by its handle, so as to leave no fingerprints, and placed it in the car as well before locking and wiping off the outside of the trunk. He would drop the keys in a trash bin a few blocks away from there. Luckily, the whole thing had happened very fast and no one had spotted the commotion.

Tanguy now had to leave Singapore, fast. It might be too late to catch the last Singapore Airlines flight to Paris, but the Air France flight left almost an hour later. It was a shame not to have been able to learn more from Darret, but at least he had found the mole.

On his way to the airport Tanguy called The Bear on a secure mobile line.

"I don't have much time. I'm in Singapore."

"What the heck are you doing there? I'd ordered you to stand down."

"I found the mole. It was Darret. He tried to kill me but now he's dead. He also killed the girl. She was obviously clean. It was messy. I'm on my way back, tonight."

Le Pan unleashed a flurry of angry expletives for a full minute, before reason took over.

"What name are you traveling under? We'll pick you up on arrival at Charles de Gaulle."

"van der Welde. Jean-Claude."

"You don't say. I'll expect a full report from you the minute you've arrived in Paris. Oh, by the way, Tanguy, we've finally tracked that Chinese operative. As it happens, she'll be in Djibouti next week. Multi-nation military drill. The Chinese have just set up a naval base there. You're going, too. We'll embed you with the French contingent. I thought you'd enjoy being back in the field for a while. The desert air will do you good. And, *please*, try not to leave a mess behind this time."

Chapter 24

Madrid, Spain, March 2016

AROUND EIGHT O'CLOCK that evening, Vikas Gupta opened the front door to his rented apartment on Calle Antonio Maura. But, to his surprise, someone else turned on the lights before he had time to do so himself. In the living room, beyond the roomy hallway, was a man he didn't know, comfortably seated on a sofa. From a distance, he looked vaguely Arabic, although on closer inspection, his eyes were somewhat slanted, like those of a Chinese person, as well as light gray in color. He was smiling.

"Who are you? And how did you get here?" Gupta asked defiantly in English, very much annoyed.

"Please, Vikas, sit down. And take a good look at this," answered the man, handing him what looked like a cheap digital camera.

"Take your time," he added.

Gupta now noticed the man wore disposable plastic gloves, not unlike those he wore himself at the laboratory. This didn't bode well. Whoever he was, he was clearly wary of leaving fingerprints, which could only mean he had criminal intentions.

"How do you know my name? Do I know you? What do

you want? I don't have any money, or even valuables here," said the scientist.

"I don't care about your money, Vikas. And no, you don't know me, just yet. But I, on the other hand, know you rather well. And I have a feeling you and I will become rather close, in very short order. Please just take a look at the camera," said the man softly.

His English was good, nearly perfect. He spoke with almost no accent, save for a slight rolling of the Rs, which, Gupta thought, might indicate that he was from the Middle East or at least might have been educated there.

The scientist grabbed the cheap SLR, which was already switched on. On the back, on the LCD screen, was a video recording. He pressed the "play" button and immediately recognized his own wife and child. They looked tired and very frightened. Gupta lost his composure.

"What does this mean? What have you done with them? Where are they?"

"Now, listen to me very carefully, Vikas, so that we understand each other well," said the man. "You don't do as I say—they die. You call the police—they die. You tell anyone about me—they die. Are we clear?"

Gupta nodded. He kept thinking he would soon wake up from what turned out to be a bad dream, but the nightmare was very real.

"What is it you want?" he finally whispered. "I'll pay whatever's needed. I have a good job, but I'm not a wealthy man," he implored.

"I'm not after your money, Vikas; I've already told you that."

"What then?"

"It's very simple, really. I want you to steal vials of a betacoronavirus for me, specifically SARS coronavirus."

The Severe Acute Respiratory Syndrome was a viral respiratory illness. It had first appeared in Asia in late 2002. Hong Kong and Singapore, among other jurisdictions, had been particularly affected. Over the space of just a few months, it had spread to more than twenty-four countries across North and South America and Europe, as well as the rest of Asia, before the global outbreak was finally stopped.

SARS usually began with a high fever. Symptoms included headache, as well as other body aches. Some people presented mild respiratory symptoms at the outset, while many also contracted diarrhea. After a few days, patients often developed a dry cough, followed by pneumonia.

Transmission of the virus occurred through respiratory droplets when an infected person coughed or sneezed. The droplets were propelled through the air and deposited on the mucous membranes of the mouth, nose or eyes. The virus also spread through close personal contact or when people touched surfaces or objects already contaminated with infectious droplets and then touched one of the mucous membranes on their own face. Transmission could include anything from kissing or hugging to sharing drinks, food, or utensils. It was also widely believed (although it had not yet been proven) that SARS was an airborne disease, meaning it could spread more broadly through the air.

In 2003, a total of 8,098 people worldwide had contracted SARS. Of them, 774 had died. While spread of the virus could, over time, be contained, there was still no known cure.

"You're out of your mind," said Gupta.

"On the contrary, I know exactly what I'm doing."

"We don't store SARS pathogens in Alcobendas."

"Bullshit! Didn't you receive a shipment of fifteen-hundred samples several months ago from the Azienda Luigi Sacco in Milan?"

Vikas Gupta was taken aback. How could the man possibly know such a thing?

"Anyway, it can't be done," he said. "The virus wouldn't survive long outside the confines of the laboratory."

Temur Khan smiled. Viruses could quickly deteriorate as soon as they left their temperature-controlled space.

"Not if they have been freeze-dried first. In sterile ampoules. Double-vial preparations. Not filled to more than one-third and then stored at below 40 degrees Fahrenheit. I'll require at least two dozen of these."

Most lyophilized viruses could be stored for years and reconstituted when required by adding sterile, double-distilled water. Temur already knew that lyophilized SARS coronavirus had shown no significant reduction in activity after being revived, and that it had demonstrated good thermal stability.

Gupta gaped at him. This man was no ordinary criminal and clearly knew quite a lot about virology, as well as reviving freeze-dried microorganisms.

"I reckon you'd be able to do it all within a few days, a week at most. Now is the perfect time: a number of your colleagues are already on holidays for Semana Santa," said Temur.

"Even if I were able to do it, and that's a big if, there's still no way I could bypass the security procedures. The BSL-4 area is protected by supermax, fail-proof protocols. It just wouldn't work. I'd get caught immediately. Besides, what guarantees do I have that you haven't killed my family already, or that you won't kill me afterward?"

"Look at the time stamp on the video. It was taken barely a few hours ago. Now, just talk me through the safeguards in place," said Temur, not addressing Gupta's other concerns. "But first, I want you to call the family in India and say there's been a minor hospital emergency, and that Deepika and Parvati couldn't come in the end. I don't want them wondering why they haven't turned up."

Once that was done, Temur looked at him with a relentless gaze.

"Talk."

"I've signed papers. I'll lose my job just for telling you."

"Right now, that should really be the least of your concerns. Now, tell me."

"All right, then. This is a US$150 million facility, state-of-the-art, *first class*, the best of the best. It's one of the safest places on the planet to handle pathogens like SARS," said the scientist. "It's also one of only a handful of integrated BSL facilities in the world, with different levels of containment. The building includes a BSL-2, as well as a BSL-3, both of which act as feeders for the BSL-4 lab."

"Vikas, don't insult my intelligence. Tell me something I don't know."

"The BSL-4 is deep within the confines of the building, on the third floor, but security measures begin even outside the perimeter of the facility. First there are concrete barriers, U.S.-embassy standard. They would stop a truck traveling at high speed from entering the grounds and crashing in through the front door, which is at a distance of over fifty yards anyway. Next, all the fences are wired for motion detection. A mouse or rat would trigger the alarm. We actually had such an incident two months ago. All the deliveries are checked, as are all shipments departing the building. If there were a blaze or explosion, which is really unlikely given the training our staff receive, even the fire engines and firemen would still need to clear security first."

"What about access to the BSL-4 itself? As you said, the building also houses areas where lower clearance levels are required."

"True, but to enter all facilities, you still have to pass an iris scan. Both eyes. And forget what you read or saw in the movies: the scanner can't read dead eyes, so don't even think of cutting mine out! Next, you must undergo the equivalent of a very thorough airport scan, with a metal detector and an X-ray machine. That's both to go in and out of the building. And there are overhead cameras everywhere. Assuming you had the time, you wouldn't even be able to dig a tunnel: all the walls are twelve inches thick, with fourteen inches of heavily rebarred concrete flooring."

"How many people work there?"

"About fifteen, just for the BSL-4. That's quite a lot. But about a hundred in total in the whole building."

"How do you access the labs themselves?"

"First, you have to undress in a cloakroom with adjacent showers. There are separate facilities for men and women.

Once you've had a good scrub, you then change into underwear that's provided by the lab. At that point, the only personal item you may be allowed to keep on is a pair of glasses. Everything else, even a watch or any piece of jewelry, has to be removed."

"Go on," commanded Temur.

"Next, you must put on a full positive pressure suit, which is connected to an overhead air supply through a one-way valve, and plastic boots. To enter the hot side, you must pass through two stainless-steel doors set up as an air lock. You must punch in a code to deactivate the magnetic lock on the first door. The keypad also alerts the building automation system, so that the airflow automatically increases the pressure in the BSL-3 area and decreases it in the air lock. This ensures that high-pressure air flows into the air lock, trapping any airborne pathogens within the lab itself. As a rule, the deeper the level of containment, the lower the pressure. Any breach in the biocontainment protocols is literally sucked in by the negativity. Once a green light flashes, you can push the second door open and enter the BSL-4 area proper."

"How do things work inside the facility itself?"

"That's where we conduct all our research. Because sixty percent of the airflow in the suit goes to the head, it's very loud inside, so we use in-suit radio communication devices. Once you're on the hot side, there are in fact several labs rather than a single one, so that we can segregate pathogens. Most of what we do includes testing on animals to study how they react to contamination by infectious diseases. We use mice, rats, ferrets and also primates, of course. We have a lot of equipment there, too: there's a PET scanner, an MRI, an X-ray machine and CT scanners. All of these can reveal how, say, a hemorrhagic fever like Ebola rips apart a body that was healthy at the outset."

"And to exit the BSL-4 area?"

"The air lock you enter through also serves as a decontamination shower. For seven minutes, water and virus-killing chemicals are sprayed all over the pressure suits, before the door to BSL-3 can open again. We also rinse all metal equipment with chemicals and then further purify everything with an autoclave bake. All the water and decontamination chemicals from the sinks and showers collect in three separate tanks. They heat the waste fluids to almost 250 degrees Fahrenheit, killing anything that might have survived the disinfectant rinse."

"What about the rest of the plumbing and power cladding?"

"All our pipes are themselves housed within other pipes, with sensors to detect leaks. Even the fire-sprinkler heads are fitted with valves to prevent viruses from swimming up the pipes. For the same reason, there are no toilets anywhere within the confines of the BSL-4. All the systems in the facility are redundant. We have three energy feeds from two power substations and two generators that can run the entire facility for a full seventy-two hours, fully loaded."

"What would happen in the event of an emergency?"

"Everything and anything that could possibly happen has already been thought of—even an earthquake! Madrid isn't directly located on a seismic plate, but the floors of the BSL-4 are flexible and can move with a different resonance from the rest of the building. In the event of contamination, the rooms will fill with vaporized hydrogen peroxide or formaldehyde, depending on where the leak happens. The walls, light fixtures and even the electrical outlets are coated with multiple layers of epoxy resin, to ease cleanup. We have overhead HEPA filters and compressors everywhere. All the air that comes in, as well as out, is filtered. I tell you, that lab is like a box within a box."

"Are there areas where there are no cameras?"

"Only in the changing areas and suit room. Everywhere else is monitored twenty-four seven. But there are of course fewer cameras in the BSL-2 and BSL-3 labs."

"How does stock management work? I know you are one of only two people with access to the master stock."

"How could you possibly know that?"

"Answer me."

"There's also a code and an air lock to access the storage area, although since all the vials are sealed, there's no need to wear a full suit, so long as the samples themselves are not manipulated—unless there's a leak, of course. There are sensors everywhere, so we would know beforehand. But we still wear full-face masks, with powered air-purifying respirators, just in case. And, of course, there are HEPA filters there, too. Most of the master stock is frozen and stored at more than minus 200 degrees Fahrenheit, although some compounds are kept in more conventional freezers or even professional refrigerators. SARS falls in the latter category, and the stock we recently received is lyophilized. Anything that goes in, or out, is logged and requires two signatures. Any samples that go to the lab for research are systematically destroyed after manipulation. There's a one-way air lock between the storage area and the labs proper to deliver the working stock."

"Well, Vikas, you and I have got our work cut out. We'd better get cracking, then, if you ever want to see your family again."

"For the life of me, man, don't you understand?" implored Gupta. "This is one of the most secure places on earth! I'm very sorry, but it just can't be done!"

Chapter 25

Arta, Republic of Djibouti, March 2016

THE TEMPERATURE WAS almost 90 degrees Fahrenheit, and all those present could feel the effect of the hot, subtropical climate. The high humidity, due to the camp's proximity to the Gulf of Tadjoura, didn't help.

The barracks' official name was the CECAD, or Centre d'Entraînement au Combat et d'Aguerrissement de Djibouti, in truth a bit of a mouthful, probably coined by an overzealous staff officer in the French Ministry of Defense. Military forces the world over very much love their acronyms, and that was a prime example. The place had previously been known as Arta Plage and was at the end of a narrow and dusty unpaved trail.

The base had gone through a number of iterations until the departure in 2011 of the demi-brigade of the Foreign Legion that had run the place uninterrupted since the end of France's dirty war in Algeria. It was now a forward operating base—and as such used to support tactical operations—under the purview of the 5ᵉ régiment interarmes d'outre-mer (5ᵉ RIAOM), a mixed regiment of the French army composed of small infantry, artillery and armored units.

Its remit was to train soldiers, whether French or other

nationalities, for combat in harsh desert conditions. It was notorious for its grueling obstacle courses, both on land and in water. One of them required first scaling and then crossing on a zip-line a formidable cliff in the Dêr Ela valley on which a giant white skull and crossbones had been painted years before above the phrase "*voie de l'inconscient*" ("the way of the reckless"). The participants were also taught counterinsurgency and anti-guerilla tactics, as well as prepared to fight in conditions they might encounter in faraway postings, such as Afghanistan.

Run by France between 1894 and 1977, Djibouti was now an independent country, even though its former colonial master maintained a visible, although much reduced, military presence. French was still one of the country's official languages, along with Arabic. The republic's position on the Horn of Africa had, however, caught the attention of other foreign powers. To the north was Eritrea. Its western and southern borders were with Ethiopia and Somalia. To the east were the Red Sea and the Gulf of Aden, with some of the world's busiest shipping routes, most ultimately leading to the Suez Canal.

In 2001, the Djiboutian government had leased the former French military base of Camp Lemonnier to the United States. This had since expanded six-fold and was now home to 3,200 troops and civilian contractors, all under the authority of the AFRICOM—the U.S. Africa Command. Permanent apartment-style barracks had gradually replaced the temporary containerized living units (CLUs) stacked atop one another under the fierce East African sun.

This was also the most important base for U.S. drone

operations outside Afghanistan, with unmanned aircraft conducting missions in nearby Yemen and Somalia. More recently, China too had started to establish a naval base there, in support of its maritime Silk Road initiative.

The increasing jostling for influence in East Africa was the very reason why the government of President Ismail Omar Guelleh had decided, at short notice, to host military exercises so that each of the participating nations could showcase its military prowess. At stake were arm sales and trade contracts and, above all, an assured entitlement to maintaining a sizeable presence in one of the world's most strategic locations. Djibouti had an appalling human rights record but, clearly, no one really cared.

"Pissing contests don't get much bigger than this," thought Erwan Tanguy, standing to attention as the white, blue and green colors of Djibouti, on which a red star was also featured, were hoisted.

The briefing was being held at the CECAD, but the exercise was set up as a multi-day competition between units drawn from the U.S., Chinese, French and German Special Forces. The U.K. did not maintain a military presence in the republic, but it had also successfully lobbied for members of one of its SAS squadrons to participate, due to the corps' considerable experience in desert warfare.

Presumably, the Germans also fell into the latter category, on account of Rommel's Afrika Korps. Not everyone might agree these were credentials worth remembering, but there was no denying the wartime exploits of the Desert Fox.

The drills had been devised by the Djibouti armed forces and were now about to be revealed to all on the parade grounds by Colonel Saheed Ali, a veteran of the war with Eritrea.

"At ease," he commanded. "Officers, non-commissioned officers and enlisted men, a warm welcome to you all! First of all, I'd like to thank the 5ᵉ RIAOM and its commanding officer, Colonel Garnier, for kindly agreeing to put the facilities of this camp at our disposal for the duration of this event. Many soldiers have passed through these gates over the years and, no doubt, a number of you will already have done so yourselves. Please be worthy of all those, living or dead, who have preceded you! I trust the Djibouti Military Challenge will be a success and, I hope, only the first of many such events in the future," he continued.

"Today, in no particular order, we are pleased to be joined by two fire teams from SEAL Team 3, from the first U.S. Naval Special Warfare Group, which will be led by Lieutenant Commander Johnson of the Naval Amphibious Base in Coronado, California. Next, representing France will be a platoon from the Commando Trepel of the French Navy's Special Operations Forces Command, led by Commandant Marc from Lorient. From China, we are pleased to have a unit from the Shenyang Military Region Special Forces Unit of the People's Liberation Army. Leading that unit will be Major Xie Wei. From Germany will be the first Kampfschwimmereinsatzteam—I hope I've said that all right!—from the Commando Frogmen Company of the Kommando Spezialkräfte Marine, led by Stabshauptmann Müller."

Xie Wei was the only woman present and, as her name was called, whispers could be heard among the audience.

Unconcerned, the colonel continued his speech.

"And finally, from the United Kingdom, we're pleased to welcome two patrols from 18 Troop, D Squadron, of the 22 Special Air Service Regiment, which will be led by Captain St. Clair from Hereford," he finally said.

"The challenge will be held over four days, starting tomorrow morning at dawn. On the first day will be a land-based obstacle course, followed by another obstacle course, in the sea this time, on the following day. On the third day we'll have a shooting competition, including a sniper course as well as exercises in a kill house. And finally, on the last day there will be a sixty-two-mile march, with a few interesting surprises, to be completed within twenty-four hours. Can I please request your respective commanding officers to meet me on the ground floor of the white building that stands behind me at two p.m. today for a more detailed briefing? Meanwhile, I trust you've all settled in all right and wish you well for what's to come. Dinner will be at six. Good luck to you all!"

Colonel Ali next called everyone to attention before saluting, and then left the parade ground. But Erwan Tanguy, embedded with the French Commandos Marine, had long stopped listening, his attention fully focused on Xie Wei, the Chinese major who had killed Saadi and his Filipino associates in Johor Bahru. It seemed she had not yet recognized him. She had no reason to expect him to be in Djibouti. He was also there incognito, under a different name and rank.

The next few days would be far from a walk in the park, but getting close to Xie, let alone finding out what she knew, might be harder still. He grabbed his equipment and walked to the tent assigned to the French contingent for a quick bite and some strategy planning. French flags were affixed on Velcro patches, underneath the word "France" on the sleeves of his combat shirt, as well as on his Bergen rucksack.

In the distance, a *muezzin* called the faithful to Zuhr, the second prayer of the day, as waves died on the nearby beach.

Chapter 26

Arta, Republic of Djibouti, March 2016

THERE HAD BEEN no chance to approach the Chinese major at dinner. This was, after all, not a social occasion and, after a courteous but brief greeting, each of the five teams had chosen to eat at separate tables in preparation for the competitive events of the ensuing days. She had still shown no inkling that she had recognized Tanguy, but that didn't necessarily mean that was the case.

Unsurprisingly, the French had quickly taken an early lead. All of them had attended training at the CECAD (or its predecessors) at one point or another in their military careers, and they were therefore familiar with the course established by their forefathers, as well as the techniques necessary to master the various obstacles along the track. Peak physical condition was obviously a must, but above all, it was really all about sheer willpower. Giving up usually wasn't for lack of strength, but rather, because of an inability to maintain a positive mindset, something for which their Special Forces training had well prepared all the competitors.

The weather and hilly terrain, however, had already started taking their toll on the participants. The operators had had to scale nets, cross deep precipices over metal beams, ropes, or perilously swinging zip-lines and rappel down impossibly steep cliffs and rock formations, all under the unforgiving African sun.

At various stations, sweaty, dehydrated and out of breath, they'd had to shoot live ammunition at targets to test their stamina, endurance and ability to react under stress. Constantly going up and down peaks around the course and under the sun made for an elevated heart rate. Succeeding came down to making a speedy recovery after each stage before tackling the next station.

This was a team event, and it was also timed, so what mattered most was the speed achieved by the last competitor within any one team. At this early stage, the scores were still close, although the Americans had already been penalized after one of the SEALs had broken a leg in a bad fall. For him, the Djibouti Military Challenge was over. War in the desert was without mercy.

Tanguy had been able to observe Xie's performance at leisure, as the Chinese team had taken over from the French on the obstacle course. She was good, very good. Even though she was unfamiliar with both the terrain and course, she had completed the latter pretty much on par with his own personal time, leading the Chinese into second position. She was certainly a formidable adversary. There was no pussyfooting, as far as she was concerned.

Following the first evening, all the meals had been taken in separate quarters and everyone had gone to bed early. It had been a long and grueling day.

On the morning of the second day, the commandos, in

full combat gear including personal weapons, had all boarded motorized rubber boats at dawn when the weather was marginally cooler and the teams had, one by one, been dropped into the ocean. They then had to swim to the wooden and metal structures of the nautical assault course, in a sea known for regular shark sightings.

Soaked and considerably weighed down by the water that permeated their combat uniforms, boots and backpacks, they'd had to climb up ropes and scramble atop floating pontoons, as well as cross underwater obstacles, before a long swim back to shore for yet more shooting at targets.

This time, the SEALs had been in their element and had passed with flying colors, followed by the French and British SAS, with little difference between them. The German unit of frogmen hadn't done too badly, but it still lagged behind. It had been a particularly bad day for the Chinese, although Tanguy had noticed that Xie herself had shone through on water as she had on land. Pain and exhaustion appeared to have no hold on her, and whispers around her now came from respect, rather than to cast a slur.

The Djiboutians, however, kept a lid on the overall tally. Not knowing where one's team stood was also par for the course. Tanguy reckoned the Commandos Marine and the SAS were probably on top, followed by the SEALs on account of their now-reduced team, the Germans and, finally, the Chinese, because of their latest setback. But there was no way of knowing for sure.

As the day came to an end, he had already decided that the sixty-two-mile march would constitute his best chance to talk to Xie. While it had to be completed in under twenty-four hours, much of the test would be about map reading and orientation, as well as the contestants' ability to reach and capture an enemy position undetected. The five teams would start at different locations, but they would encounter each other as they all neared their target. He would certainly get an opportunity to pin her down then, or even immediately after the event, when she would be no longer on edge.

By the third morning, a certain routine had emerged for the competitors, who now assembled on the parade ground. That day's events would be all about marksmanship. They would use weapons they were all familiar with, which, in theory, would even the odds.

First came shooting at still targets at various distances, with pistols and submachine guns, followed by more firing at moving boards. Most participants from the Western countries used SIG Sauer P226 or Glock 19 sidearms, as well as Colt M4 or Heckler & Koch HK416 automatic rifles. As far as sidearms were concerned, many operators favored the Glock. Its barrel height stood low above the hand, so it was easy to aim accurately because it was almost like pointing your finger at your target. For their own part, the Chinese preferred national weapons, including QSW-06 pistols and CS/LR6 submachine guns.

Next came long-range shooting, with sniper teams required to hit a variety of targets at distances varying between 985 and 2,600 feet. So many rounds were shot simultaneously that Tanguy quickly lost count. It had become near impossible to keep a tally at this stage, and no one other than the Djiboutians knew where each team actually stood.

After a quick lunch break, they all moved to the kill

house, a purpose-built building with a variety of rooms, corridors and staircases, complete with doors, windows, furniture, fixtures and fittings. Inside were man-size cardboard targets representing both hostages and terrorists. The name of the game was to eliminate as many terrorists as possible in the least amount of time, without in turn injuring, let alone killing, any of the hostages.

The teams went in, one after the other, unleashing volleys of live ammunition with a deafening roar, clearing one room after the other, as observers from the Djibouti Armed Forces kept count, impassible as always. The walls of the kill house had previously been coated with layers of rubber, to avoid bullet ricochets.

"Corridor, clear! Room, clear!" could be heard repeatedly inside, as the hours of the afternoon passed.

Pretty much all of those taking part had already been in real hostage-liberation situations, including, for some, in African countries. In 2008, Erwan Tanguy had been part of a French force that had captured Somali pirates after they had successfully taken hostage the passengers from the *Ponant*, a three-hundred-foot, three-masted luxury cruise ship, on her way back from the Seychelles. He had shot the engine of their escape vehicle with a McMillan TAC-50 rifle from a Panther helicopter flying overhead, bringing it to an immediate halt. Six men had been captured and part of the ransom recovered. The operation, off the coast of Puntland in northeastern Somalia, had been code-named *Thalathine*, which meant "thirty" in the Somali language, the number of people who had been captured at gunpoint by the pirates.

All Special Forces had their own kill houses, although

the SAS had been pioneers in this field and were, this time, expected by Tanguy to come out on top.

As they retired for the night, the mercury finally dropped below 85 degrees Fahrenheit. But lying on his cot, Erwan Tanguy was unable to fall asleep. The following morning, he would finally face the inscrutable Xie and attempt to seek answers to his questions. Beyond the dunes that surrounded the camp, a jackal called as a pink moon majestically rose over the desert. Around two in the morning, he finally shut his eyes and everything went black.

Chapter 27

Madrid, Spain, March 2016

THEY HAD BRAINSTORMED a good part of the night, trying to identify a flaw in the BSL-4 facility's security system. Gupta was reluctant to expand on what he had already revealed but, with his family abducted, he didn't really have a choice. Temur Khan had also told him he was only a cog in a much larger organization and that his accomplices would have no hesitation in killing his wife and child, should he decline to play ball. Finally, around one in the morning, they both agreed on a course of action that they reckoned had a good chance of success.

The following morning, Temur and Gupta left the apartment for about an hour. They returned with several shopping bags and a pair of Lofstrand crutches. Just after eleven, the scientist called in sick.

"Juan-Maria," he said, as one of his colleagues answered the phone. "¡Hombre! You know what? I fell in the staircase last night. Bloody stupid of me! I had go to the hospital. Bad timing, really; my wife had just left for India. I'll be fine, but thank you. Yes, a bloody plaster cast! Apparently one of these new plastic walking casts just won't do, for some reason. Pretty much half of my right leg, for at least a month, but I should be back in the office by tomorrow morning, at the latest. Maybe even this afternoon, depending on how things go. One thing's for sure, though—I won't be wearing any space suits for a least a month!"

"Perfect," said Temur. "Now, let's make that cast, shall we?"

Once Gupta had undressed, Temur donned plastic gloves, unrolled a stockinet knitted of stretch fabric and slid it over the scientist's right calf, after having cut the end with scissors so his toes could wiggle freely. He then affixed a cast padding, wrapping it tightly around the foot and ankle and stopping just below the knee. He soaked plaster rolls in a basin filled with warm water, their edges facing upward. Once they had softened all the way through, he wrung out the plaster gently before starting to apply the first roll to shape a cast.

As a trained pharmacist, Temur was very familiar with the process. He worked methodically, without any hesitation, flattening the plaster as he wrapped, ensuring that each new pass of the plaster overlapped the one before it. He then stopped wrapping the plaster before the edge of the padding, near the knee.

He applied a second and more rolls of plaster casting, much in the same manner, and finally folded the leftover padding down over the cast, wrapping the last part of the plaster over the padding to secure it. To a casual onlooker, it looked just like any other plaster cast. But, to a more careful observer, it was in truth much thicker than usual, especially around the inside of the calf. Satisfied, he instructed Gupta to remain seated, leaving the cast to dry but speeding the process with a hairdryer.

Once the plaster had dried enough, he placed the scientist's leg on a coffee table and plugged in a small cast removal saw. It was a lightweight, low-vibration tool with two oscillation speeds. A dust collection system even reduced airborne particles. With a pencil, he first drew a rectangle on the thickest portion of the cast and, working carefully, started digging into the plaster with the electric saw, following the contours of the rectangle, always taking care not to cut all the way through the padding and leaving a layer of plaster at the bottom. Upon completion, he had created a hollow compartment within the cast. It was about 4.7 inches in length, 1.9 inches wide and 1.3 inches deep.

"This should be large enough to accommodate several glass ampoules," he told Gupta. "See, no problem," he added, demonstrating how they could snuggly fit inside the cavity. "Now, let's work on the rest."

With light, water-based air-dry clay, he carefully molded a lid, pressing the putty over the compartment and ampoules. He neatly trimmed the excess on the sides with a lancet to ensure a good fit. He then gently heated the clay with the hairdryer, waiting for it to harden. Next, he coated both the inside of the compartment and lid with a multipurpose waterproof sealer and glued in thin plastic draught-excluders on the edges of the cavity to ensure a tight and secure close. Finally, he painted both the lid and the cast in the same shade of white paint, so as to render the compartment almost undetectable to the naked eye.

"Once you're all dressed up, no one will notice. It's often what's immediately before our eyes that we don't see, or rather, chose not to see. Now, try walking around with the crutches."

"You're mad," answered Gupta, making a face but doing as instructed. He hopped around the living room on one leg as he held the grip, his forearms inserted into the cuffs. "That cast is really heavy. It doesn't look natural," he complained.

"It's just perfect," countered Temur. "Just be yourself! Joke about what happened to you, and you'll be fine. They'll all pity you. They'll probably X-ray the crutches, but I can guarantee you that no one will take the slightest interest in your cast. And it has no steel components, so it won't trigger the metal detector. Now, remember that I'll need at least two dozen vials, so, at the rate of three a day…"

"I can't possibly keep doing this beyond just a few days! More than a week is plain crazy! Someone will notice!"

"Nonsense! All you have to do is go in and out of the building. Just do exactly as we discussed, and you'll be fine. I'll drive you close to the lab later today, and I'll also be there to pick you up, and the vials, of course, to avoid any material amplitude in temperature."

"You make it sound so simple! Now I'll have to keep this on for weeks afterward," said a resentful Gupta, concluding with an almost inaudible *"rowdy sheeter!"* ("hardened criminal") for good measure.

"Think of your wife and child, Vikas!" countered Temur. "It can't be easy for them either! Now, let's grab something to eat. You sound tense. We don't want you to look *too* unwell, do we?"

"Rest is fine," said Gupta, even more annoyed, as he slowly dragged himself to the kitchen, his head bobbing in a side-to-side motion.

Chapter 28

TEMUR KHAN HAD parked just one street away from the BSL-4 facility in Alcobendas. The perimeter of the laboratory was under heavy camera surveillance, and he didn't want to take any chances of being filmed. Grumpy as ever, Gupta exited the car and hopped to the front door, leaning on his crutches. He would only be at work for a few hours that day but was clearly not happy with what had been requested of him.

"I'll be here for you at eight again," said Temur, before the scientist slammed the door of the Nissan.

Gupta walked to the entrance, nervous. He paused for a few seconds and allowed the scanner to read his irises. After a couple seconds, the message "*Entrada autorizada*" ("You are allowed to proceed") flashed on the plasma screen, and the door automatically unlocked. Slowly, he made his way inside.

"*¡Señor Gupta! ¿Qué pasó?*" ("What happened?"), asked one of the security guards, who knew him by name.

"Just a small accident. Nothing to worry about, but I'll have to keep the cast on for about a month."

"*¡Qué lástima! ¡Mejorale pronto!*" ("What a shame! Get well soon!")

"Thank you, Juan."

As Temur had predicted, the guards scanned the crutches and thoroughly searched Gupta's backpack after passing it through the X-ray machine, but they did not pay the slightest attention to the cast, even helping the scientist to move forward across the metal detector. He exited the small edifice that housed security and entered the reception hall of the main building, where he was greeted in a similar manner by a few curious well-wishers. He then rode the elevator to the third floor, where the BSL-4 area proper was located, and made his way to the master stock area.

So far, so good, he thought.

He sat there for more than an hour, making small talk with his colleague, María, and catching up on the morning's work. She was genuinely concerned about what had happened to him and insisted on knowing all the details. She even fetched him a coffee, as he anxiously scanned his surroundings as discreetly as he could.

There were overhead cameras both in the office and storage areas, and he would need to find a way to escape their prying lenses. All of the security systems were redundant in the BSL-4, and the cameras could not be shut off. Finally, after sitting at his computer and looking at records for a while, he stood up and made his way to the main storage room.

"I need to take a physical count. Something doesn't quite add up. It was probably a mistake when the data was first entered. I'm sure it's nothing to worry about," he told María.

"*¿De verdad?*" ("Really?") "What virus?"

"SARS. Remember? We received a big delivery from Milan a while back."

"*Sí claro, recuerdo.*" ("Yes, of course, I remember.") "But, are you sure you don't want me to do it instead? You should take it easy with those crutches."

"I'll be fine. The Italians would have fucked things up, as usual. I'm feeling rather hot anyway. I could do with spending time in the cool room."

"As you wish, *cariño*! *Pero si necesitas ayuda con algo, sólo dímelo, ¿vale?*" ("If you need help with anything, just say so, all right?")

"Thank you, María. And while I'm in there, I'll also catch up on labeling. I recall there's still a fair bit left to do."

To a casual observer, the master storage facility might have evoked an ultra-modern wine cellar. The temperature and hygrometry were constant, with overhead UV light tubes that made for an oppressive atmosphere. But here stopped the similarities. Instead of bottles of prized Bordeaux or Burgundy, the cabinets securely housed hundreds of thousands of ampoules and vials of some of the deadliest pathogens known to man, all tightly packed in sealed boxes or ultra-low freezer racks. Every single one of them that left or entered the room had to be signed for by two individuals. Luckily for Gupta, one of the authorized signatories was none other than himself.

He donned a full-face mask with a powered air-purifying respirator and entered the room, after punching in the access code on the wall-mounted keypad. After clearing the air lock, he immediately felt the cold and a shiver ran down his spine. The good thing about walking with crutches, he thought, was that any abnormal moves he might make wouldn't raise suspicion. After all, he was now *expected* to move somewhat clumsily.

He first went to the cabinet that housed the lyophilized vials of SARS coronavirus and mentally noted the information pertaining to the latest incoming shipment. He then walked to a tiled workbench that stood in one of the corners of the facility, near the door. On it were a small sink and all manner of laboratory tools, as well as a laptop and printer, both plugged in but not connected to the laboratory network itself. They were mainly used to make labels and other records for the thousands of boxes that lay there, destined for experiments to be conducted on the hot side of the BSL-4 or for deliveries to other laboratories.

After carrying out normal work duties for a good thirty minutes, he typed on the keyboard for a short while and created a new replacement seal for one of the Styrofoam boxes. Taking great care to only show his back to the surveillance cameras, he also pocketed three sealed vials, one-third filled with a harmless saline solution.

After returning to the SARS cabinet, he unsealed one of the containers, just as he would to make a physical count, and discreetly substituted them for three actual ampoules of SARS coronavirus. Acting as naturally as he could, he slipped them all inside his cuff before he gently dropped them in one of the pockets of his white coat. He then resealed the box with the new label and promptly returned to his desk outside of the storage facility. He would now need to leave in short order. The temperature would steadily rise, and the pathogens might not remain unaffected for long.

"All clear, María. Everything's in order; it was just a typo."

"Thank God for that! Can you imagine if some of these vials ever went missing?"

"Perish the thought! Mind you, do you remember those samples that were unaccounted for in Paris two years ago? Actually, they were of SARS too, if I recall well. It looks like they had been destroyed but no one had ever bothered to make a record of it at the time. And it could never be proven."

"*¡Ay, qué raro!*" ("That's weird!")

"Isn't it just? Thank God we've got strict procedures in place here! You know what? Enough for today! I'm not used to this cast yet, and I think I need to rest."

"*¡Cuiade te, pobrecito!*" ("Take care, poor you!")

Gupta made his way out and rode the elevator to the first floor, in which the BSL-2 area was located. Security there was much more lax, with cameras accordingly few and far between. It also housed restrooms and other facilities for staff, which could easily explain his presence, should anyone bother to ask.

He walked to one of several doors that lined a long corridor. Behind it was a small handling room for laboratory equipment. The room was empty. With some effort, he sat on a stool and rested his leg on a chair. With a lancet, he carefully forced open the lid, revealing the cavity Temur Khan had dug into the cast. He then very gently placed the three ampoules, one alongside the other, into the hollow area. He was very nervous and took his time. Even though these were double-vial preparations, he did not want to risk one falling to the floor and breaking.

Next, he unlocked a large metallic jar and dipped an aluminum implement through the top opening. It very much resembled a *venencia*, used for pulling sherry samples from the aging barrels in the cellars, with a small cylindrical steel cup at the end of a long, flexible shaft. But what came out of the vessel was liquid nitrogen rather than fortified wine from Jerez. Taking great care, he poured some of the frozen liquid on top of the ampoules. It would delay any warming of the vials until Khan finally took hold of the samples.

He quickly pushed the lid firmly back into place. It was almost invisible. Whoever that awful man was, he had come up with a clever device. You had to give him that.

He went through security once more without any issues, declined the offer of a taxi and, on the dot of eight o'clock, returned to the car in which Temur was already waiting.

"Do you have them?"

"Yes, yes. I was lucky this time. But I don't know if I can keep making up stories for an entire week."

Temur unsealed the lid, revealing the three ampoules in the secret compartment, at the same time unleashing a small plume of white vapor from the liquid nitrogen as it came into contact with the ambient atmosphere. Wearing a pair of plastic gloves, he extracted them one by one from their hiding place, very carefully, and transferred them to a larger, temperature-controlled, purpose-made container in which they would now rest under optimal conditions.

"Let's go. Talk me through how you did it," he prompted, as an exhausted Gupta wiped dripping sweat from his brow.

Chapter 29

Gran Bara desert, Republic of Djibouti, March 2016

THE GRAND BARA DESERT was located to the south of Djibouti, spanning the three regions of Ali Sabieh, Arta and Dikhil. It consisted of large areas of sand flats, with sparse grass and scrub vegetation, and stood at a relatively low altitude, all below two thousand feet. Every spring, almost two thousand people, civilians and military personnel alike, took part in the Grand Bara 15K, a famed nine-mile race across that desolate expanse of arid earth, starting at the crack of dawn.

But today, twice that distance would be just the start for the participants in the Djibouti Military Challenge. Crossing the eighteen-mile-long desert would steadily stiffen their legs, as their feet hammered the harsh terrain, and their shoulders, as the heavy Bergen rucksacks, which had all been weighed to ensure a minimum load of twenty-four pounds, rubbed against their backs. Next would come tactical exercises in one of Djibouti's eight mountain ranges, each of which had peaks of over 3,200 feet. As the sun came up, water drained from their bodies through rivers of sweat, causing their throats to burn as their thirst gradually built.

The commandos had all left from separate locations.

The run across the desert itself was timed, with a few short stops along the way to shoot at yet more targets. But, as they ventured into the mountainous terrain to capture mock enemy positions, they would inevitably come across each other. The exercise would test, among other things, their navigation and camouflage skills, as well as their ability to complete a long-range tactical mission into hostile territory.

After leaving the sand flats and climbing up and down several inhospitable hills of volcanic rock throughout the rest of the day and most of the night, Erwan Tanguy and his platoon finally reached the formations of the Hemed, in the western part of the Arta region, in south-central Djibouti. They were now forty-five miles east of the capital. The summit peaked at 3,600 feet above sea level, dominating the Iskoutir pass.

Beyond it, he knew, was their objective: rusty container-ized living units and a communications mast, all supposed to represent a radio station. They would need to tread with care. The access and grounds would no doubt be booby-trapped with clusters of plaster grenades and mines.

They were near the summit, a few hours from daybreak, when a scout clenched one of his fists, signaling for the men to stop and lower themselves to the ground. Far ahead in the distance, he had spotted the Chinese. Some one hundred yards below, to the right, was none other than Major Xie herself, watching her men progress along the rock face.

Tanguy would perhaps not have a better opportunity to get to her. He indicated to Commandant Marc, in charge of the Commandos Marine, his intention to reach her. He would rejoin the platoon later. With both Tanguy and Xie held up, neither the French nor the Chinese would be in a position to swiftly complete the mission, but there were still several hours before the end of the twenty-four-hour deadline.

Leaving the group, he backed down and silently traversed the rock face toward Xie. She had seen neither him nor the rest of the French contingent, her gaze focused on her own unit. Tanguy finally found himself only twenty yards away from her. He pointed the muzzle of his submachine gun in her direction and pulled the slide backward, after moving the selector switch from the "SAFE" to the "SEMI" position.

Members of the French Special Forces, like most of their counterparts in other countries, could generally choose their own weapons. Rather than the FAMAS bullpup-style assault rifle used by other French military units, he preferred the American Colt M4 in its short-barreled version for CQB (close-quarters battle), with a foldable forward grip, which also fired 5.56-mm NATO rounds.

Xie heard the click of the slide as it returned to its full forward position, chambering an M193, ball ammunition, and quickly turned to face Tanguy.

"So we meet again," he said, smiling.

"Commandant Tanguy," she said, calling him by his true name and rank, even though his combat uniform only stated that of captain. "I was wondering when you'd finally show up for a chat."

"I was just waiting for the right moment; that's all."

She had a slightly clipped accent, but her English was almost perfect. Even in her camouflaged combat uniform,

Tanguy had to admit she was particularly good looking. Her black hair was cut short. Her nose was thin and her face well chiseled, and she had the high cheekbones of people from northern China. But most striking were her eyes. They were, most unusually, gray-green in color, and certainly not easily forgotten.

They stared at each other for a few seconds, during which no further words were exchanged. She made a half attempt to step forward, but he quickly aligned the muzzle of the rifle and the red dot of his NCStar tactical scope with her forehead, intimating for her to stay put.

"You're not really going to shoot me, are you? That would create a bit of a hiccup, don't you think?"

"It could easily be explained as an unfortunate accident. After all, we're all using live ammunition."

"True."

"By the way, your friend Darret's dead. I killed him in Singapore."

"Is that so? News to me. Well, I suppose he had it coming…"

"Was he on your payroll for long?"

"It was never about the money for Maurice. But he worked for us long enough, I'd say."

"Who else is?"

"Now, Erwan," she said with a broad smile, "you can't really expect me to answer that one. Need to know, and all that…"

"What was in that document case, in Johor?"

"May I sit? We've all been up for close to twenty hours, and I could do with a bit of a rest—if all we're going to do is chat, that is."

"Sounds reasonable. But move very slowly and, above all, don't come any closer."

"Don't worry. You know, it's the same people we're both after."

"So?"

"It looks like your friend Saadi was interested in acquiring biological weapons."

"I very much doubt the Filipinos would have been able to deliver them. Way above their pay grade."

"I don't disagree. But it appears they were in touch with people who had access to some, although perhaps only indirectly. What I found in Johor pointed to such a link."

"That sounds like a lot of loose ends, but go on," he said.

"We don't know who they might be. Whether it's a man, a woman or maybe even several people is not really clear. It might even be a sleeper cell, a splinter group of some sort or maybe just someone who's sat and waited for the right opportunity. Whoever it is, nothing's appeared on our radar before and probably not on yours, or even that of the Americans, for that matter. We also don't have any possible targets—not even a single one, let alone any timing for a possible biological strike. But there's a rumor we've now heard a few times around Xinjiang and Central Asia, about someone very deadly."

"Do you have anything concrete at all?"

"We don't have a face, or a name. Just a code, a nickname. But, again, it could just be a legend, a story created to send us on a wild goose chase."

"I don't think Saadi or Abu Sayyaf had much time to

waste, do you? There's rarely smoke without fire. The name?"

"Al-Musafir."

"That means 'the traveler,' doesn't it?"

"Yes. It's the same word in Arabic and Persian, and even Hindi and Urdu. That's all we've got."

It didn't ring a bell, but Tanguy would see what he could find.

Above them, they suddenly heard a shot. It wasn't close, but it had obviously come from an automatic rifle, although he could tell it was neither a FAMAS nor an M4.

"It looks like the taking of that radio station may have started," she said, matter-of-factly.

"Probably one of your guys losing his cool! We'd better go, now," he said.

"Tanguy?"

"Yes?"

"As I said, we're after the same people. Just bear that in mind, if we are ever to meet again."

"Good luck!" he added with a wink, before turning back and scrambling up the rocky face. After just a dozen feet, he paused and looked down, but Xie Wei had already vanished.

Chapter 30

Madrid, Spain, April 2016

VIKAS GUPTA HAD managed to successfully retrieve nine vials from the BSL-4 facility. So far, there had been no issues with security, neither within the confines of the laboratory itself nor at the entry and exit checks, where the guards continued to be helpful and treated him with much courtesy. As each day passed, he delivered his deadly cargo to the man whose name he still didn't know, but who had taken his family hostage. He was very nervous, but took things one day at a time, finding comfort in the expectation that they would now soon be freed and that he could forget about their ordeal.

Like the majority of Spaniards, his colleague María had gone on holidays for the rest of Semana Santa, and he had been able to repeat the scenario he had devised on the first day with Paul, her replacement. Paul, a Canadian from Québec, was relatively new to the facility and not as familiar with some of the protocols—so he could be more easily fooled, which obviously helped.

Gupta's confidence had grown, and Temur hoped he'd be able to carry on like this for another week. But he would probably soon need reassurance again that his wife and child were unharmed. For his own part, Temur also needed confirmation that the vials Gupta had delivered to him were indeed genuine.

On the morning of the fourth day, after driving Gupta to the laboratory, he went again to the garage in San Sebastián de los Reyes. After opening the metal door, he parked inside and closed the shutter. Within the small built-up enclosure, nothing had changed. Hearing the noise, the women stood, staring intently through the thick, one-way window glass, even though they could not actually see him.

"What do you want? How long are you going to keep us here?" asked the desperate mother.

Temur ignored her questions but unlocked the door and entered the cell, facing them. He did not wear a facemask this time. There was no need for that anymore, although he had still donned plastic medical gloves to avoid leaving fingerprints. He noted that they had drunk quite a few bottles of mineral water and also eaten some of the food. They had stored up on energy, but still looked tired and very much afraid.

"Vikas has been worrying about you," he said softly. "I believe he needs added reassurance that you're all right. Will you please give him that? I'll make sure he gets the message," he said, grinning, as he pointed a cheap video recorder at them after pressing the record button. It wasn't a cell phone, so there was no GPS. The location of the recording could never be traced, assuming someone ever got hold of the camera.

For a couple of minutes, a tearful Deepika spoke of their predicament and implored her husband to do everything the

man asked, so they could be set free at the earliest opportunity. They wanted to be with him again and put an end to
the nightmare they had endured for what felt like a very long
time. Deepika's watch had stopped. She had forgotten to
wind it up and had gradually lost all notion of time. Until
the man had returned to the garage, it had been impossible
to tell whether it was day or night. For her own part, like
many teenagers, Parvati relied on her mobile phone to tell
the time, but that had been confiscated when they had been
locked up.

They were both still in chains. Temur made sure they
were fully visible on the video recording. The drab background—a naked, gray concrete wall—added to the
oppressive atmosphere. It made for a sorry sight, which was
exactly what he was trying to convey.

"Daddy. I'm very scared! I don't want to die!" added the
daughter at the end, for good measure, between sobs.

"That was very good, thank you," said Temur, satisfied
their performance would further convince Gupta to play
ball.

He then left, closed the door and donned a full-face
mask with a respirator, as well as plastic gloves.

First, he needed to open one of the freeze-dried vials. He
inspected the blue crystal desiccant, made of silica beads. It
was neither clear nor pink in color, and he concluded that
the vacuum seal had not been compromised. He heated the
tip of the outer vial in a naked flame and squirted a few
drops of water on the hot tip to crack the glass. With a metal
file, he struck the tip to remove it in order to access the inner
vial. He finally removed the insulation and inner vial with a

small forceps and gently raised the cotton plug.

He now needed to rehydrate the freeze-dried strains of SARS coronavirus. He transferred them to a new vial and added sterile, double-distilled water. He gently shook the mixture to dilute it with the culture medium and added the virus to an agar slant in a petri dish, to act as the host cell and induce growth.

He waited for about thirty minutes and then returned to the room with a large mechanical alarm clock. It was an old-style model, black in color, which he had bought earlier from an anonymous mom-and-pop shop near the Puerta del Sol. It had a clear dome lens, which framed a Cinderella figure ("Cenicienta" in Spanish) and a steel casing. Temur had told the vendor it was a gift for his daughter. When the clock rang, a hammer alternatively struck two metal bells at high speed, causing them to vibrate loudly for a minute or so.

Ignoring the women's panic at the sight of his mask and respirator, he set the alarm for forty-five minutes later and placed the clock on the small window ledge, inside the cell but out of reach of the two women. With much care, he then positioned the petri dish on top of it. As the alarm went off, the vibrations would ultimately cause the clock to tilt and fall, taking the deadly pathogens with it. As both smashed onto the concrete floor, the liquid that hosted the virus would splash and soon contaminate the occupants of the small cell. The confinement of the space would help to speed the process.

Temur left the room again and locked the door. He then spent the next twenty minutes carefully caulking all the openings with duct tape, making sure the small room was perfectly sealed. Throughout his activities, he had not removed his heavy-duty facemask.

The two women were now anxiously looking at the clock, unsure what it meant or what was in store for them. The fact that their kidnaper had worn a mask was obviously worrying news, but he was now on the other side of the darkened window and there was no way for them to prevent whatever would soon happen.

Soon, there was only one minute left before the alarm rang, and they nervously followed the progress of the mechanical hands on the clock panel. The head and arms of the Cinderella figure energetically marked each passing second, but there was decidedly nothing funny about it.

At the set time, the hammer sprung to life, repeatedly striking the two bells. The vibrations slowly brought the clock increasingly closer to the edge of the window as it hopped on its legs, a fraction of an inch at a time. Soon, one of the legs went over. As in a dream, although it lasted only a fraction of a second, it almost floated halfway in the air before loudly crashing onto the floor.

The alarm was still ringing and, even though the cheap clock now lay on its side, it continued to drag itself on the floor with small spasms, as would the occupants of the room in just a few days' time, like dying insects doused with insecticide. After about a minute, it stopped. The petri dish had shattered into small pieces, spreading its contents over a good part of the cell.

To the women's surprise, it was as if nothing much had happened. No deadly gas appeared. The shattered petri dish had diffused its contents throughout the room, but it was completely odorless, as if inert. In fact, it very much looked like water. Maybe the experiment had just failed? Or it was perhaps just a sick practical joke.

A tiny bit of the liquid had squirted onto Deepika's dress. Without thinking, she rubbed it off with two of her fingers. She then forgot completely about it, and it soon dried off. A while later, unconsciously, she touched her face, depositing invisible infectious droplets on the mucous membranes of her mouth and eyes. As she comforted her daughter, she kissed her forehead, unwittingly propagating the deadly disease.

Through the heavy glass window, Temur had not ceased looking at them. Everything was now set in motion. If all went according to plan, within a week or so, they would either be dead or close to dying. Either way, they would never leave their cell alive. He would then know for sure that the ampoules stolen by Gupta were real.

He took a last look at them and left the garage. He didn't feel anything. They were *kuffar*, unbelievers. Just a cog in the machine, a simple tool to serve a higher purpose. Soon he would return and check on the progress of the disease.

Chapter 31

Madrid, Spain, April 2016

AFTER JUST A FEW DAYS, the two women developed a high fever and felt extreme fatigue. Recurring headaches, chills and muscle pain soon followed. They had also lost their appetite, and the gradual realization that their kidnapper must have contaminated them with the contents of the petri dish a few days before only made things worse.

On the third day, they both suffered from a dry cough and faced increasing breathing difficulties, also on account of the rarified oxygen in the sealed room. Next came diarrhea. Hygiene conditions in their cell were very basic and, along with its small size, compounded the effects and rapid spread of the infection.

There was no one to tend to them and no medication to ease their growing pain. Parvati was the first to succumb, within less than a week, dying in atrocious suffering in Deepika's arms. After that, her mother lost all will to survive and soon followed.

When Temur Khan returned to check on them, he could only note the devastating effects of what he had unleashed. Any doubts that the vials supplied by Gupta might have been tainted were instantly lifted, and he felt a tremendous sense of achievement.

He now had in his hands the ability to spread loss of life on an epic scale. Weapons of mass destruction, they called them. Indeed, the term was well chosen. That he, Temur Khan, had been tasked with the responsibility for such devastation was nothing short of a blessing and, for a moment, he beamed with pride at the idea that what he had prepared for over the course of many years would soon come to fruition. He then focused on the greater purpose it had all been for.

"Allahu Akbar!" he exclaimed, as he began to pray.

God willing, he would unleash havoc, the memory of which would remain for centuries, just as bin Laden had predicted. Soon, he would finally achieve the sheikh's vision.

Leaving the cell and its now-dead occupants untouched, he cleaned the rest of the garage as best he could with bleach, erasing all traces of his passage. Finally, he closed the metal shutter, locked it and threw away the key. There were five months left on the lease and he had paid in advance, in cash, with no questions asked. Ultimately, the landlord, or perhaps someone else, would discover the bodies but, by then, it would no longer matter.

A few days later, Temur received the last batch of ampoules from an exhausted Vikas Gupta. As he had done on each occasion, once the scientist was back in the car, Temur forced open the lid that revealed the cavity in the plaster cast and transferred the vials to a secure, temperature-controlled container.

"You did very well, Vikas," he said. "I wasn't sure at first if you'd have the courage to carry on till the end. Kudos to you."

"This has been the worst week of my life. I'm glad it's over. For the life of me, I've aged more than ten years in the space of just a few days! I'll be happy to finally see the back of you. Now, take me to my family."

"I'm afraid it's not as simple as that."

"*Suwar ki aulad*!" countered Gupta, which loosely translated to "son of a dog." "Take me to them right now!"

Without answering, Temur played the second video he had recorded of the two women before infecting them with SARS and leading them to their untimely deaths.

Gupta looked at the short recording intensely. As soon as it had ended, Temur saw that his eyes were moist with tears. He had lost both his arrogance and fighting spirit.

"You promised, you promised," was all he could say.

"Yes, I did. But now, I need you to do something else for me."

"What now? I've done everything you've asked so far, risking my job for the sake of God knows what! I haven't seen my wife and child for more than a week. What is it you now want?"

"I need you to take the vials to Mumbai for me. That shouldn't be too difficult. You can create documentation at your office. Just pretend these are vaccines, to be kept under refrigerated conditions. You must leave in a couple of days' time."

"How can I travel to Mumbai at such short notice? They'll suspect something. It's not as if I didn't cut any corners recently, you know."

"Say there's an emergency. Your family's supposed to be in India on holiday."

"And then you'll free them?"

"It's that simple. They can join you there. Take that holiday after all."

"What do you want me to do when I'm in Bombay?"

Gupta was already asking practical questions. Temur knew he'd follow instructions to a T, once again.

"I'll meet you there and just take over from you. You can then forget all about it and have your life back. *Tike*?"

"I'm not happy about this, not at all. You've already tricked me once. What guarantees do I have you won't do it again?"

"To be honest, my friend, none whatsoever. But, the way I see it, Vikas, you don't really have a choice. So, start planning. Today is Wednesday. Tomorrow afternoon, I want you to tell your office you're leaving. And on Friday, I want you on that plane. You'll arrive in the middle of the night on Saturday morning. I'll take care of all travel arrangements. You'll fly to Doha on Qatar Airways and then on to Mumbai with Jet Airways—that's the quickest. The good news is that the cast can go."

Reluctantly, his head bobbing from side to side, Gupta grumbled something unintelligible, which Temur took as an acknowledgement.

"And Vikas?" he added.

"Sir?"

"No silly games. Remember: if you talk to anyone, or if you get caught, they die."

"*Padosi ki aulaad!*" whispered the scientist in return,

which explored the possibility that Temur might have been conceived by one of his father's neighbors.

"I heard that. Now go," instructed Temur, stopping the car outside his residence and giving him a pat on the back.

Much later that same evening, Temur Khan unwrapped a box that contained a mobile telephone. It had been bought new, had never been used and would therefore not be registered by the Big Ears of the security services in the West or their allies in the war against terrorism.

He inserted a pre-paid SIM card and, once the network had been activated, dialed a number in Islamabad, Pakistan.

More than four thousand miles away, the call was answered promptly, even though it was two o'clock in the morning. The number would only be used once, and the conversation would be extremely short. Even if it were recorded by the likes of the American NSA or Pakistani Directorate for Inter-Services Intelligence, nothing remotely of interest would be said.

"Al-Musafir," he said.

"I'm afraid you've got the wrong number. And it's very late," came the answer, in Urdu.

"I'm so sorry. Let me try again," he added, before hanging up.

Chapter 32

Paris, France, April 2016

"SO YOU WERE defeated by the SAS?" observed The Bear jovially. "You must be getting old, Tanguy."

"In truth, it was by a very narrow margin only. They had the edge in the kill house; that's probably what did it. But what's there to say? They invented it, after all."

"Fair enough. And those bastards are good. Came across them in Desert Storm. You were probably still wearing nappies. They'd been parachuted days ahead before the fun and games began in earnest, to map out batteries of SCUD missiles. We later took them on one by one, as if on parade. We learned a lot from them."

"They're good all right, but the SEALs trailed far behind. One of them even broke a leg early on."

"And the Krauts?'

"They struggled. And the Chinese certainly didn't cover themselves in glory this time."

"Sounds like desert warfare's not their thing, then."

"Not yet, no. And neither was the nautical assault course. But they've come a long way in a short span of time. Xie, however, was impressive. She's tough; that's for sure. On top of being quite a looker, I might add. No doubt she's given a major bollocking to her men after the event. Djibouti's strategic for them."

"As it is for everyone, nowadays. Did you see what the Americans did with Camp Lemonnier? Looks like a bloody theme park! When I was last there, it had not changed since before the last World War. Anyway, great tan! Now, back to what's really of interest. What could you find about al-Musafir?"

"Well, as you know, it means 'the traveler' in Arabic. But it could also be a Persian, Hindi or Urdu phrase."

"Why Persian? Saadi and his accomplices were Sunni."

"That still leaves a lot of possibilities. To start with, we don't know of any group by that name. It doesn't appear in any of our databases or watch lists. We checked with the Brits and the Americans too, but *zilch*."

"Could Xie have bullshitted you?"

"I doubt it. She kept repeating that we both faced the same threat."

"What else?"

"*Musafir* is also an Internet-based travel agency in Beirut."

"That's more like it."

"But, as far as we know, it's totally legit. It has Dutch shareholders, and they are beyond reproach. We've also found a number of websites, although none appear to be propaganda-related. There are also various hotels by that name, and quite a few Hindi movies too."

"Looks like this is going nowhere."

"Afraid so. It's a rather common word and, as noted, in more than just one language. We've applied filters to monitor communications and have asked our allies to do the same but, as you can imagine, it's really looking for a needle in a haystack. And it'll only get worse. As the pilgrimage to Mecca nears and everyone in the Muslim world boards a plane to Saudi, there'll be hundreds of thousands of leads to look into. Travelers galore, so to speak."

"Well, that Great Migration doesn't start until September this year. Maybe something will turn up. You know as well as I do that this is a game of patience. Actually, patience and plenty of luck! What about those biological weapons?"

"I was actually very surprised. I doubted these guys were that sophisticated. An attack with a crude chemical bomb would be much easier to put together. Much of that stuff you can even buy on Amazon these days. Well, at least in the U.S. A dirty bomb combining radioactive material with conventional explosives would be simpler too. It wouldn't generate much in terms of radiation, and the actual nuclear fallout would be negligible, but the panic created as a result would probably be worth the effort. And getting your hands on some nuclear waste is not all that difficult in some countries. But a biological weapon, that's something else altogether."

"I agree. As a first step, procuring pathogens would be far from a walk in the park," said The Bear.

"There are fewer than sixty facilities around the world that store viruses for which there are still no known cure. Of course, they might try their hand at something more conventional, but it wouldn't be the same as attempting to spread, say, Ebola germs."

"Agree again. If you're going through the trouble of

making biological weapons, then you might as well go all the way. Why bother with just spreading the flu?"

"Now, fifteen of these so-called BSL-4 labs are in the U.S. There are also a few in Latin America. The FBI and the CIA are on the case there. The Brits and the Australians are also looking into the matter on their end. Since the intel came from the Chinese, they'll already have done their homework in Asia. That leaves Europe and Africa. We're currently checking for anything untoward: changes in personnel, abnormal events, major shipments. The usual. We've also alerted all of these facilities to carry out extra stock-taking and checks as a matter of urgency, as well as a security audit of all their procedures."

"How long will it take?"

"We're treating this as an absolute priority. A number of teams are on it, but we're lucky that the Easter holidays have just come to an end and the labs are being very responsive. Hopefully within a few days we should have a clearer picture, maybe even before, if anything gets flagged as a red light."

"Well, keep going. We don't have much else to pursue for now."

"What about Southeast Asia, now that Darret's gone? And also that girl, Lilly Ling?"

"It's not as if we had extensive operations there in the first place. Asia's always been a bit of a backwater for us, as you know—since Điện Biên Phủ anyway. So any risk should be fairly easily contained. We're double-checking everyone's background again, and new case officers have been assigned to the agents Darret was running. We're also looking into all of them to see if what they've been feeding us over the years was kosher. I'm sorry about Ling, by the way. I misjudged her. She was obviously on our side."

"Xie said Darret didn't betray for money."

"He was always an old Asia hand. Born in Hanoi, you know. We've already established he had a brush with the Chinese while in college. Cultural exchange trip of some sort, in the post-Mao years. For some reason, that didn't register on our radar at the time. It was years ago, but that's probably when he decided to start working for them. You think you've got it all covered, and then something like this happens. Thankfully, even though he'd been around for a long time, he was always small potatoes. Anyway, we're in damage-limitation mode now. Not to worry. You did the right thing taking him out."

"It's not as if I had much choice."

"End-of-story. Focus on the labs. And report anything that sounds remotely suspicious. We can't afford a new terrorist attack, and especially not one involving WMDs. Next year's an election year, for fuck's sake!"

Tanguy sighed as he left the room. Politics always took precedence, especially in their shadowy world, and in France, perhaps more than anywhere else. Some things never changed.

Chapter 33

Dubai, United Arab Emirates, April 2016

"IN THE NAME of Allah, the Most Beneficent, the Most Merciful, I declare this meeting open. Thank you all for coming," said Ismail Khan.

The Pakistani fixer for much of the world's Muslim terrorist population was now in his late fifties. His hair had turned gray, but he was still active, raising funds and helping rally supporters to the cause. Inevitably, he'd had a few close calls over the years, including in 2001 during the battle of Tora Bora, in the White Mountains of eastern Afghanistan. He'd barely escaped with his life from the complex of caves, as tribal fighters backed by U.S. Special Forces, British commandos and even troops from the German KSK (Kommando Spezialkräfte) overran al Qaida's secret bunkers.

Since then, he had largely remained below the radar of the West's intelligence services, due to a combination of tradecraft, extreme caution and mistrust for anyone but a very small group of people—among them, Temur Khan, whom he had first taken under his wing more than twenty-five years ago and whom he had taught much of what he knew about jihad.

The meeting had been called in one of the city's tallest buildings, a swanky five-star hotel by the Dubai Marina with breathtaking views of the Persian Gulf in the distance. Offshore, reclaimed islands continued to emerge, proof that the Emirate was now back in full swing after the blow dealt by the latest financial crisis, which had seen Dubai's highest tower renamed after the ruling family of Abu Dhabi, as thanks for helping to keep it afloat financially.

The small gathering was held on the top floor, the entirety of which had been privatized for this purpose. Security guards preventing unauthorized access were posted at each exit.

Each of the eight men who had been invited wore the typical Arab national dress: a white *dishdasha* or *thobe*, which was a loose, ankle-length robe made from fine white cotton. Only one, an Omani, stood out, his own garment sporting a tassel. There were differences in their respective headdresses: most wore the distinctive head covering known as a *ghutra*, with a plain cloth held in place by an *agal*, a black "rope" that was originally a camel tether, above a white skullcap. Two of the cloths, also known as a *shemagh*, were red in color, indicating their owners were from Saudi Arabia, whereas most of the others were just white, as was the fashion throughout the Emirates. One of the men, however, was obviously from Qatar: his more African-style headdress featured two long "tails" reaching down the back.

All, however, were deeply religious and long-time financial supporters of *wahabbism*, the extreme branch of Sunni Islam, and jihad, the armed struggle advocated by myriad terrorist groups from the Middle East to Indonesia. All were immensely wealthy, their combined financial power largely exceeding that of many a medium-sized central bank.

"It goes without saying that everything that will be discussed here today must never be repeated outside these walls," added Khan. "The whole of this floor was swept earlier this morning for listening devices. I'm glad to report that none was found. As an additional security measure, it would also be best if you all left separately, just as you've all arrived here," he continued.

"I'd like to convey my thanks and appreciation for your arranging today's proceedings," said a man with a neatly trimmed beard, a Saudi in his forties, in Arabic. "In this business, discretion is key, and our brother understands that more than anyone," he added, sipping a very dark and bitter coffee.

"And that is probably why I'm still alive and kicking," said Khan, as some of the participants let out a few laughs.

"Brothers," he added, "I'm pleased to say that we now have the capability to strike the enemies of Islam on an unprecedented scale. It has already been fifteen years since those dreaded twin towers came down in New York, but we are now able to repeat such a feat. The *kuffars* will perish in their thousands."

"And how do you propose to achieve such a thing?" asked the Qatari.

"Brother, it's best that none of you be made privy to any operational details. Not that you cannot be trusted; far from it, but this is an elementary security precaution to ensure our plans are ultimately successful, Inch'Allah. I'm sure you all understand and accept that. In addition to killing our enemies, however, this could also be a golden opportunity to generate substantial profits, not just for our cause, but also for each and every one of you."

Khan now knew he had their full and undivided attention.

"I need not explain to you gentlemen that the easiest way to achieve wealth is knowledge, and good information. By knowing when and where to strike, we have a unique ability to move markets and beat the unbelievers at their own game. This is a zero-risk investment. By placing bets that we are sure to win, we can reap many riches and, what's more, over a very short span of time."

"Brother, what exactly do you have in mind?" asked the Omani.

"I propose that we pool your resources, with a minimum ticket of US$200 million per head. An investment fund of sorts, so to speak. The money will be invested offshore at the optimal time, and the trades closed once we have spread havoc throughout the world's financial markets."

"I understand that the international consortium of journalists investigating that leak from the law firm in Panama is now very close to releasing their findings. Offshore companies will soon come under intense scrutiny. Are you sure about this, Brother?"

"The money will be invested through hundreds of separate vehicles run by a number of purposefully created hedge funds. These are all legitimate. Only a handful of people will know that they are, in fact, acting in concert. There will be many layers of intertwined companies, making them most unlikely to unravel and, most importantly, it will be impossible to identify the ultimate beneficiaries. I have worked on this for close to three years. Brothers, the time has now come for us to harvest this manna."

"What are your conditions?"

"I propose a one percent management fee, as well as a profit-sharing arrangement of twenty percent, above a hurdle rate of eight percent, which we are virtually certain to achieve. These are standard private equity commissions, as you will know, although instead of waiting for five or seven years, you gentlemen can cash in your profits within this calendar year, Inch'Allah. I also hasten to say that I won't accept any of these fees for myself. All the money will ultimately be used for the greater good of the Ummah."

"Half a percent," said one of the sheiks, who had been used to haggling since he'd first uttered a word as a toddler.

"Deal," answered Khan, who had already anticipated this. "Are all of you gentlemen in agreement? If so, may I please ask each of you to write down on the sheet of paper in front of you the sum you wish to entrust me with? I will contact you separately with practical details, to ensure maximum confidentiality."

"And how are we to refer to this so-called 'investment club,' among ourselves?" asked one of the Saudis.

"Since it will involve many jurisdictions, I thought of calling it the Musafir fund, not that such a name would ever appear anywhere."

"Al-Musafir. I like it."

"*Shukran.*" ("Thank you.")

"One more thing, Ismail," added the Qatari, his piercing eyes now like those of a desert snake.

"Yes, Mawlānā?" ("My Lord?")

"Don't disappoint us. Never forget that."

Khan felt a chill down his spine. While they were not men of action, their incredible means allowed them to satisfy any desire, any craving, and to achieve anything they longed for: women, luxury yachts, Lamborghinis or mansions in Mayfair. In the event of failure, their desires might well include his very own head, served on a silver platter.

"Never, Mawlānā," he answered, bowing respectfully, his hand on his heart.

Chapter 34

Mumbai, India, April 2016

VIKAS GUPTA WOKE up early. He had arrived a few hours earlier, in the middle of the night, at Mumbai's Chhatrapati Shivaji international airport, after a stopover in Qatar. He had headed straight for the Oberoi Hotel on Nariman Point, entering the black marble lobby to check in and heading straight for his room, which offered a view of the Arabian Sea.

The flight had been tiring but without issues. He had traveled business class, accompanied by a portable cool box for the transportation of vaccines. It was a small but rugged medical container, with an LCD temperature display. The outside of the device was composed of metal and plastic, preventing air inflow and helping to maintain the temperature within. There were added rubber shock absorbers to protect the contents if the ride got bumpy. Inside was a small insulating shell that contained several compartments in which the ampoules were stored. It worked with sophisticated batteries, which ensured its contents remained stored under optimal conditions for up to sixty-five hours. Every now and then, one had to top off the power bank by plugging it in. It was a simple but reliable device, mostly used for fieldwork and vaccination campaigns by NGO medical teams in Africa or remote parts of Asia.

When checking in at the airport, he had shown a forged certificate from his laboratory. He had previously written hundreds, if not thousands, of them and was very familiar with the procedure. No issues arose. The box was sealed and had revealed nothing untoward when passed through an X-ray machine, so he had been able to board without further ado. He had kept his eyes firmly focused on the package for the entire duration of the flight.

He had left Europe late on a Friday. There probably wouldn't have been anyone left at the lab in Madrid to confirm the story anyway, but no one even bothered to check. And it had been way too early in the morning for anyone at the laboratory in Pune that was, according to the certificate, supposed to receive the shipment, to do the same. The customs officers were bored and tired and had waived him through, only bothering to check that the right stamps had been printed on his luggage tags.

He had then made his way to Nariman Point in the comfort of one of the hotel's chauffeured cars. He had limited confidence in Mumbai's taxis and did not wish to take any risks of an accident, or losing the box—not with his family's lives at risk.

The container now rested on the hotel room's coffee table, the LCD display indicating an optimal low temperature, its deadly cargo soon ready to be used.

Gupta had decided to take all his meals in the room as he waited for the man to call. Temur Khan had not said when he might arrive in India, but he reckoned it was probably a question of hours, or a few days at most.

The sun had just risen. He walked to the window and pulled the curtains open, letting in the bright rays of sunshine. Down below, the day's activities had started on and around Marine Drive. He saw tourists jogging along the length of the promenade, kids attempting to sell them cheap souvenirs and an old fisherman precariously stepping onto boulders to cast lines out over the water with bamboo rods. It wouldn't be long now. The nightmare would soon be over, and he could go back to his comfortable expat life in Madrid.

Vikas Gupta had just finished a late dinner, a chicken curry doused in a fiery sauce, when the telephone rang. He lowered the volume of the television and picked up the receiver.

"Gupta."

"Any trouble?"

Sure enough, it was the man.

"None at all. I have the box here with me. I can't wait for you to come and pick it up. I've had quite enough of this. When will my family be released?"

"Soon enough," said the man. "I'm now on my way to Mumbai."

"Oh, you're not in town yet. I thought…"

"Take a boat to Elephanta Island tomorrow morning. Bring the box with you. I'll see you there."

"But…"

At the other end of the line, the man had already hung up.

Elephanta Island was one of several islands located to the east of the city's harbor. A monolithic basalt sculpture of an elephant discovered by the Portuguese had given its name to the place, previously known as Gharapuri Island. The statue was now at the Victoria and Albert Museum in London.

Boats left from the Gateway of India, opposite the Taj Mahal Hotel and only a short drive from the Oberoi, for the seven-mile trip across the water. It was a popular tourist destination, particularly because of the archeological remains dotted around the island. There, caves, some dating from the second century B.C., had been dug out from the rock, a number of them featuring ancient statues of Indian deities, in particular a twenty-three-foot-high carved masterpiece of Shiva.

The island had an area of six square miles and was thickly wooded with palm, mango and tamarind trees. Some 1,200 people lived there, in three villages. It would be busy on a weekend. No one would pay much attention to him or the man to whom he would, at last, hand over the package. Everyone would just assume they were tourists, lost in the crowd.

Gupta looked at a guidebook he had found in his room. The first ferry left at nine in the morning, and the last one at two in the afternoon. The first boat back to Mumbai would leave at noon. Tourists weren't permitted to stay overnight, and the last return ferry left at five-thirty in the afternoon. With luck, all his troubles would be over by dinnertime the following day.

He gobbled up a piece of crispy *poppadum* and then another, and turned the volume of the television back up. On Zee News, a good-looking girl in Western clothes reported on a number of fatalities in the nearby state of Gujarat. A mad shooter had been caught by the police and was now being paraded in front of the media's cameras.

Gupta looked at the container on the coffee table and felt increasingly uneasy. He silently prayed to Ganesh, the Hindu God of good luck, never to find himself in such a predicament.

That's when he realized the battery of his mobile had died. He plugged in the charger. After a few minutes, the screen of the iPhone turned on again. He slid his finger to unlock it and typed in his personal safety code, unleashing a popular Bollywood tune. He then saw that he had five unread messages on WhatsApp. He clicked the green icon and immediately realized they were all from his office, and all urgent requests to call back Diego Morales, the head of security.

He felt a chill. Drops of sweat flowed from his forehead and neck, and he knew he was in trouble. Big time.

Chapter 35

Paris, France, April 2016

"WE MAY HAVE something," said Tanguy.

"Already?" asked The Bear.

"We got lucky, I guess. We started looking into all the BSL-4 labs in Europe, in alphabetical order. As it happens, the first one we probed was Alcobendas, in Spain. It's just outside Madrid. Together with our friends at the CNI (Centro Nacional de Inteligensia), I managed to get in touch with their head of security, a guy named Morales. Diego Morales. By chance, he's ex-CESID (Centro Superior de Información de la Defensa). He's a bit thick, probably an ex-Francoist henchman, but efficient. He's almost retired by now, but he's been very responsive so far."

"Thank God for dictatorships," said The Bear, probably sincerely. "So, what's the score?"

"There's a scientist there. He's worked for them for several years. He was previously with the Institut Pasteur, among other employers. He's one of those in charge of inventory."

"Jesus! What's his name?"

"One Vikas Gupta. He's got a clean record, though. As you can imagine, people who work in such labs undergo a thorough vetting process. He's Hindu, too, not Muslim. Not a known militant, either. In fact, no one's ever heard of him, other than to confirm he was clean when he first moved to Europe. That was years ago. By the way, he carries a French passport. He was naturalized after working in Paris for a number of years. He's originally from Pondicherry, so there was some logic to that move. India doesn't allow dual nationality, so he had to relinquish his passport, but he's still an Overseas Citizen of India, which waives the requirement for a visa when he travels there. To be honest, he looks kosher. Not the terrorist type."

"But do they ever? Could he be a sleeper? Him being Hindu and all might just be a cover. He might have been recruited elsewhere years ago, and only activated just now."

"That's always a possibility. We're combing his past, but so far, he looks legit. Now, here's the story. Gupta recently broke a leg, just over a week ago—or so everyone thought. For the last week or so, he's strutted around his office with a pair of crutches and a plaster cast. Then, out of the blue, he calls his bosses and says he needs to take a trip to India. Family emergency. His wife and daughter—both of them also French, by the way—were known to be on holiday there."

"So far, that doesn't amount to much."

"Wait: it gets better. First, we've established that his family never left the country. His wife and daughter were supposed to fly to Mumbai via Paris about ten days ago, but the flight left without them. Second, they didn't fly there at a later date either. Third, no one answers the phone at his residence and his flat is empty. Our people in Madrid have paid a discreet visit, but found no one."

"So, Gupta left the country and we don't know where his family is?"

"Correct."

"That's a bit thin. He could have referred to issues with other members of his family, and his wife and daughter may well have changed their plans at the last minute. For all I know, they could be staying with friends in Barcelona, or wherever."

"True. Gupta himself left on Friday night. Under his real name and using his own passport. The thing is, we have a video of him walking through security at Barajas, but he no longer had a cast. He seemed to walk normally, too. Not even a limp."

"Looks like an amazingly quick recovery! Maybe his injury wasn't all that bad, after all?"

"He'd told colleagues he needed the crutches and cast for at least a month, maybe longer."

"Ah, that's different. Carry on."

"He also traveled with a high-tech freeze box. Vaccines, apparently, with a certificate from the lab. It doesn't quite square with what he told them in the first place. And nothing was due to be delivered to India, either. They know nothing about it."

"Just being devil's advocate for a moment—if there really was a family emergency, it might well be of a medical nature. Maybe he took it upon himself to bring whatever was needed, and bend the rules to make sure everything went smoothly. Not good, obviously, but not a disaster either. What vaccines were they, allegedly?"

"Japanese encephalitis. Quite common. Contrary to popular belief, India has very good hospitals. Surely there was no need to bring these over."

"You've got a point, Tanguy. Was he traveling on his own?"

"He checked in alone and doesn't seem to have interacted with anyone, at least not at the airport. We're still tracking down the flight crew to see if anything happened on board. The good news is, we've gone through the passenger manifests and found a red flag."

Tanguy passed a couple of color photographs to The Bear. The mugshots showed both a front view and a side view of the face of a young man in his mid-twenties. He was unshaven and looked Arabic in origin. He had an angry gaze and stared defiantly at the camera.

"Looks like a thug. Who's he?"

"Reda Darkaoui. French and Algerian dual-national. Small-time dealer from Marseille. He was arrested a few times and also did time at La Santé two years ago. Robbery. Since then, he's been on our radar, after he browsed some Islamist websites. But, other than that, he looks like small fry. Still, his traveling alongside Gupta could be bad news."

"I agree. It's usually the ones you don't worry about at first that end up spreading chaos. There's no smoke without fire, and the coincidence is certainly troubling. Has anything disappeared from Alcobendas?"

"Morales is looking into it. But that might take a while. There are literally thousands of references to check. Gupta could also have substituted vials for others to muddy the waters, although it's still unclear how he could have taken anything out of the lab. These are maximum security facilities."

"Security was also pretty good at the Twin Towers and the Pentagon—until some guys started thinking outside the box, that is. Where's Gupta right now?"

"He first flew to Qatar and then transferred to another flight bound for Mumbai. We know he arrived there yesterday early in the morning but, afterward, the trail went cold. We don't know if someone picked him up at the airport or where he went after that. Morales tried calling him several times, but there was no answer. He also left a number of messages, but received no reply. There was a brief blip last night showing he was within the city center, but it wasn't long enough for us to identify his exact whereabouts. And his mobile has since been switched off. With no battery."

"Shit. And what about that…Darkaoui?"

"Same story. He was on both legs of the flight: Madrid to Doha, then Doha to Mumbai. After that, we lost him too. We don't have a mobile number for him. He might be using a pre-paid SIM card, if anything."

"They can't have gone too far. Get the Indians to help track them down. These two guys were French, so our request is legitimate. Boissard would know who to call. Gupta probably has family there, so he might be staying with them. They should also check all the hotels. If one of them is carrying vials of infectious diseases, then we're all in for a hell of a ride."

"It's already in hand. But today's Sunday. And we're struggling to get through to the right people."

"Jesus. And then you wonder why a bunch of hoodlums can land unmolested on a beach, with backpacks full of grenades and AK-47s, and set the Taj Mahal Hotel ablaze. Mumbai remains a prime target for Islamic terrorists."

"That's for sure."

"On the other hand, Gupta, or Darkaoui, or both, might have caught a flight to somewhere else. Look into that too. Personally, I doubt it. Gupta at least would have done so immediately, rather than make his way to the city. Unless he had something to pick up or deliver there first. But he could have done so at or near the airport. Anyway, get the Spaniards to look into his wife and kid—we might track him down that way, too."

"Will do."

"And don't dismiss the other labs just yet. While this looks promising, other facilities may also have been targeted. But Gupta and Darkaoui must take priority."

"Roger that."

"And get ready to fly to India on short notice, just in case."

Chapter 36

Elephanta Island, India, April 2016

VIKAS GUPTA HAD taken the first boat from the Gateway of India to Elephanta Island. There were two types of vessel one could take to get there, but he had opted for the cheaper version, which meant he didn't get an upper deck seat.

It was busy, with a mixed crowd of Indian and foreign tourists, but probably more discreet too. He would blend in and be largely anonymous among them, save for his distinctive container, although it could readily pass for some sort of picnic or drinks cooler. A couple of times, he even had to rebuff curious approaches by people who thought he might sell cans of tea or cola. Such annoyances came with the territory.

Bollywood music was blaring on a speakerphone, and it was also hot and humid. The launch had left at nine in the morning and would arrive at Elephanta Island at ten. The boat ride itself wasn't particularly memorable, although it offered a fine view of the harbor, Gateway of India and iconic Taj Mahal Hotel in the distance. Nothing he had not seen numerous times before. Along the way, they passed a few ships as well as Butcher's Island, with a mooring jetty for oil tankers and a whitewashed fort.

The boat finally alighted at a dock located on the north of the island, and soon offloaded its cargo of eager visitors. On the jetty was a toy train that took tourists to the base of a hill. He ignored it, preferring to walk the short distance along the pier to the entry of Gharapuri village. There, he paid the five-rupee entrance fee at the security gate, waived away two men who offered to carry him in a sedan chair and climbed the one-hundred-and-twenty steps that led to the plateau where the caves were located. He had not yet seen the man who had abducted his family.

Along the path were many souvenir shops that offered curios, guidebooks and T-shirts, along with a good number of beggars. He ignored them all and joined the queue at the Archeological Survey of India ticket counter. Having paid again, he finally followed the crowds to the main cave.

There were six imposing granite columns at the entrance, and the rock-cut architecture sheltered massive panels carved into the inner walls. Dominating them was a huge statue detailing three aspects of Shiva: the Creator, the Preserver and the Destroyer.

It had been years since Gupta had last visited the place. The memory of it slowly brought tears to his eyes. It had been with his wife and then infant child. He walked into the cave to take a better look at the pillars and sculptures. After a couple of minutes, he finally saw the man, waiting in one of the rear corners. He was smiling.

"I see you've got the box. Did anyone follow you?"

"No."

Gupta had debated whether to tell the man about Diego

Morales' attempts to reach him. On the one hand, the man had said he would not hesitate to sacrifice his family, should he fail to deliver the vials of SARS virus. On the other, he had succeeded and safely brought the ampoules to India. The fact that what he had done might now have been uncovered also clearly posed a threat to both of them. On reflection, he thought it best to be upfront.

"But there might be a problem," he added, almost tear-fully.

The man made a face and grabbed him by the arm.

"Let's move over there; it'll be quieter. What happened?"

"The office tried to reach me. I received five messages from them yesterday. They were all from Morales, the head of security."

"What did you do?"

"Nothing. I didn't call him back and switched the phone off. That was yesterday evening. For all I know, he might have called again since. There was no way of telling you before this morning."

"You did well. Did you take the battery out?"

"I couldn't. It's an iPhone."

"Pass it to me. People can still trace you and even listen to your conversations when the phone's switched off, so long as the battery's charged."

"I didn't know that," said Gupta, handing over the phone.

"That's all right," said Temur, destroying the handset with the heel of one of his shoes, shattering the bits of metal and glass across the barren earth floor just outside the cave.

"That was uncalled for!" said Gupta. "The battery was dead anyway," he added, before saying "sorry."

Temur Khan ignored his protest.

"We must leave."

"What am I going to do? They obviously know. Or at least, they might have found something suspicious. For the life of me, I can't imagine how. I swear I didn't tell anyone. You know that. I wouldn't do anything to endanger my family. You have to believe me."

"I believe you, Vikas," said Temur, as they walked toward one of the smaller caves along the path. It wouldn't be as crowded there, and they'd be able to talk discreetly for a few more minutes.

"We'll take the first boat back to the city, at noon," he added. "But you have to understand something. You can never go back to your previous life now. All that probably awaits you in Madrid is a prison sentence. Besides, you're now a major security risk to me, and I can't let you compromise what I'm set to accomplish."

"I understand. I understand," said Gupta. "I'm sorry, truly sorry. Really. What about my family?"

"I'll see to it that they join us where we're headed."

"And where are we going?"

"You don't need to know that, just yet."

"But surely they can track me—I mean, us—through passport controls."

"You don't need to worry about that. We won't be catching a plane."

But were they going to leave the country, or to remain in India? Only time would tell.

"I'll pick up my stuff at the Oberoi as soon as we dock. There's not much. Do we have time?"

"Absolutely not! They probably already know you're in Mumbai. It's surely a question of hours before they find out where you've been staying. You can't go back there. Give me your passport and your wallet. From now on, you can't use your credit cards either. Anything that leaves a trace has to be discarded."

"But…"

"It's not up for discussion! Listen to me! You're now a wanted man, whether you like it or not. And your best chance to slip through the net and leave the country is to do exactly as I say. Think of your family."

So they were going abroad; that much was clear now. But would it be by boat or by land? In the latter case, there were a number of options: Pakistan, China, Nepal, Bangladesh…even Bhutan, Tibet and Burma, if they made their way to the eastern states of Sikkim, Assam or Nagaland. But the man had said a passport was not important. In that case, they would probably travel in some of the more remote areas. Either way, it would surely be a long and arduous journey. His troubles were far from over, and there was no way of knowing what might be in store for him and his family.

"When…when will I see them again?" he asked, almost sobbing.

"All in good time. Let's go now; the boat's leaving soon," said Temur, grabbing the box from his shoulder.

"I'm coming, I'm coming," said Gupta, dragging his feet on the dusty path and following behind like a tame animal that had lost all willpower.

Along the way, he nonchalantly put his hand in the back pocket of his trousers to retrieve a handkerchief. Instead, what he found inside was his Overseas Citizen of India card. For some reason, he had not returned it to his wallet with the other documents after checking in at the hotel. Defiantly, and unbeknown to Temur Khan, he decided to hang on to it.

Chapter 37

A FEW DAYS had passed, and India's Research and Analysis Wing had finally managed to trace both Vikas Gupta and Reda Darkaoui. In the case of Gupta, however, what they had uncovered was only his last known location.

He had checked in at the Oberoi Hotel shortly after landing and had only spent two nights there. He had not yet checked out, but was last seen carrying a large bag a few days before and traveling in a hotel car to Apollo Bunder, the pier on which the Gateway of India was built. He had not resurfaced and, to all intents and purposes, was now considered a missing person. All attempts to reach him, or to locate him through his mobile phone, had also failed.

Things were quite different, however, in the case of Darkaoui. In the spirit of cooperation, the RAW had informed the DGSE that his current whereabouts were a cheap hotel by the name of "The Goddess Palace" in the suburb of Kurla in West Mumbai. The place, which was particularly rundown, was a palace only in name and was located close to the railway station, one of the busiest in the city. "The Godless Palace" would perhaps have been more appropriate.

If there was a link between Darkaoui and Gupta, the former had clearly drawn the short straw. Not only had he traveled economy class, while the scientist had flown business, but his lodgings were also a far cry from the luxury and comfort of the Oberoi, with its marble lobby, restaurants and bars, not to mention its location in one of Mumbai's swankiest neighborhoods.

Darkaoui had booked the room for five days and, unlike Gupta, had so far always returned to spend the night at the hotel. Rather than run the risk of losing his trail as well, The Bear had instructed Tanguy to fly to India to check him out.

The Indians had been more than happy to facilitate things and let their French counterpart have a quiet word with the Franco-Algerian. India was just about to finalize the purchase of Rafale fighter jets from France and had been grateful for the tipoff. Security and military cooperation between the two countries was on the rise.

Should anything untoward be uncovered, they would arrest Darkaoui and, most likely, extradite him at the request of the French authorities. But for now, there was no warrant out for his arrest, so everything had to remain off the books.

Erwan Tanguy had traveled a few times to India, although Kurla was not an area he was familiar with. In fact, even though it formed part of greater Mumbai, there was no reason for it to be on the tourist trail. A large part of the district was made up of industrial estates, including an automobile assembly plant and a dairy factory, while hundreds of thousands of workers passed each day through the railway station to catch commuter trains on the Central Railway Suburban Line or Harbour Line.

The RAW had given him an hour face to face with Darkaoui before they would take matters into their own hands—or not, as the case might be.

Tanguy walked up a filthy staircase and knocked twice on the door to Darkaoui's room.

"Coming!" said a voice inside, in a strong French accent.

As he opened the door, Tanguy shoved him inside the room and slammed the door shut.

"What…what is this?" asked Darkaoui, taken aback.

"*Assieds toi!*" ("Sit down!") commanded Tanguy.

"*Putain, mec, t'es qui? Tu veux quoi? T'es ouf?*" ("Who the fuck are you? What do you want? Are you off your trolley?")

"You're in deep shit, Reda! So just do as I say, and answer my questions. And then maybe, just maybe, things will be all right, as far as you're concerned."

"I…I don't understand. I'm here as a tourist. Who are you, anyway?"

"I'm the one asking questions. Don't make me waste my time. Where's Gupta?"

"What's Gupta? I'm here on holidays."

"As if. Where are the vials?"

"What vials? I'm clean, dude."

"If you don't want to talk, I'll make you talk. And, believe me, you don't want to go there."

"I'm not scared, dickhead! Come, I'll give it to you!"

Tanguy slapped Darkaoui and, grabbing him by his collar, led him to the tiny, grimy bathroom. The Franco-Algerian quickly realized he didn't have the upper hand.

As part of his commando training, Erwan Tanguy had endured what was known in the French military as *le coxage*.

It was meant to give the Special Forces operatives in training a taste of what they might endure, if ever captured by the enemy. It had taught him a great deal about pain and ways of inflicting it. Everyone had his or her own limits but, beyond a certain level, all ended up talking.

Le coxage usually started late at night, at the end of what had seemed like one of the usual tactical exercises on an island off the coast of Brittany. One by one, the men had been wrestled to the ground by the instructors and re-strained, a crude hood placed over their heads, their wrists bound behind their backs with thick cable ties.

They had then been forced to walk in line, for more than an hour, through a thick forest, tripping on roots and shrubs before reaching an abandoned fort. There, they had been told to wait in the cold and dark for a good part of the night, with nothing to eat or drink, standing or crouching in uncomfortable positions.

Next had come the questioning. Each of the recruits had been subjected to "enhanced" interrogation techniques, including being slapped and punched as well as waterboard-ing. It had been drilled into them that the only answers they could give to any question were their name and service number.

It had been particularly unpleasant, but Tanguy had gone through it without much consequence. It did hurt, but it was not so much about the pain; more the will to go through it and face what might come next. Not all had been so lucky. Some had panicked, unable to process what was happening to them.

Then had come what had been termed the *parcours eva-*

sion (escape drill). Already tired, hungry and dehydrated, the trainees had been dumped into a completely dark room and told to find the exit to the building in which it was located, within a set period of time. This had meant feeling one's way through dark, narrow passages, ending with a crawl across a damp, smelly tunnel, before they could finally emerge at dawn in the open air. There, a senior officer had greeted them with food and water, whispering a few words of encouragement.

"Where's Gupta?"

"I don't know!"

Tanguy wrestled Darkaoui to the ground and placed his back at a small incline, his feet resting on the edge of the shower cubicle. He put a small towel over his face and started to slowly empty a bottle of water over it.

Waterboarding was also known as simulated drowning. One's life wasn't really at risk most of the time, but one experienced the sensation of drowning as water made its way inside the nasal passage. It caused a gag reflex, often leading the prisoner to vomit.

Tanguy applied water continuously for about twenty seconds and then removed the cloth to allow Darkaoui to breathe two or three times. He then repeated the procedure. The small-time hooligan was now experiencing full-blown panic, wide-eyed and awestruck. He finally vomited all over his chin and chest. He inhaled some of it as it traveled up his esophagus and coughed violently.

"Stop! Stop!"

"Where's Gupta?"

"Man…I really don't know! You have to believe me!"

Tanguy pressed on for another round. Darkaoui's legs were restless, flapping away, as water trickled down his nostrils.

"Talk!"

"I don't…know…any Gupta!"

Tanguy made preparations to continue, but Darkaoui raised a hand, imploring him to stop. For a suspected terrorist, he was surprisingly weak and now a sorry sight.

"I…I came to India to buy weed…" he finally said. "I have a contact in Crawford Market, an Afghan guy. He can arrange shipping to Europe too. The stuff arrives in a container in Marseille, hidden among cheap furniture. It's almost foolproof. I don't know any Gupta. His name is Aabdar. I know nothing about the vials you mentioned, either. Please stop! Arrest me if you want, but I don't think I can take any more of this!"

He sounded sincere.

"You browsed Islamist websites recently. What was that all about?"

"I was just curious, man. Honest! But these guys are nuts. No fucking way I'm heading to Syria! That's not me! I'm happy just dealing shit in France."

Tanguy pondered for a minute. In all likelihood, it had been an unlucky coincidence. The *modus operandi* of Gupta and Darkaoui had been very different. Darkaoui also lacked the edge to be involved in something as sophisticated as the smuggling of infectious viruses. They had obviously gone down the wrong path.

"Go back to France, kid!" he said finally. "And do that soon. Get a proper job. But be aware you're now under watch. If we ever find you dealing dope again, let alone being involved with crazy motherfuckers like ISIS, you won't be so lucky next time. Are we clear?"

Darkaoui briefly nodded to indicate he had understood.

Tanguy left the hotel room and walked down to the gritty hotel reception.

"What about it?" asked his contact from the RAW, who was waiting in the lobby, smoking a cigarette.

"False alarm! Let him be. He's clean. Well, almost. You may want to look up a guy by the name of Aabdar in Crawford Market, though. Afghan. Drug dealer. But I'm still very keen to locate Gupta, as a matter of priority. We don't yet know what exactly he's smuggled from Europe, but it could prove to be extremely dangerous."

"We're doing our very best, but it's as if he's vanished into thin air."

Chapter 38

Arabian Sea, off the western coast of India, April 2016

THE PABLO SUÁREZ was a compact container ship holding the equivalent of 500 twenty-foot units (TEUs), with a total length of just over three-hundred-and-thirty feet and a beam of sixty feet. She had a relatively shallow draft, and her covered holds contained fifty-two refrigerated containers, each connected to electricity feeds, in addition to many more intermodal boxes of cargo on her upper deck.

She was old, rusty and rather slow, with a speed of only fifteen knots. But what she lacked in performance, she more than made up for in discretion and anonymity. There were many similar ships cruising the world's oceans, and there was little to distinguish her from thousands of others, many of which made the route between Europe and Asia.

Like many of her brethren, she was registered in Panama, but unusually enough, her captain was Egyptian. Ali Ahmed was also a former operative of Ansar Bait al-Maqdis, perhaps better known as the Supporters of the Holy House, a terrorist organization that had recently pledged allegiance to the Islamic State of Iraq and the Levant (ISIL). He had been delighted to welcome on board the quiet Asian man with strange eyes who had made contact months earlier, and who seemed to have impeccable credentials and connections. He had no way of knowing the man had been groomed by the competing al Qaeda organization, and he had not hesitated for a minute to help a Brother and fellow believer in jihad.

Al Qaeda's strategy was global, with the aim of spreading terror not only to its historic bases in Afghanistan and Pakistan, but also to Yemen and the Horn of Africa, as well as across the Maghreb, Egypt, parts of Asia and, occasionally, the Western world. By contrast, the Islamic State of Iraq and Syria (ISIS) and its sister organization ISIL had chosen the path of creating their own state, spread over parts of Syria and Iraq. This meant they were increasingly facing relentless attacks from their enemies, who now threatened their hegemony, unlike that of al Qaeda, which continued to operate covertly. As they came ever more under pressure, it was now likely that ISIS' and ISIL's strategy would mirror that of al Qaeda in a not too distant future.

What was not part of the plan, however, was the nervous Indian man, obviously a *kafir*, who had accompanied Khan as they had departed from JNPT, or Jawaharlal Nehru Port, the largest container port in India. It was located east of Mumbai, in the state of Maharashtra, and provided access to the Arabian Sea via Thane Creek. Every year, it handled a volume of almost four-and-a-half million TEU, with vessels of all sizes docking at one of the three berths along its quay.

All the same, Ahmed had agreed to hide them both in one of the containers until they were safely at sea and had found them small but not uncomfortable lodgings in two cabins reserved for occasional passengers in the white bridge castle, which was located at the stern. They would take most of their meals there, and he had instructed the crew to have as little interaction with them as possible. They were scientists, he had said, and were not to be disturbed. In any event, the sailors were busy enough not to pay much attention to them.

The sea had been rough just outside the port on account of the wind, and there had been much rocking and rolling. Vikas Gupta had slipped and bruised his head against a porcelain washbasin in his quarters. He had wiped the minor bleeding with a tea towel he had found in the cabin, pocketing it in case more blood trickled. The name of the ship was embroidered in faded green letters on one the towel's corners. It sounded vaguely Spanish. Could they be headed back to Spain? That hardly made any sense. Perhaps to Latin America, then? But in that case, why travel from Madrid to India in the first place? Everything was still very confusing to him.

But for now, since they had just reached the safety of international waters, the two passengers were both outside on the container deck, although away from view of the crew.

"Did you hurt yourself?" observed Temur, matter-of-factly.

"It's nothing. I just slipped, as the boat hit a large wave. Not to worry. But thank you for your concern."

The wind was still blowing strong. After a few minutes, he added:

"I still can't imagine how they managed to find out. I took great care not to leave any gaps in the inventory."

Temur Khan did not answer. In truth, the change of

plan had hardly turned things upside down as far as he was concerned. He had always assumed the disappearance of some of the lab's stock would ultimately come to light. But the speed with which it had happened had still come as a surprise.

Gupta had obviously made a mistake at some point and was now a marked man. He had planned to get rid of him, back in Mumbai, but it had been impossible to stay there any longer and he had been forced to leave the country with Gupta in tow. Luckily, Ali Ahmed had agreed to set sail slightly earlier than planned. What happened to Gupta next was unimportant. The vials of SARS virus were now safely hidden in Temur's cabin, and that was all that mattered.

Chances were that the trail had ended at the Oberoi, and that the nature of the pathogens smuggled out of Alcobendas had not yet been discovered. He still had everything going for him, and he no doubt had a good lead over his pursuers. By now, he assumed, intelligence agencies were likely involved. But they would hardly have the full picture. He allowed himself a faint smile.

"Where are we headed, anyway?" asked Gupta. "How soon will you arrange safe passage for my family?"

"We still have a long journey ahead of us," answered Temur. "But our final destination is Hong Kong."

"Hong Kong, Hong Kong," repeated Gupta pensively, looking at the horizon.

He had never been there. It was almost on the other side of the world. Could he start a new life in China? It wasn't as if he had much of a choice now. And was it there that the man planned to spread the deadly disease, assuming that's what he had in mind?

Ahead of them, sea birds dove into the water to feed on a shoal of small fish.

While Gupta wasn't looking, Temur Khan put his hand in his pocket and retrieved a folding knife.

It had a four-inch upswept blade with ambidextrous thumb studs. The finish was black, and it had once belonged to a U.S. Marine from the 1st Reconnaissance Battalion that had been deployed to Trek Nawa, in the contested Helmand province in eastern Afghanistan. It was sturdy, made of cryogenically treated steel and extremely sharp—a lethal weapon designed for hand-to-hand combat. He had acquired it in the Bab-el-Barhain souk in Manama, in Barhain, while still living in Oman.

He silently flicked it open and locked the blade into position with the manual push-button safety.

"Yes, Hong Kong," he said. "But you won't be joining me there. So long, Vikas," he added, plunging the blade into the Indian's external carotid artery.

Vikas Gupta didn't utter a sound, his eyes wide open and his arms flapping as blood gushed out of the wound. Within seconds, his face went pale as the life quickly drained out of him. Temur didn't wait for him to die, but threw his body straight overboard.

It landed in the sea below, head first, and disappeared under the mass of boiling water stirred by the Pablo Suárez's massive propellers.

Chapter 39

San Sebastián de los Reyes, Spain, April 2016

SOMETIMES, IT'S the little things that significantly change the course of events. One late morning that April, in a residential building in San Sebastián de los Reyes just outside central Madrid, it came in the shape of a domestic gas pipe, badly connected to a rusty but functional cooker, in an aging kitchen.

The pipe was galvanized, something that the municipal code normally never would have allowed, but the installation had been done on the cheap by an unregistered plumber many years before, and the zinc coating applied to the steel had long since started to strip off. Over time, flakes had traveled through the pipe and gotten stuck in its orifices. That day, as pressure inside the tube built up to previously unseen heights, the end of the gas line started to develop a leak.

No one was at home that morning and able to take note of the unfortunate development. In any event, the owner of the apartment, known to all in the building as Doña Carmen, was elderly and had poor eyesight. Had she been home at the time, she probably wouldn't have noticed anything untoward about the appliance.

The lethal mixture, made up of hydrogen, methane and carbon dioxide, with a small amount of carbon monoxide, nitrogen and oxygen, was lighter than air. It began to propagate sideways throughout the flat, seeking the path of least resistance. All the windows were closed tight, and the mixture slowly started to accumulate, saturating the air to a level of about ten percent within less than an hour. Some of it even found its way under the front door of the flat, reaching the second floor elevator lobby of the building, which had seen better days.

Doña Carmen's next-door neighbor wasn't in her prime, either. As she returned from her daily grocery shopping, she flipped on the light switch in the dark stairwell. Her mundane gesture triggered an ignition, followed by a powerful explosion that not only killed her immediately, but also ripped apart the entire edifice.

Within ten minutes, firefighters had arrived. They immediately evacuated the nearby buildings, some of which had also been badly shaken. There was always the possibility of secondary explosions, and they didn't want to take any chances.

On the ground floor of an adjacent development that had also been partly hit, there stood what looked from outside like a garage. It was quite rundown, and the metal shutters covered with a green peeling paint were closed with a padlock. One of the firefighters inserted the pointy end of his axe in the catch and swiftly broke it with a strong twisting motion.

Rolling the shutters and stepping inside, he first saw that the premises were much larger than he had first expected.

Proceeding with caution, he then discovered toward the back some sort of room, built out of concrete blocks, with a relatively narrow tinted window. He approached and looked through the gap, and immediately saw two bodies.

They were two women—or, more precisely, a woman who had probably been in her forties, and what looked like an adolescent girl. They were quite obviously dead and had been so for perhaps several weeks.

He was about to tear down the door to take a better look when he saw the duct tape that had been applied all around the edges. In fact, all the openings to the room had been carefully caulked, effectively sealing it from the outside world. Inside, a small lamp was switched on, although the light was feeble by now. He concluded that they had not died from gas poisoning.

Fortunately, many years before, the fireman had served in the 2nd Spanish Legion's Engineer Battalion in Viator, near Almería in Andalusia. As one of those known as the "bridegrooms of death," he had received training in chemical, biological, radiological and nuclear (CBRN) defense. It had been quite cursory, but he still recalled well what he had been taught and immediately instructed everyone to back off.

He then took it upon himself to evacuate and seal off a good part of the entire neighborhood. Although he could not know it at the time, his initiative probably saved the lives of several hundred people that day.

Within an hour, the CBRN units of the National Police and Spanish Civil Guard had arrived at the scene, soon joined by the Military Emergencies Unit. A few hours later, they were seconded by a platoon of the country's first CBRN regiment, stationed in Valencia, which had been flown to Madrid in a hurry by helicopter. It had been created in 2005, following the train bombings in the Spanish capital, and each year it participated in a realistic large-scale training exercise, known as Grifo ("Griffin").

After a thorough briefing about what had been discovered so far, its members donned two-piece protective suits, manufactured in Germany by a firm called Blucher GmbH. The suits gave them twenty-four-hour protection against environmental threats. Next, using technology known as Bioaerosol Triggers, they collected samples to identify and confirm the nature of the threat. The virus was then isolated in a cell culture, and a sequence was obtained by a polymerase-chain-reaction-based random-amplification procedure. Genetic characterization indicated that the virus was related to known coronaviruses, and it was soon recognized as SARS.

They then sealed the entire surrounding area under a large plastic tent and deployed an air filtration system to remove any deadly particles from the air, much as the HEPA filters did at the BSL-4 facility in nearby Alcobendas.

Pictures and DNA samples were taken of the victims, before their bodies were destroyed with powerful flamethrowers and the place subjected to a thorough and lengthy chemical wash.

Within less than a day, the woman and girl were positively identified as Deepika and Parvati Gupta, the wife and daughter of the scientist who had been reported missing only a few weeks before.

A check of the inventory at the Alcobendas laboratory, at the behest of Diego Morales, the head of security, finally identified Gupta's fingerprints on no fewer than twenty-four vials in a sealed Styrofoam box of SARS virus, held in a refrigerated storage facility. The other ampoules in the batch, however, were clean and had therefore probably been untouched. Further analysis established that the twenty-four glass containers only contained a harmless saline solution and had obviously been substituted for the real samples.

By the following morning, most major security agencies in Europe, as well as some of their closest allies and correspondents around the world, were informed of the nature of the threat. One of their worst nightmares, and a scenario they had envisaged for years—but without really believing it might one day happen—had just become painfully real. A suspected terrorist was at large, with samples of a deadly pathogen for which there was no known cure.

The ampoules had last been sighted in Mumbai, India, but all traces of them had since disappeared, and there was no way of knowing where the terrorist, and perhaps potential accomplices, planned to use them.

National emergency plans were immediately triggered, and police and military patrols increased in all the sensitive areas of major cities, including airports, train and metro stations, as well as large commercial centers and thorough-fares. But, to avoid panic from spreading, the truth was withheld from the public.

What still remained a mystery, however, was who exactly had killed the two women—and the whereabouts of Vikas Gupta.

Chapter 40

Indian Ocean, April 2016

THE PABLO SUÁREZ had continued her journey toward southern China, the routine of the voyage bringing little in terms of surprises or novelty. The never-ending rumble of the powerful engines and breaking of the waves on the bow gradually became familiar sounds at all times of the day and night. After a while, all those on board even ignored them completely. They all adapted and became part of the self-contained universe that was the container ship.

Temur Khan spent most of the days in his small cabin, planning for what would come next and only emerging after lunch for a short walk outside to take the air. As a fellow Muslim, Ali Ahmed had lent him a prayer mat, and he faithfully recited the Salat five times daily, starting before sunrise and ending between sunset and midnight. A fixed Qibla locator was quite useless when at sea, but there was a small compass in his cabin that allowed him to find the direction of Mecca for his devotions. The course of the boat was also straight, at least most of the time. He could tell the direction he was facing by simply looking at both the sun and his watch, or the stars at night.

The ship had stopped en route in Cochin, a major port

on the Arabian Sea-Indian Ocean route and also the largest transshipment facility in India. There, a number of containers had been unloaded from the hull, to be replaced by yet more boxes, both in the covered holds and on the upper deck.

All those on board had assumed the Indian man who had accompanied Temur had disembarked then. He certainly wasn't seen anymore after the ship's stop, vanishing without leaving any trace. The captain had doubts about this—he had found a few remaining items of clothing in the cabin he had assigned to the man—but thought it best not to ask any questions. In the shady business of Islamic fundamentalism, it was always wiser not to be too curious. The Asian man had a mission, and the less Ali knew, the better, as far as he was concerned. Besides, the Indian man was a *kafir*, an unbeliever, and what had happened to him was the least of his concerns. In any event, some things were probably best left unsaid. The small crew, mostly composed of men from the Philippines and Kiribati Islands, had never socialized with him, as they had been instructed, and didn't really care one way or the other.

The Pablo Suárez was now well on her way to rounding the southern tip of the Indian subcontinent. There were a few additional stops scheduled along the way to Hong Kong, and the men all looked forward to a few hours of rest and recreation on dry land before boarding again for the ensuing passages. It meant an opportunity to buy souvenirs for the family, cigarettes or a small treat to vary the monotonous diet churned out by the ship's kitchen. For some, it was also a chance to get drunk in the local bars, since the consumption of alcohol was not permitted on board, or for cheap and hasty intercourse with local prostitutes. After all, stopovers catered to the most basic of human needs.

Next would come ports of call at Colombo in Sri Lanka, Singapore and Ho Chi Minh City in Vietnam, before they at last reached their final destination in the Pearl River Delta.

"We should arrive there in less than three weeks, Inch'Allah," Ahmed had said. "She's not that fast, but we're making good progress and the weather's favorable," he had added.

Temur had followed the news on the Internet, which could be accessed in clear weather through a satellite connection on the bridge. From what he had read, it looked like security measures had been reinforced in a good number of major cities across the Western world. The threat of terrorism, following the recent attacks in the Brussels metro system as well as at the city's Zaventem airport, was generally mentioned as the reason for beefing up such security plans, although nothing specific was stated. He obviously knew better. In his cabin, the twenty-three ampoules of betacoronavirus looked harmless enough, resting in their portable container, which was plugged into the mains for additional safety. But what they contained was capable of killing hundreds, maybe even thousands, of people in the space of just a couple of weeks.

Nonchalantly, in the safety of his cabin, he unfolded the *ikat* fabric belt given to him in Kashgar by the bazaar merchant Farruck Durdona, some twenty-seven years before. It had never left him. The belt brought back memories of his childhood, as well as of the journey to Kyrgyzstan that he had first taken with his mentor, Ismail Khan. Much had changed since then, but there was no turning back. He refolded the garment and returned it to his backpack.

Next, he carefully studied a thick and already well-thumbed document, created on AutoCAD software. It included technical drawings, documenting the architectural design of a building in Hong Kong. He had already gone through it many times, but he needed to become completely familiar with the perspectives, floor and site plans, elevations, cross-sections and isometric and axonometric projections. He had never seen the building in real life and, when the time came, he could not afford to hesitate.

He closed his eyes and mentally walked through the various elevator lobbies, underground garages, upper floors, technical areas and even the rooftop. The success of his plan would ultimately depend in no small measure on his thorough understanding of the construction's most intricate details.

And then, once he was finally ready, he would strike. Without mercy.

Chapter 41

Paris, France, April 2016

"SO, THERE WAS no link between Darkaoui and Gupta, in the end? Talk about bad luck," said The Bear, in a foul mood as always.

"Indeed. He was a thug all right, but mostly a small-time dope dealer. A bit of a loser, really. Nothing for us to worry much about. But he gave me the name of a bigger fish, an Afghan, who exports some of the stuff to France, via Marseille. The Indians are on the case, as are the DGSI now," answered Erwan Tanguy, who had returned to Europe after the trail in Mumbai had gone cold.

The Direction Générale de la Sécurité Intérieure, only established in 2014, was the domestic equivalent in France of the DGSE, as MI5 was the counterpart to MI6 in the U.K., whose real name was actually the Secret Intelligence Service, or SIS. It was charged with counterespionage, counterterrorism, countering cybercrime and the surveillance of potentially threatening groups, organizations and social phenomena.

"And Gupta's now vanished for good?"

"Sadly. We lost him after he left the Oberoi, without checking out, I might add. We haven't found any traces of him leaving the country, though. Chances are he might still be in India."

"Or he could also have crossed into Pakistan, or half a dozen countries by land. In some of these areas, the borders are rather porous, obviously. If he's made it to the badlands, we'll have a hell of a time trying to get to him."

"He could also have left the country by boat. That's another possibility. After all, he was last seen on the banks of the Arabian Sea."

"Then God save us all! He could be anywhere by now."

"The minute he surfaces at an immigration checkpoint, checks into a hotel or uses one of his credit cards, we'll know. But until then, there's very little we can do."

"I doubt he's that stupid. He's probably using a new set of papers already, as well as an offshore bank account. Fuck, that's what I'd do! But there's still something I don't get. Why kill his wife and daughter? He very much seemed like the family man. And, as you'd already mentioned, he hardly was the terrorist type either."

"I've been asking myself that same question. Maybe there was someone else? Someone who might first have kidnapped his family? That would make sense. At the very least, it would explain why they didn't make it to India and failed to catch their flight. Then, it would have been a question of convincing Gupta to steal the vials and bring them there. As to how exactly he did it, that remains a mystery."

"Meanwhile, the man (or men) behind the kidnapping happily tested the virus on Gupta's wife and child to make sure he had been supplied with the genuine article."

"And then made up a story to explain why they had not yet been released. Gupta would have had to remain convinced they would eventually be set free to play ball," said Tanguy.

"But, assuming we're right, after killing them, there would hardly have been any further need for Gupta, would there?"

"One would still need to reactivate the virus. It was in lyophilized form, remember?" said Tanguy.

"Well, if I've followed well, he obviously managed to do that in Alcobendas. On the safe assumption that Gupta had no part in it, we have to believe the other man is more than capable of doing so by himself."

"You're right. In which case, Gupta may still reappear, but only dead as a dodo."

"That's my biggest concern," said Colonel Le Pan. "He's the only real lead we have, after all. How does that virus spread, anyway?" he asked.

"Some believe it's airborne, although that was never proven, apparently. Otherwise, it spreads by contact with mucus membranes; that much is known. Do you have any idea how often we touch our face, our eyes, our mouth, or just scratch our nose, in any given hour? Let alone in the course of a day? Or maybe just shake hands with someone or kiss people we're close to? Just serving contaminated food or drinks in, say, an international airport would be enough to propagate the virus around the world in no time. Or it could be released into an air conditioning system and spread that way, if the airborne theory is correct. Doing that in some sort of transportation hub would surely have devastating consequences."

"They did manage to contain the infection in Asia, didn't they?"

"They did, but it still took a few months. Meanwhile, almost eight hundred people died from the disease, amid absolute chaos. And it's not just about the loss of human life. Arguably, the impact on the economy of many a country would be equally significant. Healthcare facilities and hospitals would fall under a huge strain—no pun intended. The transportation sector would virtually grind to a halt. Many businesses would shut down. Share prices would collapse, at least for a period of time."

"And all that because someone stole a few vials from a laboratory."

"Actually, not that it makes a huge difference, they must now be down to twenty-three after testing one of these on the two women a few weeks ago. One would have been reactivated, as you just said. Fragments of a petri dish were found in the women's cell. Intel says that it wouldn't have taken all that long for the virus to get to work. The room was also completely sealed with duct tape. They would have suffered a horrible death, with oxygen slowly thinning out in that enclosed environment and the virus gradually taking hold of their bodies. Apparently, they were gone within a week, tops. The daughter died first, then the mother, shortly after."

"What about Musafir?"

"We don't have enough to shrink that haystack just yet. What the Chinese gave us was very little. At the very minimum, we need to establish a pattern before we can follow that lead. Like that name appearing several times in suspicious phone calls, or at the very least, through the same caller or receiver. We're hardly there. Our Big Ears are listening. The NSA and GCHQ are also on it. But so far, we've drawn a blank."

"Any idea when they might attempt to strike?"

"I'm afraid not. If we can narrow down the target to a city, or even a country, we might be able to come up with an educated guess. But, for now, we're far from it."

"I've never felt so helpless. Knowing there's nothing you can do to change the course of events is just the absolute worst feeling! I suppose we must pray for Gupta to finally turn up somewhere, or for whoever's behind this to make a mistake at some point."

"I'll keep monitoring the situation and let you know the instant we get any clues," answered Tanguy.

"Meanwhile, keep the Chinese informed. After all, much of what we know came from them in the first place. They may well come up with something that could have sunk below our radar. It's also a good opportunity to reestablish relations on a better footing, after that fuck-up with Darret. As it happens, the damage he did wasn't all that extensive. And word from the powers-that-be is not to rock the boat, at least not too much. The sad reality is that we need them more than they need us. I thought I'd never live long enough to say that, but here you are."

Erwan Tanguy stood briefly to attention and left. He had the uneasy feeling he would come across Major Xie Wei again before too long. And so far, she had hardly proven to be the bearer of good news.

Chapter 42

LOKMANYA TILAK MUNICIPAL General Hospital was better known in Mumbai as the Sion Hospital. It was a general, municipal healthcare facility located on Dr. Babasaheb Ambedkar Road, in the Sion Koliwada suburb of India's financial capital, one of the city's earliest settlements.

The hospital's location was fairly close to the international airport. It had first opened with only ten beds, in 1947, the year India had gained independence from the British, but it had since grown into a multi-specialty center that could welcome up to 1,400 inpatients. It was also one of eight hospitals in Bombay where autopsies could be conducted.

In charge of the postmortem was Dr. Vijay Banati, a no-nonsense man in his fifties with a white mustache, who had conducted several hundred, if not thousands, of such examinations since graduating from university. That day, he wore a green gown with matching shoe covers and plastic gloves and was joined by a young and eager assistant with a broad smile but rather bad skin.

Also in attendance was Atul Jain, an intelligence officer from India's Research and Analysis Wing. Not as used to the smell of decaying bodies as the two medical professionals, he first conscientiously applied a generous layer of Vicks VapoRub under his nose to mask the stench of the cadaver that had been brought earlier into the examination room. In the background was a faint odor of formaldehyde and bleach. The procedure had not even started, but he already found the atmosphere disturbing.

Vikas Gupta, or rather, his badly damaged remains, were still in a body bag. Dr. Banati removed the seals to allow for his identification. Even though the body was in a sorry shape, the odds were that the face matched the one featured on the OCI card that had been recovered by the beat policeman from Chowpatty Beach. A number of photographs were taken of the corpse while it still lay inside the bag. Further matching would be conducted with the DNA records obtained from his latest employer, a high-tech laboratory in Alcobendas, Spain.

The physician described aloud the body's appearance on a voice recorder. At this stage, Gupta was still clothed. The ripped and soiled rags would be removed later. His hands, most of which appeared to have been eaten by marine animals, were still wrapped in evidence bags. The bags were removed to cut the fingernails, but there were hardly any left to be collected. Samples of hair and fibers were also taken.

Above the body, Dr. Banati lit an overhead UV lamp to locate secretions on uncovered skin and the few items of clothing, before taking several X-ray shots as he and Jain retreated behind a thick partition wall.

"I take so many of these I should have more powers than Superman by now, on account of the radiation! Not that my wife would agree," joked the physician.

The assistant carefully removed the body bag and emptied Gupta's pockets. The only item that he found was some sort of tea towel or handkerchief, with words embroidered on a corner in neat but faded green letters that read "Pablo Suárez." Jain made a mental note to check it out later.

Gupta's body was then undressed and cleaned, before being weighed and measured. Once this was done, Banati donned a full-face plastic mask and Gupta's body was moved to a canted aluminum table whose raised contours allowed for the drainage of blood and bodily fluids. It now lay face up, and the physician placed a rubber block behind the back to make the chest protrude forward. This would enable him to cut more precisely during the course of the examination.

But, first, he carefully noted details of the skin, arms and legs, searching for tattoos, birthmarks and other remarkable characteristics.

"I'd say M. Gupta, assuming this is him, was in his mid to late forties," he volunteered.

"That tallies with the records from IVFRT. He was forty-six," said Jain.

"A fair bit overweight, too. I see from the OCI card photograph that he was wearing glasses. Were any found?"

"Sadly not; they were probably lost at sea."

"That figures. Oh, there's a sharp and deep cut toward the external carotid artery. Our man didn't die solely from drowning; that much is clear. Look at the neck."

Jain came closer to examine a nasty wound.

"Yep. He was stabbed, all right."

"Undoubtedly."

Banati then made a deep, Y-shaped incision, starting from the left and right shoulders and meeting at the breastbone, and continuing all the way down to the pubic bone. He then peeled back the skin, muscle and soft tissue with a scalpel to reveal the rib cage, further cutting down the sides for better access to Gupta's internal organs.

Jain remained silent, focusing on his breathing. The procedure was not for the fainthearted. It was not the first autopsy he had attended, but he knew he'd never really get used to what would follow next.

Banati detached the larynx and the esophagus, followed by the arteries and ligaments, before cutting the organs from the spinal cord, bladder and rectum, skillfully extracting the entire mass of internal organs virtually in one piece.

"Careful now," he said under his breath as he pulled the entrails out, before weighing and dissecting these further as more samples were taken.

Next, he cut open the stomach, weighing and examining its contents. By then, the stench had reached another level, and Jain could barely control his urge to vomit. Banati spoke again, but Jain heard very little of what he was saying, totally focused on suppressing his gag reflex.

It seemed nothing remarkable had been noted.

"So far, I don't see anything to alter my initial observations," said the doc. "Step aside a little, now. I need to access the brain."

Jain was only too happy to oblige.

The rubber block was moved from Gupta's back to his neck, as Banati cut open the forehead with a scalpel, from one ear to the other, like in a scene from a horror movie. He then pulled away the scalp and cut into the skull with an electric saw to expose the brain. A dust collection system reduced the amount of airborne particles, but a good many still splattered everywhere, including over the front of Jain's protective gown. Quickly, he wiped them off with a flick of the hand, onto which some remained stuck, much like pieces of nuts and dried fruits atop a *phirni* milk pudding.

Dr. Banati next severed the brain from the spinal cord before lifting it out. It was also carefully examined and, like the other organs, weighed.

"Right," he finally told Jain. "I still have to go through the samples I dissected earlier, as well as the toxicology report. Expect that within a few days. But, quite frankly, I don't believe this will shed any further light on what happened. It looks like our friend Gupta was killed at sea, most likely as a passenger on a boat. He would have been stabbed in the throat by a knife or dagger. A very sharp one for sure, with a blade of perhaps 3.7 to 4 inches in length, probably military grade and with a single cutting edge. He wasn't yet dead when he went, or, more likely, when his body was thrown overboard, but he would have lost a lot of blood in a very short space of time by then, and death would have followed within a matter of minutes—perhaps even sooner. But he would have been completely unconscious at the point when he dropped into the water."

"What about the time of death?"

"The body was remarkably well preserved on account of the water temperature. Rather chilly for the season this year. But, judging by the damage inflicted by marine life, I'd say perhaps up to three or four weeks ago or so. It's difficult to be more precise. He really is in pretty bad shape, as you can see."

"Definitely not a suicide?"

"Clearly not! On top of being an odd way to end one's life, unless perhaps if you're Japanese, and a rather traditional one at that, he wouldn't have been able to thrust the blade into his body with that much force and at such an angle. It was clearly murder, a killing or an execution, whatever you want to call it. What did you say he did for a living again?"

"He worked for a laboratory. Virology."

"Well, it seems no one's safe these days. At least the bugs didn't get to him. You're welcome to take his personal belongings for further analysis, of course. Just sign for them when you leave. Varun will see you out. I'll get back to you as quickly as I can. What about the body?"

"As soon as you've reverted, the family should be able to take it away for cremation. I believe he had relatives in India. We'll notify them, assuming nothing new surfaces. Sorry, odd choice of words for a body found at sea."

"Understood," said Banati, with a mischievous smile. "Talk soon, then."

Later that day, Atul Jain sat in his cramped office, a stone's throw from Sion Hospital, to conduct further research into the case. On a wall behind him was a framed picture of the Ashoka Chakra—the twenty-four-spoke wheel featured on the Indian national flag—and some script in Sanskrit, on a saffron background. It read, "The law protects when it is protected." This was the RAW's motto.

After an hour or so, Jain first discovered that the Pablo Suárez was in fact a container ship that had departed from Jawaharlal Nehru Port only a few weeks earlier. The timing seemed to coincide. It was probably the vessel on which Gupta had been fatally stabbed and then dumped at sea. It had to be. For some reason, Gupta would have pocketed a piece of laundry on board. It had been sheer luck, although clearly his demise would have been far from peaceful.

According to Lloyds' insurance records, the Pablo Suárez had just docked in Hong Kong barely a few hours earlier, after a long passage that had taken it first to southern India and then to Sri Lanka, Singapore and Vietnam. Its cargo was a mix of frozen food in reefer containers deep in the hull, and large appliances and other electronics carried on the upper deck. The manifest didn't seem to include anything of note, and the crew was quite thin in number. It was a compact vessel, not one of those Panamax, let alone post-Panamax, behemoths.

The captain was, oddly enough, an Egyptian, one Ali Ahmed. Further probing revealed he had a somewhat shady past and was rumored at some point to have supported a terrorist organization by the name of Ansar Bait al-Maqdis, although that could never actually be established beyond a doubt.

Ansar Bait al-Maqdis had since rallied to the cause of ISIL, which was more than enough of a red flag. The Pablo Suárez was scheduled to remain in Hong Kong for another couple of days at most, before leaving for Busan in South Korea.

At least it now looked like India was probably not the target of a possible biological attack. After obtaining the green light from his superiors, Jain called the Frenchman who had visited a few weeks before. The consulate had already been informed: Gupta had left the bosom of Mother India years ago and had since become a French citizen. The man would no doubt be pleased to receive news of the discovery of the body, as well as further information on what Jain had just uncovered.

Clearly, the trail no longer ended with the scientist. Whoever had killed him would instead now become one of the world's most wanted men.

He picked up the receiver and dialed the IDD code, followed by thirty-three, the country code for France.

Chapter 43

Kwai Chung, Hong Kong, May 2016

THE PABLO SUÁREZ had just docked in Kwai Chung, where the city's busiest container port was located. Established in the 1970s, it had significantly expanded throughout the 1980s, when much of the commercial port had relocated there from Yau Ma Tei. It was now the fifth-busiest container port in the world. With the exception of Singapore, which now ranked second, all the others were in China.

Located on the South China Sea, most of Hong Kong's traffic was devoted to trade in containerized, manufactured products, rather than raw materials or passengers. The natural shelter and deep waters of Victoria Harbor provided ideal conditions for the berthing and handling of all types of vessels. Five companies operated its nine terminals and ninety-two quay cranes, alongside almost 4.3 miles of water frontage. At all hours of the day and night, thousands of people loaded, unloaded and transported modular boxes, in a frantic ballet played by dockers and lorries across the many container yards and freight stations.

They had arrived late in the afternoon. Temur Khan had offered thanks to Captain Ahmed and then cleared immigration using a perfectly forged Canadian passport that would allow him to remain in the Special Administrative Region of China, with no need for a visa, for up to ninety days. It was more than enough for what he had to accomplish. The important thing was that he had been able to enter the city unmolested. If everything went according to plan, he would have no need to clear immigration again later.

Carrying the cool box and a small backpack, he had taken a red and white urban taxi and given the driver an address near Shek Tong Tsui, on the northwestern edge of Hong Kong. Until fairly recently, it had garnered something of a bad reputation, having been home to many of the brothels that catered to sailors and those serving in the British military. In more recent years, however, it had experienced a revival, gentrification slowly creeping in with the expansion of the mass transit railway network. Fashionable restaurants, bars and nightclubs had opened, as had trendy boutiques, gradually replacing commercial printing and Chinese medicine shops.

Temur Khan had rented a small apartment there, using his Airbnb Internet app. All that was needed was a Facebook account and a credit card. It was far more discreet than staying at a hotel, and he had not even been required to produce an ID. The credit card was linked to an account in Dubai, opened under an assumed identity that matched the passport he had shown the immigration officer earlier. The booking had been made months in advance. He had no plans to use the card again in Hong Kong, where everything he might need would be paid for in cash.

Cash was best. It was untraceable, and he had yet to find people—and certainly not in Hong Kong—who turned down this method of payment.

The owner was happy for him to stay for two weeks. Everything had already been pre-paid. A cheerful British expat with a blonde bouffant hairstyle had met him at the door, shown him around the first floor flat and given him the keys to the building and front door.

"I look like a mess! Can't stand the humidity! What is it you do again, Peter?" she had asked.

"I'm a chemist. I work on flavors and scents for the food and beverage and cosmetics industries," he had answered.

"Oh, that explains it! I was wondering what was in the cool box."

"Only samples, for canned products. Nothing too exciting, I'm afraid! And you needn't worry: these are for delivery to my office. I won't be turning your kitchen into a lab! In fact, I probably won't even use it at all—I like to eat out. I love Cantonese food!"

"Well, then, have a lovely stay! Just put the keys in an envelope and pop it into the letterbox when you leave."

The property was small, but clean and functional and, best of all, anonymous. No one would pay attention to his comings and goings there. It was also moments away from the Hong Kong University Mass Transit Railway (MTR) station, only a few stops away on the Island Line from the hustle and bustle of Central.

After the owner had left, he plugged in the cool box and unpacked his bag, took a shower and prayed. He then walked around the area to familiarize himself with possible exit routes, in the unlikely event he might need to depart in a hurry. He couldn't leave anything to chance. Not at this stage, when he was so close to his goal.

He next took the escalator down to the MTR station. He bought a single ticket at one of the vending machines and caught an eastbound train to Central. After ten minutes, he walked up to the Pedder Street exit. He turned left and immediately saw the skyscraper in the distance.

The International Finance Centre, known to everyone in the city as IFC, was a prominent landmark on Hong Kong Island's northern waterfront and an integrated development that included two office towers and a giant commercial mall as well as the Four Seasons Hotel and serviced apartments.

Number Two IFC was the tallest of the two towers and the second-highest in the city, after the International Commerce Centre, or ICC, in West Kowloon, which faced it on the other side of the harbor, creating a giant gateway of sorts for passing ships and ferries.

Completed in 2003 at a cost of US$770 million, Two IFC was 1,300 feet in height and had eighty-eight floors, a particularly auspicious number in Chinese culture. In truth, however, it fell somewhat short of that number, as several floors ending with a four, a word that sounds like "death" in Cantonese, had been omitted to address local superstitious beliefs. *Feng shui* still very much mattered in Hong Kong.

The Hong Kong Monetary Authority, the city's central bank, occupied the highest floors. Among other tenants were many investment and private banks, including UBS, BNP Paribas and Nomura, as well as a galaxy of hedge funds and "long-only" institutional investors. There were no fewer than twenty-two high-ceiling trading floors, with panoramic views of the Hong Kong skyline and harbor. The building, with double-deck elevators, was equipped with advanced telecommunications, raised floors for flexible cabling management and nearly column-free floor plans.

He had not chosen Hong Kong by chance. It was a unique target in that it almost seamlessly blended East and West, as it had done for more than a hundred years. Many expatriates still worked there—American, British, Australian and numerous other nationalities—including a growing number of entrepreneurs from continental Europe, fleeing a morose economy.

The territory had returned to the Chinese motherland in 1997. The latter increasingly administered it in much the same way as any other Chinese city, despite the guarantees of relative independence included in the Basic Law, Hong Kong's *de facto* constitution, set to expire in 2047. There was no love lost between the Cantonese who lived there and their masters up north, as the Mandarin language and simplified Chinese script increasingly crept in, changing their way of life forever. In spite of often vocal opposition, all the important decisions related to Hong Kong were now firmly made on the mainland. Striking the city would therefore send a strong message both to the West and to Beijing.

But what had most attracted Temur Khan to the Two IFC tower was that many of those who worked in this glass and steel skyscraper spent a great deal of time traveling. As international financial executives, their jobs dictated that they frequently visit colleagues and clients, from Mumbai to

Tokyo to Sydney and beyond, not forgetting regular trips to headquarters in London or New York.

Three MTR lines and two stations met under the complex. In particular, underneath the mall was the Hong Kong station for the Airport Express train line. There, as well as in Kowloon, passengers could check in, receive their boarding passes, drop off their luggage and travel directly to the airport unencumbered. Trains left every twelve minutes until late at night, and each one had a dedicated baggage car. All checked-in luggage was scanned in bulk by a mechanized automatic explosives-detection system. On average, every day, forty-three thousand passengers traveled to the airport in this way. Many worked in one of the complex's office towers, the bulk of them in Two IFC.

It would not be easy, but unleashing SARS pathogens in the building would not only contaminate its tenants, but also shoppers throughout the mall, many of whom were tourists from the Chinese mainland, as well as travelers to the airport aboard the shuttle trains. In his refrigerated box, Temur Khan possessed the ability to spread death and havoc on an unprecedented scale.

A ray of sunshine touched a glass panel on the skyscraper, its crisp edges suddenly gleaming across the sky's blue palette. Temur Khan smiled and walked down Pedder Street in its direction, for a reconnaissance tour.

Chapter 44

Central, Hong Kong, May 2016

TEMUR KHAN CROSSED Des Voeux Road and walked up the stairs to the elevated walkway that led to the waterfront, a good twenty-three feet above the motorized traffic. Hong Kong seemed to have plenty of these sheltered bridges, linking office towers and shopping malls and shielding locals and tourists from the harsh sun or rain showers that were a feature of the weather in the territory.

On his right was Jardine House, home to the headquarters of one of the city's oldest conglomerates and nicknamed the "building with the ten thousand assholes" by Hongkongers, on account of its many round, 1970s-style windows. He followed the walkway for a short while after passing the General Post Office and finally turned left, entering the IFC mall.

It was an eight-hundred-thousand-square-foot, four-floor shopping center, with many luxury retail brands, a cinema, a high-end Japanese supermarket and a wide variety of restaurants.

Near the entrance lurked parallel traders from mainland China, offering for sale boxes of brand new smartphones and the latest iPads they had previously queued for at the nearby Apple flagship store. Some of these would also be taken across the border in large wheeled suitcases for resale there. They sat in full view of everyone, including the security guards, who didn't seem to mind. No wonder their northern neighbors increasingly exasperated some of the locals.

Temur turned right and walked for about a hundred and fifty yards before reaching the entrance to the Two IFC office tower, the twenty-fourth-tallest building in the world. In the daytime, the public had open access to the giant lobby. It spanned two levels, and large wall-mounted television screens played Bloomberg Television almost continuously, as was the case in each of the elevator cars. Female anchors, many sporting an attractive physique, commented twenty-four seven on interest rates and equity market swings, for the benefit of traders and hedge-fund managers.

After seven in the evening, giant sliding partition doors were shut and one needed an access card to proceed beyond the reception desks manned by "concierges," as the developer liked to call them. In truth, they were just glorified receptionists. Visitors were required to register there by showing an identification document, and to provide a mobile telephone number that no one ever bothered to call.

There were a number of separate elevator lobbies, depending on the floor one wished to access. For the upper levels of the tower, one also needed to change cars at one of the transfer lobbies, meaning there were often significant queues at lunchtime to accommodate the fifteen thousand or so people who worked inside the building. The developer had boasted an average travel time of only thirty seconds from any point in the building to the ground floor, but that assumed you could readily enter an elevator car in the first place.

To access each of the individual elevator lobbies, irrespective of the time, a card was needed to unlock glass turnstiles. All those who worked in the building had been issued an Octopus card. It was a contactless smart card, used by virtually everyone in Hong Kong to pay for public transport or parking and to shop at outlets such as 7-Eleven or Starbucks, where it effectively replaced bills or coins. It could be topped up with cash at "add value" machines at any MTR station, and every day some twelve million transactions were made throughout the system.

The company that owned the Octopus card managed the metro system and was also one of the developers of the IFC complex. It had naturally imposed the use of the Octopus card to grant access to the premises. In turn, the tenants used separate magnetic passes to access their own offices within the tower.

Temur walked slowly across both the upper and lower reception lobbies that were linked by two escalators, on the west and east sides, respectively. He carefully noted the location of all overhead cameras and observed people leaving and entering some of the sixty-two individual elevators. On a wall was an array of analogue clocks showing the time across a number of financial centers around the world.

In addition to the "concierges," the two main lobbies were patrolled by uniformed guards, most of them Nepalese, as well as former Gurkha servicemen in the British army. They wore red military-style berets, gray pants with heavy black leather boots and blue shirts with epaulettes. Some also held a dog on a leash, trained to sniff out explosives.

On the upper level, on the east side—largely hidden from view to the public—a small staircase led down to the control center, where yet more guards monitored all strategic locations within the building using a vast network of CCTV cameras. There, they could remotely close or open access to all floors, or one of the six underground levels in which visitors and residents could park in one of seven hundred and fifty parking spaces and where commercial deliveries were made. They could also monitor the integrity of the high-bandwidth fiber-optic wireless network and verify that the building, cooled in part with seawater, remained at an optimal temperature.

Satisfied he had seen everything he wanted to see, Temur exited at level P1, the main floor, and returned to the mall, where he spent the following ninety minutes walking through each of the individual levels to understand their respective floor plans and possible exit routes.

He finally left using the southwest entrance, which led to the Mid-Levels Escalator. It was a moving walkway that took residents from Hong Kong's hillside boroughs down to the business district of Central throughout the morning. After lunchtime, it switched directions, taking them back up to their high-density condos.

He passed a few beggars, including a fake Buddhist monk, and walked down to Queen's Road, which he followed all the way to Shek Tong Tsui, where his rented flat was located.

There, he grabbed a quick bite in a rundown but tasty Thai restaurant, before retreating for the day to plan the rest of his week.

Chapter 45

Admiralty, Hong Kong, May 2016

ERWAN TANGUY HAD arrived a few hours earlier at Chek Lap Kok airport, on the island of the same name, located to the northwest of central Hong Kong. He was now on his way to a meeting with Mortimer Tse Wong-chung, the city's commissioner of police (CP), who presided over the careers of more than 29,000 officers and 4,500 civilian personnel.

After receiving the call from Atul Jain, the RAW officer he had met in Mumbai, he and The Bear had debated on what to do next. It seemed most likely that Gupta had been murdered aboard the Pablo Suárez, shortly after leaving India's financial capital. That same vessel was now docked in Hong Kong, but scheduled to leave that very evening.

The city had a high, although fast-falling, degree of autonomy compared to other Chinese cities, but it now undoubtedly belonged to the People's Republic of China. They had therefore decided to directly inform their Chinese counterparts about the possibility that bacteriological materials might have been smuggled into Hong Kong or, at the very least, might still be found on the container ship. They also mentioned the shady background of the captain, as well as the fact that a French citizen had been found murdered, with linen presumed to have come from the ship found in one of his pockets.

The information had been promptly processed, and the Chinese had agreed to allow Tanguy to travel to Hong Kong to assist with the case, but only as an observer. He had been picked up upon arrival by a familiar face, Major Xie from the Chinese Ministry of State Security. He wasn't surprised to see her there, even though she was not based in the Special Administrative Region. They had stopped at his hotel for a few minutes so he could freshen up, and now both headed to the police headquarters at Arsenal House, in the Admiralty district, in a marked police vehicle.

They entered the complex made up of several towers and surrounded by high walls topped with razor wire, and then rode an elevator to one of the higher floors, where Mortimer Tse's rather lavish offices were located. The panoramic harbor view was stunning, but Tanguy wasn't there as a tourist. The CP, in full police uniform, waited for them behind his desk.

"Ah, Commandant Tanguy, welcome to Hong Kong! And thank you for alerting us to this rather nasty state of affairs," he said. "Please sit down."

"Thank you, Sir," said Tanguy. "At the risk of being direct, if I may, I believe time is of the essence. The Pablo Suárez is currently scheduled to depart from Kwai Chung tonight, heading for Korea."

"Yes. We already know that. Rest assured, she will not be allowed to leave Hong Kong waters, unless and until we're satisfied she doesn't carry any dangerous cargo."

"With respect, Sir, there's also the important matter of the murder of a French national. Everything points to him having been killed at sea, on that same vessel. The two cases are linked, you see. The man was a virologist and likely had a part in stealing the virus from a laboratory facility in Spain."

"This seems to be getting more complicated by the minute. I assume proper documentation for all this will follow? What is it that you suggest in the meantime? I lived through SARS in 2003 and hardly want to repeat the experience."

"First, that the ship be prevented from leaving Hong Kong at all costs. Second, we must search for any vials that may be on board. Third, we must detain the crew, and especially the captain, with a view to understanding what Gupta—that's the name of the murdered scientist—was doing on board and who may be responsible for his assassination. And lastly, we should ascertain whether any other passengers were also on board and might have disembarked in Hong Kong. Or indeed, at any of the previous stops in Cochin, Colombo, Singapore or Ho Chi Minh City."

"Sounds like a comprehensive plan. From what I understand, she's a fairly small cargo ship with a limited number of seamen. There are clear rules about the manning of vessels at port to avoid incidents, so I assume most of them would be on board. Especially if she's now about to leave."

"Sir," said Xie, "the captain is a known extremist. May I suggest that Commandant Tanguy and I question him separately, while your men and Customs do the same with the crew and also conduct a search of the vessel?"

"Major, as you know, under the Basic Law, officials from the mainland have no jurisdiction here. Technically, you're both in Hong Kong as observers or facilitators, but nothing else."

"I fully appreciate that, Sir," answered Xie, "but, on the other hand, our French colleague and I both have extensive experience in dealing with such individuals. It's of course all to your credit that Hong Kong has never had to face a terrorist attack. But you're hardly equipped for a threat of this nature—even your own Special Duties Unit. I should know; I personally trained the PLA's Special Operations Company here in Stanley. We're talking weapons of mass destruction, not sticks and knives! As was previously said, time is of the essence, and I respectfully ask that you consider my suggestion. Besides, no one needs to know. Think of it simply as international cooperation between security forces, which this is, in any event."

The CP thought deeply for thirty seconds. He knew she was right. He also could not afford an open conflict with a senior officer of the Guoanbu.

"Hmm, very well, then. But don't go shooting people around. This isn't Xinjiang, Major! Superintendent Ip from the Security Wing will be in charge of this operation."

The Security Wing was part of the police's "B" department, which dealt with crime and security. More specifically, it was responsible for a range of security-related matters, including VIP protection, counterterrorism and security coordination.

Tse glanced at his watch. The CP continued, "The time now is four-thirty p.m. You will leave immediately. The

Marine Department has already been notified that any departure of the Pablo Suárez must be prevented."

Minutes later, three Mercedes-Benz Sprinter police vans left Arsenal House for Kwai Chung, all sirens blazing. Additional personnel would meet them there, including from the Hong Kong Customs and Excise Department. The Hong Kong Police Force had a habit of staffing operations with more constables and officers than was strictly necessary. Not that this was a bad thing in this particular instance. Even though the ship wasn't very large, there could still be many places where vials of pathogens might have been hidden. The search would take time and be labor-intensive.

In one of the vehicles were Xie Wei and Erwan Tanguy. She grabbed a black tactical backpack as he donned a bulletproof Kevlar vest with the words "Hong Kong Police" written in both English and Chinese characters on the back and front. She had already done the same earlier.

She opened her backpack and retrieved a QSW-06 firearm. It was a polymer-framed, short-recoil-operated, semi-automatic pistol used by the Chinese Special Forces. It was chambered for DCV05 5.8x21-mm subsonic rounds, which created less noise than standard pistol ammunition. It used a double-column, double-feed, twenty-round magazine and had a rail under the barrel, to which a variety of sights, flashlights and other accessories could be attached. It normally came with a detachable suppressor that could be screwed onto the barrel, but none was included on this particular model.

She handed the pistol to Tanguy, together with a soft-shell holster made of ballistic weave. There was no safety catch, to allow for a fast draw in close-quarters situations.

"You may want to carry this. You never know."

"I assume this is not sanctioned by the CP?" he asked.

"I think he'd be more embarrassed if anything ever happened to you! It's only for protection. Better safe than sorry. It's a recent model, 2006, one of our best. I'm sure you'll like it. But please be a good boy; I'd like it back."

Tanguy smiled and took the pistol from her. He held it appreciatively in front of him and looked through the iron sights with three-dot luminous inserts.

"Thank you," he said. "I'll remember that."

"Three minutes," said an officer at the front of the van, flashing three fingers to make his point. "We've almost arrived."

Chapter 46

Central, Hong Kong, May 2016

"KELVIN, CAN YOU come over for a minute?" asked Derek van Deen. It wasn't really a question; more of a request, and Kelvin dutifully walked over to the desk of his boss, a managing director and the regional head of equity capital markets with Global Securities Asia, GSA for short.

Kelvin was a lowly ranked associate, with only a couple years of investment banking experience under his belt. He was a smart, twenty-something Hong Kong Chinese man, who had graduated *summa cum laude* with an MBA from one of the top universities in the U.S. His tiger mum had seen to that.

He didn't earn big bucks just yet, although his package was clearly way above those of his contemporaries who worked outside the financial industry. But it was still clearly peanuts compared to the almost two million dollars his boss took home every year, in both salary and discretionary bonuses.

His experience, however—even though it was still limited—meant that he could generally be trusted and largely left to his own devices when it came to putting together the pitch books that helped win the mandates that brought in many millions of U.S. dollars in underwriting fees. Over the last several months, he had drafted perhaps fifty of these, for IPOs, placements, block trades and even a few rights issues.

"We just received another RFP," explained Derek van Deen.

Everyone within the bank and at competitor firms called him DVD, not just because of his initials, but also for his uncanny ability to spin stories in order to secure mandates from potential clients.

An RFP was a request for proposals: a long list of questions, several pages in length, that companies and their advisers sent to a number of investment banks. Based on the quality of responses, they would select a handful of them to act as lead underwriters. They would oversee all the execution work, from documentation and valuation to marketing shares to end investors.

"It's one of those second-tier, Chinese commercial banks again," said the head of ECM. "The submissions are due next Tuesday."

"Bugger," he added as he read further through the document. "They want it in both English and Chinese."

Kelvin made a face. That meant only six days to come up with several hundred pages of answers. He looked at the document, which totaled a dozen pages in length, all in small typeface, requesting information on anything and everything from an analysis of market conditions to a comprehensive valuation of the business. Clearly, his plans for a boozy and leisurely weekend on a motorboat were now dead in the water. He would need to spend many hours putting together the PowerPoint slides. And worse, they would then need to be translated into Chinese, which he would have to carefully check, character after character.

"That's very short notice," he observed.

"I know. But most of what they're asking for, you can easily recycle from other presentations. They always ask the same questions anyway. What they really, really want to know is how much they can raise and what it's going to cost them," answered Derek. "Same old."

"And what's that?" asked Kelvin.

"Lemme think," said his boss, scanning for a good thirty seconds the one-pager appended to the RFP, which included a small compendium of financial statistics. "You know what? Just say they can comfortably raise one billion U.S. dollars and probably more, depending on market conditions. With a twenty-five percent free-float, we estimate the fully distributed valuation of the business to be in the region of four billion, post new money. No, say 3.8 to 4.2. That would sound better. We can't be too definitive."

A fully distributed valuation ignored any IPO discount, to account for the fact that the issuer was coming to market for the very first time. It was a way of hedging one's bets. If investor demand ultimately turned sour, the actual valuation upon listing would be much lower, and the bank couldn't so easily be held accountable for its advice. Not that CEOs and finance directors had any clue about all that.

"Okay. And the fees?"

"Ah, yes...the whole world and their dog are going to pitch for this, so we need to be competitive. Let's say 1.5 per cent, with a fifty basis points discretionary incentive on top. I'll clear it at the new business committee."

"Got it."

"Good. Are we done?"

"I think so."

"Can you get me a first draft before close of biz on Friday? I'll have a look before leaving. I really don't want to spend any time on this over the weekend."

That left less than forty-eight hours to produce an initial, although still comprehensive, proposal.

"No problem. Can I use Mabel to help with statistics and stuff?"

Mabel was seventeen and had worked at the bank as an intern for a few weeks. Her father was the CEO of one of Hong Kong's largest conglomerates, and very keen for her to get work experience. It might come in handy as she later joined him on the board of directors. With her long, slick black hair and gentle smile, she was quite a looker, too. And with her pink Chanel suits, flashy jewelry, huge collection of Hermès bags and seemingly endless pairs of Louboutin shoes, she didn't go unnoticed on the trading floor. The bank had only been too happy to oblige.

Unbeknown to financial regulators, GSA had put in place a program known as SND, which stood for "Sons and Daughters." Its sole objective was to target the offspring of tycoons for internships or even junior employment, with a view toward ultimately influencing their genitors to award the firm lucrative mandates. Some might say it was borderline illegal but, in the cutthroat environment that was investment banking in Asia, management saw it as plain common sense.

"Can't do. Interns can't work weekends anymore. You

know that. Besides, she's playing golf with the head of Equities on Friday. Use the Indians," countered DVD.

Kelvin sighed. There was no point in arguing. The rules for interns obviously didn't apply to full-time associates. He would have to slave alone over the next few days, including all of Saturday and Sunday, on the dreaded proposal.

The "Indians" the head of ECM had referred to were an outsourcing firm based in Hyderabad, in Andhra Pradesh. It was staffed by highly qualified, but vastly underpaid, business school and engineering graduates who crunched numbers and compiled much of the statistics the bank included in its pitch books—at all hours of the day or night. It was a cheap and efficient way of processing a mammoth amount of information, freeing time for junior bankers to focus on the more "value-added" parts of a proposal. Or so they said.

This arrangement gave potential clients the impression that the bank had done an enormous amount of work on their behalf, to support what they thought was honest and carefully considered advice. This couldn't be further from the truth. Much of the information they received was produced mechanically, without much thought behind it. What mattered most was the number of pages, rather than what was actually written on them.

"Christ, it's so hot!" said van Deen. "We're only just in May, and it's already well over eighty-five degrees! The aircon's on maximum strength. It's usually freezing, but I can barely feel it. Ask Amy if they can do something, will you?"

He had been used to hot, sweaty summers in his previous posting, in New York, but it had been nothing like this.

"Well, Chief, I'll leave you to it," DVD finally said. "Call if you need to, but don't bother me with anything trivial," he added, leaving the trading floor for a long liquid lunch at a Michelin-starred restaurant with one of his counterparts from another firm.

GSA's offices were located at almost the very top of Two IFC, just below those of the Monetary Authority. They occupied an entire floor, offering panoramic views of the harbor and Kowloon peninsula on one side, and the northern shore of Hong Kong Island, from Kennedy Town to Quarry Bay, on the other. A massive trading floor that often buzzed feverishly took up most of the space. Research analysts, sales people and traders were continuously on the phone, or moving from one station to the other, buying, selling or hedging shares, bonds, foreign exchange and even commodities. It smelled of money—and lots of it.

Van Deen opened the top button of his cutaway-collar shirt and loosened his tie, which had been hand-woven in Naples, Italy, by Marinella. He swiftly shined the top of his Berluti loafers on the calves of his bespoke suit trousers, swept his hair back and wiped a bead of sweat from his forehead as he exited the elevator car on the ground floor of the skyscraper.

He didn't pay any attention to the Asian man with strange, clear eyes who followed him as he walked across the mall to the restaurant. He didn't notice either when the man sat at a nearby table, seemingly oblivious to his conversation but, in reality, very much focused on every word.

Chapter 47

Kwai Chung, Hong Kong, May 2016

THE THREE POLICE vans had parked on the quay. A dozen officers from the Customs and Excise Department joined them as they prepared to board the ship. Xie Wei and Erwan Tanguy made their way to the white bridge castle located at the stern to see the captain. The rest of the men proceeded to round up the crew and initiated a search of the vessel.

"What's this?" protested Captain Ahmed. "We're just about to cast off."

"I'm afraid your passage will have to be delayed, Captain," said Xie. "Please sit down now, and listen carefully to what we have to say."

Realizing he was powerless to stop them, Ahmed did as instructed.

"Are all the crew on board, or are any still on shore leave?" asked Tanguy.

"Everyone is now on board. As I said, we're planning to sail for Korea before dusk—or at least, we were."

"Good. Captain, we've reason to believe you may be carrying hazardous materials on board," said Tanguy, without elaborating on the nature of that cargo.

"That's ridiculous!"

"I'm afraid we'll have to search the vessel."

"It will take forever! Time is money in this business! We can't afford to be late!"

"Captain, don't make things any worse for yourself," said Xie. "Did you take on any passengers in or after departing from Mumbai?"

"Of course not! This is a cargo vessel, not a cruise ship!"

"Well, we'll have to see if your crew share the same recollection. That shouldn't be too difficult to establish," countered Tanguy.

Ahmed swallowed uneasily. The conversation could end up being more difficult than he had first envisaged. If any among the crew mentioned the Asian man or the Indian passenger, he'd be in deep trouble. That's when Tanguy noticed a small towel on the chart table. In one of its corners, the name of the vessel was embroidered in green letters.

"You must be very proud of your ship, Captain."

"Who wouldn't be? She's old and slow, but she's never failed me."

"Where did you have these made?" asked Tanguy, holding out the piece of cloth.

"These? In Singapore, a few years back. I bought a large batch then. It was a good value. I've put some in all the cabins and common areas. But what does this have to do with your search?"

"The issue, Captain, is that one of these pretty towels was found a few days ago in the trousers pocket of a French national—a French national of Indian descent, to be more precise. His name was Vikas Gupta."

"Never heard of him."

"M. Gupta, you see, was found murdered. His body washed up on a beach in Mumbai. It was in a rather bad state, but the postmortem examination established, beyond any doubt, that he had been stabbed. One of his carotid arteries was slit with a knife."

"I'm sorry to hear that, but I don't know anything about it. Maybe one of the crew left one such item in Mumbai, perhaps in a shop or a restaurant. As I said, I got a large number of these made."

"M. Gupta wasn't just anyone, Captain. In fact, up to the point when we recovered his body, he was one of Interpol's most wanted men. He was involved in the theft of dangerous materials in Europe. And, between you and me, we're talking about stuff that could be used in weapons of mass destruction. So, let me ask again, and please think about your answer very carefully this time: what do you know about Vikas Gupta?"

Ahmed swallowed again nervously.

"I've already answered you. That man was never a passenger aboard the Pablo Suárez."

"I never suggested he was, Captain. So your latest answer puzzles me, to say the least."

The captain silently cursed himself. They'd be relentless now. Ultimately they'd find out, and he'd be held accountable.

Superintendent Ip suddenly appeared, asking to have a word with Xie Wei.

"Will you please excuse me for a moment?" she said. "It

seems we might have an interesting development."

Within a minute she was back. She flashed a wide smile.

"Well, Captain, as we suspected, your crew appear to have paid more attention than you to the comings and goings of passengers aboard your ship.

"You see, according to them, it now seems that two men boarded the Pablo Suárez in Mumbai's JNPT. One was Asian and the other, oddly enough, an Indian man, with glasses, and whose description fully matches that of Vikas Gupta. Even more interesting, the latter was not seen on board after your stopover in Cochin, maybe because he got off there? Or, more likely perhaps, because his body was dumped at sea, just after you left Mumbai? Does that now ring a bell? I might add that you allegedly instructed the crew that the two men should be left undisturbed."

"I remember now," said Ahmed, after what seemed like a very long pause.

"Good. Could you please enlighten us, then? We're all ears."

"There were two passengers, all right. Both disembarked in Cochin. Something must have happened there and the body was thrown into the sea. End of story."

"Now, I find that rather hard to believe," said Xie. "You see, Captain, from Mumbai to Cochin is a distance of more than eight hundred nautical miles, and that's as the crow flies. Given the marine currents in the Arabian Sea, it would be a physical impossibility for a corpse to drift from south to north in the manner you suggested, especially at this time of year, and in such a short span of time. The pathologist who examined the deceased was adamant that the body would have been thrown into the ocean only a short while after leaving Mumbai, perhaps as soon as the vessel entered international waters. But let us come back to that later. From what we gathered from the crew, the Asian man remained on board and alighted in Hong Kong only two days ago."

"I think you might be right. I was confused. It was a long passage. I may have mixed up some of the facts."

Xie Wei had now lost all patience. She pointed an accusatory finger at the captain and raised the tone of her voice.

"Listen to me carefully, asshole! You've no idea how deep in shit you are! If you don't tell us everything you know, right now, and without omitting any of the details, I'll break your fingers one by one," she said, holding her automatic pistol by the barrel, ready to use the butt as a makeshift hammer.

"And that'll be just for starters," she added. "Next, you'll be taken to a black site, on a small island off China, from which you'll never return. The Americans are not the only ones having fun with your lot, you know? Guantanamo's just a walk in the park, compared to what we've got. We know all about your little friends from Ansar Bait al-Maqdis and ISIL in Egypt. Now, talk, or I'll put my hand so deep up your ass it'll make your lips move!"

"This is Hong Kong. China has no jurisdiction here," he protested, but his attempt to sound unshaken was betrayed by his quavering voice.

"Do you really want to test me, *chan tou*?" she asked, now screaming her head off.

Captain Ahmed was fully taken aback. That policewoman, or whoever she was, was in a real fury. He needed to backpedal, big time. He had dug himself into a very deep hole, and it was obvious they now knew enough to make his life very difficult from hereon. The prospect of being held up for months on end was most unappealing, and probably also very real. And, after all, all he had done was take a couple of passengers on board. Anything else that had happened, he had played no part in. He thought it best to confess.

"All…all right. I never knew their names, honest. They didn't tell me, and I didn't ask. It's true I knew people in Islamist circles in Egypt. But I never took part in any violent action, and lost contact after the Brothers pledged allegiance to ISIL. You have to understand: life wasn't much fun under Mubarak. And the army robbed us of a legitimate victory when el-Sisi took power."

"We're not here to hear about Egyptian politics. Please return to the matter at hand," instructed Tanguy, matter-of-factly.

"A few months ago, an Asian man contacted me in Oman. I thought he might have been from Central Asia, but he never said where from exactly. He was also a Muslim, a good Muslim. He knew of my political ideas. He dropped all the right hints and then asked me about the shipping routes I sailed. He asked me if, one day, I wouldn't mind taking him on board, as a passenger, from Mumbai to Hong Kong, as a service from one Brother to the other. I had no reason to refuse."

"When did he contact you again?"

"Just a few weeks ago. He called me. He had my number. He knew the boat's schedule, and told me when he'd come on board, as we'd previously discussed. Except that there were two of them."

"The Indian?"

"Exactly. That was not part of the plan. It was obvious the other man was a *kafir*, too. To be honest, I was rather annoyed, but he said it was important, so I took them both in. I gave them cabins and told the crew not to bother them. In truth, they were both very discreet."

"How did Gupta die?"

"I don't know! I swear on the Holy Quran! From one day to the next, we just stopped seeing him. His cabin stood empty, except for a few items of clothing that were left behind. I thought it best not to ask. Ultimately, I managed to convince myself he had perhaps disembarked in Cochin, although he hadn't been seen for some time already by the time we arrived there. Deep down, I think I knew better."

"What did the Asian man carry, in terms of luggage?"

"Very little. He had a small backpack. And some sort of icebox: a portable container with a square shape, like something for a picnic. But more high-tech."

Tanguy and Xie exchanged a quick glance.

Or something to carry vials of medicine, or vaccines, thought the Frenchman.

"Did he give you a parcel to look after, or for you to conceal?" asked Xie.

"No, not at all; he left with the same baggage, just after we docked in Hong Kong. And you'll find nothing on the boat either, Inch'Allah—at least, nothing that I know of."

"Ip," said Xie, calling the superintendent. "Can we urgently get someone to check all arrivals at the immigration checkpoint here in Kwai Chung? For the last forty-eight hours? We'll need pictures and copies of the passports. You can ignore non-Asians, as well as seamen's ID books, if they've returned from shore leave. There can't have been that many people."

"I'll put someone on it right away."

After about an hour, the police officer had returned.

"There were only seventeen passengers. Here are copies of the documents and disembarkation cards."

"Captain Ahmed, please look at these very carefully. Which one belongs to our man?"

Ahmed perused the photographs for a few moments, before pointing to one. The man was perhaps in his mid-thirties. He was barefaced, his hair cut short. His eyes were unusually bright for an Asian, a combination of gray, green and light blue.

"That's him, definitely. I see this says he traveled on the Coonawarra. It was docked next to us and left yesterday. He'd probably said as much to muddy the waters. But he definitely came to Hong Kong on the Pablo Suárez."

"You're a hundred percent sure?"

"As Allah is my witness, that's him all right."

"Peter Tremblay. Canadian. It's probably a fake pass-port," said Xie. "Ip," she continued, "can we urgently confirm his bona fides with the Canadian consulate? And put all border points on high alert, in case he plans to leave the city? He might even have already left, especially for the mainland. Let's look into that too—you never know. We should also check all the hotels and guesthouses and circulate his photograph to all of the force's officers. That man is actively wanted for the murder of a French national and suspected of carrying sensitive materials. He's extremely dangerous. If located, do not attempt to apprehend him. This is one for the Special Duties Unit or the PLA's Five-Minute Response Unit. This is to be treated as a number-one priority."

"Roger that. What about the ship?"

"Continue the search, although I doubt we'll find anything. As for the vessel itself, it's to be impounded, of course. But the crew can leave, if nothing untoward is found onboard."

"Very well. And what about him?" he asked, vaguely pointing in the captain's direction with his chin.

"That man is to be placed immediately under administrative detention, for endangering the security of the People's Republic of China. Can I please request your assistance for a high-speed interception craft to take him to Shenzhen?"

"That's quite irregular. I'll need to refer it to the CP."

"You'll find him to be most agreeable to my request," she said, as she grabbed her cell to dial a number in Beijing.

Chapter 48

Dubai, United Arab Emirates, May 2016

ISMAIL KHAN WAS now ready to spring into action. Over the last few weeks, he had collected more than US$2 billion from the wealthy patrons who had agreed to back the Musafir fund. The money was now sitting in a variety of banks and broking accounts, and was about to be put to use.

Over several years, he had created a galaxy of impenetrable vehicles, all established in opaque, offshore locations. None could be traced to him, nor to the men whose capital he was about to invest. Assumed identities and fake certificates and addresses, as well as numbered accounts, had seen to that.

In recent years, it had become increasingly difficult to hide or launder money around the world, as financial regulators and tax authorities made ever-greater inroads into the erstwhile secret world of global wealth and asset management. But money still greased the wheels of corruption. So long as they believed they wouldn't be caught, many financiers were still happy to bend the rules, for a fat fee or an anonymous cash payment. And money wasn't something Khan or those in his circle lacked—far from it.

Others had more simply been caught in a web of black-mail, and left with no other choice than to offer Khan and his shady associates services that, only a few years before, would have been considered par for the course. Their vices, whether drug or sexual habits, had—often by chance, although sometimes by design—been uncovered. Keeping them secret meant becoming party to ever-more secret transactions. Once in, once guilty of malpractice, there was no turning back.

Timing was crucial. In just a few days' time, he knew he would receive the signal from Temur. It would, of course, be coded, as before, to fool the Big Ears of the American National Security Agency (NSA) and British Government Communications Headquarters (GCHQ). When the call finally came, he knew he would have a day, two at most, to get to work.

Within about a week, the virus would have spread so widely that much of Asia would become virtually paralyzed. Transportation would grind to a halt. People would remain confined to their homes, not daring to venture outside. Hospitals and health facilities would be overwhelmed, and even the financial sector would be affected for an extended period of time. And all throughout a continent that was now the world's engine of growth.

Most importantly, stocks would quickly collapse, espe-cially for airlines, airports, train and shipping lines, hotels and insurance companies. On all of these, he already had pre-placed large, highly leveraged sell orders, ready to be executed. He would then wait for the securities to reach a low point before buying them back, generating a flurry of riches, both for his investors and for the cause he backed.

In 2007, hedge-fund manager John Paulson had raked in US$15 billion in just a few months by betting against the U.S. property market and predicting the collapse of sub-prime mortgages. Of that, US$4 billion had gone into his own pocket. He had correctly read the writing on the wall, and it had only been a matter of time for him to be proven right. But personal enrichment wasn't what was on Khan's mind.

In this business, it often paid to be a contrarian, to go against established trends and beliefs. In spite of a slowdown of China's economy and all the naysayers, Asia was still very much the place to be for global investors.

They remained cautious about the U.S. in what was, after all, an election year, the outcome of which was full of uncertainties. Europe remained perpetually stuck in deflation and kept facing one issue after the other, from the near-collapse of Greece to Brexit and terrorism, to the never-ending migrant crisis. Australia and the Middle East were still severely impacted by the collapse of commodities prices. Yes, Asia was definitely still it.

And so, its fall from grace would be even more spectacular. The consequences would also be felt in the West, a dreaded enemy and now also Asia's major trading partner. China, for all its arrogance and might, would be taught a lesson it would not easily forget as the longstanding oppression of its Muslim people finally came back to haunt it. Best of all, Khan's backers and others they supported would reap major benefits, and all in a very short time span.

On several computer screens stacked three high, he

monitored the world's markets, aided by a handful of traders who shared his ideas and whom he trusted. Prices flashed in green or red as buy and sell orders were matched across the world's major financial centers.

Like many others, the fund operated from anonymous offices in the DIFC, Dubai's International Finance Centre on Sheikh Zayed Road. But that was just a front, the emerging part of this most secret of financial icebergs. From there, its tentacles extended to a network of jurisdictions from the Caribbean and Latin America to the Channel Islands to Labuan, in Eastern Malaysia and even to tiny nations in the Pacific, whose economies revolved entirely around offshore dealings.

Only Khan knew the full extent of the scheme and its inner workings. Control was power. Those who aided him were only privy to well-defined, isolated portions of this elaborate construction. Had they known its range and magnitude, they might well have taken fright.

In fact, the game was no different from clandestine operations of the kind he had known for much of his adult life. Unknown to each other, a number of cells worked in isolation to seed chaos while perhaps only one individual or, at most, two or three, had a clear overall picture of what could be unleashed on the path to destruction.

Today, Khan was that man. When The Traveler called him, he would free the forces of annihilation like a new cohort of horsemen of the apocalypse. For the first time, the East and the West together would pay dearly and learn to submit to Allah's will and yoke.

Outside the steel and glass cube that housed the fund's

offices, a *muezzin* called the faithful, his voice rising across the desert maze that was Dubai. Respectfully, he closed his eyes and silently prayed for the success of his enterprise.

Chapter 49

Wan Chai, Hong Kong, May 2016

TEMUR KHAN WAS walking along Lockhart Road, in the district of Wan Chai. The area was better known as one of the city's red light districts, home to countless bars and nightclubs. In a good number of these, customers could buy drinks from working girls, many of whom were from mainland China or Southeast Asia, before taking them to one of several cheap hotels that charged by the hour, after paying the *mama-san* the compulsory bar fine.

That, however, was not what was on his mind and, in any event, it was still early. Most of the vice dens were now closed. The action generally didn't start in earnest until much later, around mid or late afternoon and lasting until the early hours of the morning.

The area had prospered after World War II, in particular thanks to the clientele brought by the U.S. Navy. The mama-sans had then catered to sailors on shore leave and had never looked back. Nowadays, however, stopovers by American ships were few and far between, and they were also subject to the whim of the Chinese authorities. Every now and then, the latter prohibited vessels from their rival superpower from docking in Hong Kong, just to make a point, or perhaps as a negotiating tactic for trade agreements or foreign policy matters.

These days, most of those who frequented the Wan Chai bars were expatriate businessmen, many working in the financial industry, or Chinese self-made men with more money than sense.

Still, a couple of establishments had already opened that morning, and Temur silently passed the velvet curtains and rows of girls sitting on plastic stools outside the blacked-out bow windows. All of them wore skinny tank tops and impossibly short skirts or shorts. A couple of girls, heavily made up even at that hour, called out to him as they smoked cigarettes on the pavement, but more by force of habit than to make a trade.

"Hey, Mister! You buy me drink? We can have good time, together. Long time, short time, whatever! You choose—you pay, lah!"

Temur ignored them. Aside from the drinks business and sex industry, Wan Chai was a heaven for contractors of all stripes. The parallel thoroughfares of Jaffe Road, Lockhart Road and Hennessy Road, which stretched from Admiralty to the west to Causeway Bay to the east, and every street in between, harbored shops that sold plumbing supplies, paint, power tools, air compressors and more. Virtually everything and anything that might be needed to build, tear down or renovate a house could be found here, all within an area of just a third of a square mile.

What he was after wasn't so easily found in Hong Kong. The high humidity, especially during the summer months, meant that dehumidifiers were readily available everywhere, from portable units that could process a gallon of water in a small removable tank, to a man-size version for large offices and commercial facilities. Without dehumidifiers, mold soon developed in the warm, wet air and grew on anything from walls to clothes, shoes and archived records. New arrivals to the city often learned about it the hard way and then wasted no time investing in this essential piece of equipment.

However, what Temur was looking for was exactly the opposite: a portable humidifier and, more specifically, an ultrasonic fog or mist-maker. These were occasionally used as an alternative to pest control services, the fog they created containing a powerful insecticide. Others were used in dance clubs or for home decoration or landscaping. Since they could generate a high level of humidity very quickly, they were also commonly used in germination rooms or green-houses to promote plant growth.

Each of these units had a water tank. They also used a piezoelectric transducer with a resonating frequency of around 1.6 MHz. It created ultrasonic waves and high-energy vibrations that turned the water into a fog-like cloud. The waves produced tiny water droplets less than five microns in size that could penetrate the tiniest of spaces but would not turn into stagnant water. These devices were sturdy, with few moving parts, and required no special temperature or pressure conditions.

The mist would be the perfect medium for the SARS pathogens, after the freeze-dried microorganisms had been revived. Temur would send the particles into the Two IFC air conditioning system, from which they would then spread throughout the units and rooms, across its eighty-eight floors and common areas, including elevators, stairways and lobbies. It would be quick, invisible and extremely lethal.

After a long search, he finally found a shop that carried what he needed.

He ignored the smaller models. These worked on batteries, but their tanks had a very limited capacity that wouldn't be enough for the scheme he had in mind. Conversely, the high-capacity units were too bulky and heavy. They had wheels and were cumbersome to move from one area to another; they would hardly be inconspicuous if carried into the skyscraper. Setting them up would most certainly attract unwanted attention on the part of the building's security.

All the larger models had to be plugged in to function, but that wasn't an issue. He had carefully studied detailed blueprints of the building and knew there were a number of power points near the air conditioning intake wells.

He spotted a model with a five-gallon tank, but it topped fifty-five pounds and was therefore too heavy for his purpose. Finally, he saw a smaller version that could be loaded with just over 2.5 gallons of liquid. It was still relatively heavy, but it could be concealed in a large backpack fairly easily.

He carefully noted the exact dimensions of the apparatus, paid cash and even obtained a small discount, which he had not asked for in the first place. In Hong Kong, many shops gave discounts for good luck or to secure the patronage of repeat customers. He exited the shop and hailed a taxi, which took him back to Shek Tong Tsui, where he dropped the humidifier unit at his rental accommodation.

Next, he traveled by MTR to Yau Ma Tei, in Kowloon,

and left the station through Exit A2. From there, he walked to the intersection of Dundas Street and Sai Yeung Choi Street and entered a building by the name of Park-In Commercial Centre. Hidden among its higher floors were a number of military surplus suppliers. They sold combat gear, heavy-duty hiking shoes, a wide range of knives and daggers, and even a whole assortment of firearm replicas, many of which were produced under licenses granted by the likes of Glock, Smith & Wesson or Heckler & Koch.

It was almost impossible to acquire a gun in Hong Kong. Even purchasing a hunting rifle came with so many restrictions that, in practice, no one ever bothered. Conversely, the city had a thriving airsoft community, whose members collected gas or electronic-fired replicas of automatic pistols, rifles and even submachine guns and fought mock battles in converted industrial buildings or the wilderness of the New Territories, shooting at each other with harmless 6-mm plastic ball ammunition. These weapons were similar in all respects to real firearms except for their lethal power and, generally, lighter weight.

Temur first chose a large backpack into which the humidifier unit could fit. He deliberately stayed clear of models made of camouflaged fabric or military-style MOLLE modular lightweight, load-carrying equipment, with rows of heavy-duty nylon stitched onto them for attaching compatible pouches and accessories. They were very popular among Sunday warriors, but perhaps not ideal for going about unnoticed in a high-end office tower.

Instead, he selected a backpack of the type an adrenaline junkie of the corporate type might bring into the office, to carry his suit, tie and document case back home on a long run after a working day on the trading floor. There were many such action men in the financial community in Asia. They ran marathons, climbed rocky cliffs barehanded or kicked sandbags with their feet and elbows, in sweaty gyms manned by boxing champions or former military types.

He then spent time looking at the weapon replicas. They would be useless for shooting anyone, but one might come in handy for keeping an inquisitive security guard at bay. Even at close range, they seemed very real. Once held at gunpoint, someone could then easily be neutralized with a knife or even barehanded.

One of the weapons caught his attention. It was a Japanese-made SIG Sauer P226 railed-frame automatic pistol. It was a dummy, not even a gun that shot plastic pellets, but it was extremely well made. It was a shell-ejecting replica that came with fake metal bullets. They could be loaded into the magazine, chambered and ejected with each cycling of the slide, just like a real gun but without the actual deadly bang.

The replica was made of heavyweight plastic that felt cold to the touch and was quite deceiving, even to a careful observer. Of course, its actual weight was lighter than real steel, but he didn't plan on letting anyone other than himself hold the gun. Best of all, each metal bullet could be unscrewed to insert a gunpowder cap that would actually cycle the gun on firing.

Again, he paid cash for both items and returned by MTR to his flat. He was now ready to proceed to the next step of his plan. Then, he would send word to his mentor, Ismail Khan, and afterward, all hell would break loose.

Chapter 50

ERWAN TANGUY, XIE WEI and Superintendent Ip were back in Mortimer Tse's office, in Arsenal House, the city's police headquarters, after the raid on the Pablo Suárez. Twenty-four hours had elapsed since then. Much had been done in that short space of time, but what they had to show for it in terms of results was actually quite meager.

"The good news is, we now know who smuggled the SARS virus into Hong Kong. Well, almost," said Tanguy. "We believe he's known in fundamentalist circles as Musafir, which means 'the traveler' in Arabic."

"The traveler?" asked Tse, incredulous.

"It's just a nickname, of course. He used a fake Canadian passport to pass through immigration under the name of Peter Tremblay. That document was very well made. Top quality. But we've since established through the Canadian consulate that no passport was ever issued to such a man. They couldn't reconcile the identity and the serial number," added Ip.

"Christ! And what about the bad news?" asked the commissioner of police, not missing a beat.

"To put it simply, we've lost him," said Xie. "We're still

checking all the hotels, guesthouses and even serviced apartments but, so far, we haven't been able to find him. It looks like he hasn't left Hong Kong—at least, he hasn't gone through any immigration checkpoint. But he could have traveled onward on a pleasure craft. It wouldn't be the first time. Not all of these get controlled; far from it. There are also more than one-and-a-half million arrivals of Canadians into Hong Kong every month. Of course, many of them are locals who acquired a Canadian passport after 1997. But the fact that he's Asian doesn't make it any easier. He's been quite clever and is probably well hidden. Deep underground. And Tremblay is also one of the most common surnames in Canada. We've got a name and a picture, but trying to find him calls for a lot of manpower and, so far, we're not winning."

"If we have a face and a name, why not publish them? Members of the public might recognize him—that would make our job easier," observed the CP. "After all, he's also the alleged murderer of a European citizen."

"No doubt about it. And we debated that. But he's also extremely dangerous. And we don't want to create a full-blown panic among the public at this stage, by letting the media know he's carrying vials of SARS," said Tanguy.

"But we could keep that a secret. Just mention the killing. That would do."

"True. But, Sir, with respect, he doesn't yet know we've already identified him. In that sense at least, we're ahead of the game. There might still be a chance to catch him before he decides to act. Were we to release that information, it might spook him and maybe even lead him to speed up his plans, whatever they are. We don't know when exactly he's planning to act, but what we're doing now is probably best in the circumstances."

"I see. I think you're right. That makes sense. Please carry on."

"We've run his photograph through all our databases, both in the SAR and on the mainland, but found nothing. Commandant Tanguy has also passed it on at his end but, so far, without any results either from our friends in the West. No one seems to know who this man is," said Ip.

"Any purchase he makes with a credit card in that name will be flagged," said Tanguy. "And we're still filtering all calls and emails making any reference to a Peter Tremblay, or to Musafir."

"I doubt he's that stupid. He's probably buying anything he needs in cash right now, and under our very noses," said the CP. "What about possible targets?"

"The airport and all MTR and train stations are on alert to look out for any suspicious activity. Water tanks, filters and pipes, as well as the air conditioning systems there, could be especially vulnerable and are under watch almost twenty-four seven," answered Ip. "There are more than a hundred-and-fifty sizeable malls in the territory, and surveillance of them has also been reinforced. Their management companies have all been notified. I doubt, though, that he'd go for any of the smaller ones. If there's to be a terrorist attack, he'd probably go for something spectacular."

"I agree. But don't hold your breath about property managers being on top of utility systems. Remember how lead was found in the soldering iron for water pipes only earlier this year. And that was in public housing, and we only found out by chance! God save us all if that's what he's going after. What about the Peak, Disneyland resort, Ocean Park and other tourist attractions?" asked Tse.

"Same thing there, but thank God there are not so many of these! And many of them are also outdoors, which wouldn't work well for a biological strike. We're prioritizing the city's transport infrastructure and the larger malls for now. That's where most tourists—and residents—can be found anyway."

"What if we finally locate him?"

"The SDU and the PLA's Five-Minute Response Unit are ready to intervene at a moment's notice," said Xie. "They've all had a refresher course on CBRN threats. I've seen to it personally. High-speed interception craft and intervention vehicles are ready to take them anywhere in the territory, immediately."

"The Five-Minute Response Unit is technically not subordinated to the Hong Kong authorities. There could be…unpleasant political implications if we were to use them. I'll need to think about it. Well, it seems we've got all possible angles covered, at this stage," concluded the CP. "Please keep me informed the minute that…Musafir surfaces. The chief executive is very anxious, as is Beijing. As you know, the chairman of the National People's Congress Standing Committee is due to visit our city soon. We can't afford any incident at that time. And, unfortunately, that also means a significant number of law enforcement personnel will need to be redeployed, as part of the security operation for the state visit."

"That's most unfortunate," said Tanguy.

"If anything happens to Zhang Dejiang, we can all kiss the rest of our careers goodbye—for good. Be in no doubt about it, Commandant; our lords and masters would be merciless. This is not France! Personally, I have no wish to spend the rest of my life laying bricks in western China."

"I fully appreciate that. But we're not there just yet! Thinking aloud for a moment, could the chairman be the target? And all that SARS business and Musafir just a decoy, to lead us in the wrong direction?"

A deadly silence followed.

"I can't discount that possibility, unfortunately. But I pray for it not to be the case! Well, it seems we're caught between a rock and a hard place. Just find him and eliminate the threat. I've never said this, but kill him if you have to. Dismissed."

Chapter 51

Mid-Levels, Hong Kong, May 2016

DEREK VAN DEEN lived in a 2,500-square-foot apartment in Hong Kong's Mid-Levels district, which was home to many expatriate residents. It mainly consisted of often ugly high-rise buildings and towers, densely packed in along the steep roads that ran down from the lower peak. The rents were expensive, and homes often boasted a number of facilities such as swimming pools, in-house libraries or function rooms. Hong Kong residents often didn't entertain at home, on account of the relatively small size of their dwellings, although that clearly wasn't a concern for van Deen's.

That Sunday morning, he had just gone for an hour-long run on a brand-new Technogym treadmill, complete with cable television and Internet connection, in the building's communal gymnasium. It was quite convenient: he just had to take the elevator down to the second floor. He didn't even have to change there: he could go already wearing his sports gear and return to the comfort of his home to shower.

There were a number of exercise machines, all kept clean and in good condition by the property's management office. Few residents bothered to visit the gym. The swimming pool was more popular, especially with families that had children. As a bachelor, he avoided it like the plague. He couldn't stand the screams and whines of the army of toddlers, all loudly encouraged by their admiring parents, as they splashed about the water in their life preservers.

It was starting to get hot by the end of May, so running outside—on Bowen Road, for example, which stretched from the Mid-Levels all the way to Wan Chai, high above the concrete jungle of Hong Kong Island's northern shore—was increasingly not an option. It wouldn't be so again until perhaps October, when lower temperatures and, above all, a more palatable level of humidity, returned to the city.

In the gym, even with the air conditioning on full blast, he had sweated heavily. A boozy Thai dinner the previous evening in Lan Kwai Fong had probably not helped.

"Issan food packs a wallop," one of the other guests, a South African, had said, and indeed it had. But he had enjoyed the exercise earlier that morning and already felt much better.

His demanding investment banking lifestyle in Asia, where constant travel was required, was starting to take its toll, he thought, as he inspected his face in a wall-mounted mirror. He wondered for a moment for how long he could continue to go on like this, but the thought quickly went away. The money was too good. And, besides, his skill set was rather limited: there wasn't much he knew besides pitching clients to execute their equity offerings. And he was rather good at it.

On the television screen in the gym, he had just learned of a thwarted attempt to disturb the forthcoming visit to Hong Kong of a dignitary from the PRC. It had involved drones, which seemed to be quite a novelty for pro-democracy protesters. Traffic and access to the Central business district would probably be hell over the following days.

His thirty-fourth-floor apartment offered a panoramic view of Victoria Harbor. He gulped half a bottle of mineral water as he watched, for a few moments, a regatta unfold on the water. It was a perfect day to be sailing. He was about half undressed when the bell to the front door suddenly rang.

It was unusual. He wasn't expecting any visitors. Very few people, bar the odd local girl he picked up from time to time in a bar or nightclub, actually came to his apartment. And most of the time, they left after a few hours. In fact, he could not recall any one of them spending the entire night there. He liked to sleep alone, after the deed was done. Maybe it was someone from the building's management? They turned up on occasion to flag issues with maintenance, or deliver parcels, although the latter would be unlikely on a Sunday.

He opened the door wide to find a man he had never seen before. He was carrying a small backpack. He assumed the man must have taken the elevator to the wrong floor, or mistaken van Deen's apartment for that of his next-door neighbors. Clearly, he did not work in the building. He was Asian, of average height, but what was most remarkable were his eyes. They were slanted but very bright—blue or gray; he couldn't really tell. The rest of his face was hidden behind a surgical mask. The man slowly raised his right arm, revealing that he was holding an automatic pistol, whose barrel now pointed at van Deen's forehead.

"What...what's this?" asked the banker, taken aback.

"M. van Deen, would you please take a few steps back, so that I can close the door?"

The stranger had addressed him by name. Whoever he was, the man had not rung at the wrong door. The tone of the voice was calm, almost gentle, in sharp contrast to his intentions, which were obviously far from friendly. He was fully composed and that, for some reason, sent signals of extreme fear to van Deen's brain. The banker was a bit of a loudmouth and could also be supremely arrogant, but his swagger and any semblance of self-importance had suddenly evaporated.

"Who're you? And what do you want? I don't have any valuables here. And I carry little cash in my wallet. You're welcome to take it all. And then please leave. How did you get into the building anyway?"

"I'm not after your money, M. van Deen. Are you alone, right now?"

"Yes...I live alone. There's no one here other than us."

"Good. Listen to me carefully now. I'll need your Octopus card, the one that provides access to your office, in IFC. And also your pass for the GSA office. I assume both are in your wallet, which I can see on that table, over there? Please get them for me, but move very slowly and keep your hands where I can see them at all times."

"Yes...they're in my wallet," he said. "What's this

about? Office robbery? Even if you managed to get in, there are cameras everywhere in IFC. And there's nothing to steal there. Nothing of commercial value, anyway."

"That's for me to worry about."

"You understand that the minute you leave, I'll report them stolen. All access will be blocked. You won't even make it in time to enter the building," said DVD, his cockiness finally taking over.

"That, I doubt very much, M. van Deen," answered Temur Khan.

He placed the gun in his trousers, at the small of his back, and then swiftly retrieved his trusty folding knife from his pocket. He flicked it open, with a quick push on one of the metal thumb studs, revealing the black upswept blade. He then pushed the small button to lock it into place.

"Hey…easy now! You don't need to do this!" pleaded van Deen.

But before he could utter another word, Temur was on him. He grabbed the banker's shoulder, making him pivot and lose his balance. In the blink of an eye, he had fallen to his knees, his back now facing his assailant. Khan quickly lifted and tilted back his jaw with his left hand, and cut deeply across his throat with the blade. In doing so, he severed van Deen's external carotid artery, as well as two of his five jugular veins. He also sliced through the vocal cords, preventing him from screaming for help.

He knew that even though van Deen would still take a few minutes to bleed to death, he would collapse long before that happened, due to the brain's finely tuned pressure-control system. When the area around the carotid arteries experienced a change in blood pressure, the human body initiated a fainting reaction, collapsing to bring the heart and brain to the same level.

At first, even though he had been mortally wounded, van Deen felt only a sting, just like a bad shaving cut. Next, he sensed the equivalent of several cups of warm water rapidly flowing down his chest, as blood oozed away from his throat. Within a fraction of a second, he also felt very dizzy, as if standing up too fast from a lying position. A wave of severe nausea followed. His vision quickly blurred and then he fainted, never to regain consciousness. He died, not only from the loss of blood but also from the equivalent of a massive stroke and oxygen deprivation of the brain.

Temur held on tight, waiting from him to stop thrashing about, although at this stage, much of it was due to the body's reflexes rather than attempts by the banker to defend himself. He had long passed that point.

Finally, Khan let go of him.

"*Allahu Akbar!*" he whispered.

He first gave thanks for the life he had sacrificed. He then wiped his hands clean, searched the wallet and retrieved the Octopus card and office pass. Next, he went to a nearby bathroom and found a couple of towels, which he used to soak up some of the blood that had poured onto the wooden floor, careful not to step into the red pool that had started to form. More blood still flowed out of van Deen's wound. The varnish on the floor was cracked in a few places. The volume of blood in a human body totaled almost 1.3 gallons, and he could not take the risk of some trickling down and leaking through the ceiling of the apartment below.

Once he was satisfied with his damage-limitation exercise, he located van Deen's cell phone and turned it off, before wiping clean with a soft cloth all the hard surfaces he had touched. Some of the blood had spurted onto his own clothes. That was almost inevitable, and he quickly changed into a new polo shirt he had carried in a small backpack. He then inspected the rest of the apartment before leaving through the front door, wiping any fingerprints he had left from the door handle.

He had not been stopped earlier. The property was part of a complex of three towers, and the residents changed often. Every year, dozens of new faces came in, replacing those who had left due to either a rise in the rent they paid or because they were posted elsewhere. Walking in with a quiet air of confidence rarely elicited any questions, and the guards had simply assumed he lived there. He left, still unchallenged, by the security staff. Once on the street, he hailed a red and white taxi.

Chapter 52

Central, Hong Kong, May 2016

TEMUR KHAN HAD picked up the ultrasonic mist-maker at his rental flat in Shek Tong Tsui and was now on his way by MTR to the Two IFC office tower. The apparatus, carefully wrapped, was in his backpack, as were two large-capacity bottles of double-distilled water. It made for a heavyweight load, but he did not have to walk over too long a distance, and it would save him from carrying them the following day.

His dress was of the smart casual variety, as would be that of an investment banker working in the office on the weekend: a pair of jeans, a Ralph Lauren polo shirt and branded Japanese trainers. He alighted in Central and walked through the maze of underground corridors that led to the IFC mall. Because of the hot weather, it was busy, as residents and tourists sought the comfort of its air-conditioned arcades to do a bit of shopping. While many visitors from the mainland now preferred traveling to Taiwan, Singapore or even Japan, not all of them had given up on the attractions of the Special Administrative Region. Entire families, some pulling heavy wheeled suitcases, stocked up on luxury goods and pharmaceutical products, either for themselves or for resale north of the border.

He soon reached the entrance to the Number Two tower. Because it was a weekend, all the sliding doors but one had been shut, leaving only a relatively narrow entrance for those executives unlucky enough to have to work on such a day. As one came in, one had to check in at the reception desk to be allowed to proceed onward to one of the elevator lobbies.

Temur retrieved from his pocket the Octopus card he had taken earlier from Derek van Deen and placed it on the reader. The system did not check the face of the owner against a photograph, let alone his identity. It simply acknowledged the card was valid, granted access and recorded the visit.

He took one of the walking walkways down to the lower floor, where the elevator lobby for the higher levels was located. There, he swiped the card again through another reader and the glass turnstile opened, granting access to the elevators. It seemed he was the only visitor at that time. He rode the elevator to the thirty-fifth floor transfer lobby and then took another to the sixty-seventh floor, where GSA's offices were located. It had all taken just over a minute.

The corridor was quiet and no one was around—at least, no one that he could see. Unbeknown to him, slaving away at his desk was Kelvin Ma, the equity capital markets associate who worked for the late Derek van Deen, busily putting the final touches to the Chinese translation of his lengthy pitch book.

Temur ignored the entrance to GSA's offices and went straight to the men's restroom down the corridor. He pushed open the door and first ascertained that all of the stalls were unused. He then entered one and locked the door behind him. He placed his backpack on the floor, unzipped it and carefully retrieved its contents.

He took off his shoes, flipped down the toilet seat and stepped on it. He easily reached up to the ceiling and dismantled a couple of white plastic panels. They simply dropped into a grid-work of metal channels in the shape of an upside-down "T" that were suspended on wires from the overhead structure, hiding piping, wiring and ductwork. Once he had created enough space, he lifted the ultrasonic mist-maker and bottles of distilled water and placed them inside the false ceiling.

He would need a few additional water containers later, but this would do for now. They were relatively heavy, but not enough to loosen the metal channels or show through the plastic panels. He then carefully replaced the ceiling tiles in their original positions.

He stepped down from the seat, put his shoes back on and grabbed his bag. He was just about to exit the cubicle when he heard the unmistakable sound of footsteps. They quickly stopped. He heard a zipper being opened and then the flushing of water from a nearby urinal. Finally, after a few seconds, he heard a man relieve himself. Next, he heard the zip again, followed by running water from a tap and, at last, the stranger left.

He waited a couple of minutes before exiting the cubicle. He was just about to pull open the door that led back to the corridor when someone pushed it from behind and it almost flew into his face.

"Oh! Sorry, dude!" said a young Chinese man with a thick American accent. "Didn't see you! Forgot my phone," he added, as he walked to the nearby sink to retrieve a Samsung handset.

"No worries! I was wondering who might have left it there."

"Oh really? Well, you now know! Hey—that's a pretty big backpack you've got! What do you carry inside? Body parts?"

"Nothing of the sort! Just a bag of rice! Twenty-two pounds. I'm training for an endurance race later this year, in Mongolia. It's the easiest way to create a heavy load."

"You're training *in this weather*? Better you than me! But, say, I've never seen you before. Who do you work for?"

"Derivatives trading," answered Temur, making things up as he went along.

"Oh—you're on Tjun Kim's team?"

"That's right. Just transferred from New York."

"That explains it, then. I'm Kelvin Ma, by the way. ECM. Anyway, gotta go!"

And, with that, he left, as abruptly as he had arrived.

It had been a close call. Temur looked up, toward the ceiling panels, but there was nothing to betray what lay hidden behind them. He had left no tracks. Bar a ruptured pipe and water leak, which was most unlikely, the mist-maker and containers would be safe there until the following day.

He walked back through the corridor and called the elevator. He rode it to the thirty-fifth floor, changed to another lift, and exited at the ground-floor level. He then took the escalator back up to level P1, swiped his Octopus card on the reader as he exited and found himself back in the mall, just outside the office tower. He followed the arcade to the elevated walkway that led to Pedder Street and walked down to the Central MTR station.

The following day, he would return to the skyscraper and make his way to the sixty-seventh floor again, hidden among the dense flow of workers, back from their lunch breaks. If all went according to plan, most of them would quickly fall prey to a dangerous disease, and many would ultimately die.

Chapter 53

Shek Tong Tsui, Hong Kong, June 2016

BACK AT HIS APARTMENT later that afternoon, Temur Khan's next task was to revive the freeze-dried SARS virus. Conditions in the flat were far from ideal and certainly didn't match those of a laboratory, but they would have to do. Unlike in the experiment he had conducted in the garage in San Sebastián de los Reyes in Spain, he now had to open many more ampoules and work on a much larger batch of microorganisms.

He was acutely aware that he most certainly would become contaminated as a result, although that was something he readily accepted. Working with such a large quantity of pathogens, it couldn't really be avoided, not in this crude, unprotected environment. But any signs of contamination wouldn't appear for at least a few days. He was in good physical condition and now needed less than twenty-four hours for what he had to do. As far as he was concerned, what happened afterward was irrelevant. After all, this was all about jihad, and for years he had waited to sacrifice his life for the cause he believed in. All the same, perhaps by force of habit, he chose to wear eye protection as well as a facemask and plastic gloves. He had also changed into a cotton shirt with long sleeves, to avoid any droplets spilling onto his naked skin.

In the safety of their temperature-controlled container lay the ampoules he had smuggled from Spain. Twenty-three of them were left. All were double-vial preparations. The outer vial was made of soft glass, while the virus itself was enclosed within an inner vial. At the bottom of the outer vial was a freeze-dried pellet, situated above a small wad of cotton and a crystal desiccant made of silica beads. The desiccant was still blue in color. This indicated that the vacuum seal had not been compromised and that the material contained in the vial was accordingly fit for revival and culture. The ampoules had survived the journey without apparent damage. Otherwise, the beads would have turned pink, or even become completely clear.

Above the inner vial was a cotton plug, held in place by an insulator. At the top end of the glass ampoule was a pointed tip. Temur took the first ampoule from the container and gently heated the tip of the outer vial in a flame. He had decided to use the gas ring in the kitchen of the apartment for this manipulation. Once it had been heated, he squirted a few drops of water on the tip to crack the glass. He then struck it with a metal file, without excessive force. The tip neatly broke.

He removed the insulator with a pair of forceps. Next, he slowly raised the cotton plug and then pulled out the entire inner vial. He scored the glass container he had extracted once, with the metal file, about a third of an inch from the tip. He disinfected the inner ampoule with an alcohol-dampened gauze and wrapped the latter around it to break it at the scored area. He had taken care to ensure the gauze wasn't too wet, to avoid allowing alcohol to be sucked into the culture when the vacuum broke. He pushed with his thumbs, pulling outward with his forefingers, and heard a gentle crack. He then immediately dropped the material in the vial into a glass test tube. He added a dash of double-distilled sterile water to rehydrate the microorganism and started the incubation process with an agar slant as a base. He then sealed the test tube with a rubber stopper and placed it in the kitchen fridge.

So far, so good, he thought.

He wiped a bead of sweat from his forehead with the sleeve of his shirt, and then took another ampoule from the cool box to repeat the process. He worked methodically but slowly, to avoid the risk of dropping one of the glass vials onto the floor. Every ampoule counted, and he could hardly afford to lose one. It had been pretty quick in Madrid, but he knew the incubation could take up to a few hours. There was no rush. He would work late into the night, until he had processed the entire batch.

He was halfway through when he decided to take a short break. He could only focus for so long and was now in need of a drink and something to eat. But, after forty-five minutes, he was ready to start again. He heard the siren of a police car in the street down below as he picked up yet another vial from the cool box, ready to heat the tip on the naked gas flame. Even though it was now dark, it was still hot and, above all, humid. He had decided not to switch on the air conditioning. The damp atmosphere would probably help the revival process.

It was almost midnight when he finally emptied the contents of the last ampoule from the batch. He checked on the first tubes he had filled, but unlike with fungi, it was difficult to visually confirm whether the culture had started to grow. He was confident in his skills, however, and in all likelihood, the preparations that now lay in the fridge had been successfully activated.

In the morning, he would transfer their contents to a larger glass container, enclosed in a metal outer vial sealed with a screw top. In turn, the culture would later find its way into the tank of the mist-maker, where it would be diluted into a larger quantity of distilled water. He would then switch on the machine to spread the contaminated droplets within the office tower's air conditioning system.

Once he was done, he emptied a bottle of bleach into the kitchen sink to sterilize the empty and broken vials, as well as the tools he had used, before discarding them in a large Ziploc plastic bag. He then carefully washed his hands and wrists with a solution of water and bleach as an added precaution. Finally, he showered and prayed. He gave thanks to Allah for all that had been achieved so far.

He lay in his bed for a while, but his mind was feverish and he didn't manage to sleep for more than a couple of hours. He awoke just before six o'clock, as he had intended. He retrieved a mobile handset from his bag, removed the battery and inserted a new pre-paid SIM card in the slot. Like the SIM card, the handset had never been used before. He powered it on and dialed an international telephone number. The country code was ninety-two, for Pakistan. It had never been called before and, like that of the caller, the number would be used only once.

After roaming, and a few ring tones, the call was finally answered in Dubai, in the United Arab Emirates. The time there was exactly two in the morning.

"Al-Musafir," said Temur Khan.

"I'm afraid you've got the wrong number. And it's very late," came the answer, from what sounded like a sleepy voice, in Urdu.

"I'm so sorry. Let me try again," he said, before hanging up.

After the call in Dubai, Ismail Khan immediately went to work. Pre-programmed short-selling orders were swiftly executed, starting with Japan and the rest of the Asian time zone. The process would continue throughout the day, as financial centers around the world became active, one after the other.

In Hong Kong itself, this was tricky. Only stocks designated on a list maintained by the exchange could be sold short. And selling a stock one did not own was also prohibited under Hong Kong law, unless one had an exercisable and unconditional right, such as the holding of options, warrants or convertible notes, to sell the shares. Accordingly, short-selling there often entailed entering into stock-borrowing arrangements with existing shareholders, but this required significant collateral. In addition, shorting stock in Hong Kong could only be executed through the exchange's automatic order matching and execution system. But there were still plenty of securities to be found in the region, and beyond, to generate substantial profits, once all hell broke loose in the city's financial district.

There was no turning back now. The following day, around lunchtime, Temur Khan would return to the office tower and implement what he had been working toward since his teenage years.

Chapter 54

DEREK VAN DEEN had not lied before dying. He had indeed lived alone, in his trophy apartment fit for a high-level expatriate executive. From the large windows of the living room, one had fine views of the national day fireworks or cruise ships that regularly crisscrossed the water, usually before and after weekends. But, what had completely slipped van Deen's mind, and what he had not told his murderer—something that was, after all, understandable at the time one was about to meet one's maker—was that a domestic worker came to his flat every morning to take care of chores.

Unlike many people in Hong Kong, at least beyond a certain income bracket, van Deen had not cared for a live-in maid. But he had still required one to clean his apartment, do his laundry, iron his shirts and shine his shoes in the daytime, while he worked in his office or traveled around the region. Like other equity capital markets practitioners, van Deen had started work early, usually turning up between seven and seven-thirty, in time for the morning Equities briefing on the trading floor. Much of his job had entailed conveying to corporate clients the mood of the market. Hearing firsthand what the firm's economists, strategists and research analysts said and thought had therefore been essential for sharpening his pitching abilities.

That's why, at eight o'clock on this Monday morning in early June, Grace entered van Deen's apartment on the thirty-fourth floor. As usual, she did not expect him to be there. He was usually long gone by the time she arrived. It was therefore quite a surprise to find him half naked, on the floor of the living room that morning—and all the more so because he was lying in what looked like a wide pool of half-congealed blood.

She had experienced her fair share of violence in Manila, in the Philippines, but it had been nothing like what she had to take in that morning. Van Deen's throat had most obviously been slit clean, and he had bled to death. His face was very pale, as the blood had almost completely drained from his body.

The door had been locked, and it didn't look like any windows were open, at least none that she could see. But, all the same, she did not wish to check the other rooms in the apartment in case the killer (or killers) might still be around. Shocked, breathless and in a panic, she immediately left the apartment, took the elevator down to the main reception desk on the ground floor lobby and went straight to the security guards to inform them that she had just found M. van Deen murdered. She was formally employed by his next-door neighbors, but, with their tacit agreement, worked for him on the side to earn extra cash. It was not strictly legal, but all the maids did it, and she reckoned that she'd hardly get into trouble. The authorities would have bigger fish to fry with his killing today.

The police arrived quickly, within about fifteen minutes. Murders were rare in Hong Kong, one of the safest cities in Asia and even in the whole world. They were even less common in the Mid-Levels, a residential enclave for wealthy expatriates, where most buildings had guards, cameras and security patrols at all hours of the day and night. Bar the odd domestic dispute that occasionally took a turn for the worse, it was as safe as living abroad could get.

A couple of inspectors and half a dozen uniformed constables arrived, in addition to the crime scene team, clad in white overalls. They immediately went to work to secure the perimeter, study the body and question the neighbors, as well as anyone who might have seen or encountered those responsible for the financier's murder.

The time of death was estimated at around nine o'clock the previous morning, with a margin of error of about two hours earlier or later. The maid had a cast-iron alibi. While Sunday was her rest day, she had left her employer's residence well after at noon on that day and had been seen there throughout the morning by the entire family.

In addition, the security cameras in the building soon clearly showed a man entering the building around that time and riding the elevator to the thirty-fourth floor. He had left after about fifteen minutes in the same fashion. Much of his face had been hidden by a mask, of the type locals wore when they had a cold. That man was clearly the killer; there was little doubt about it.

What was less clear, though, was why the banker had been executed in such a brutal fashion. He lived alone and appeared to be a high-profile financier. Local girls apparently sometimes came there, according to the security guards, but none was known to have been a regular girlfriend. His apartment had not been ransacked, and all items of value were still evidently there, including his wallet, in which a wad of cash was even found. A number of jewelry items, including a rather heavy, limited-edition Big Bang watch by Hublot as well as a computer, were similarly uncovered. Whatever it was, the motive had clearly not been stealing money and valuables.

No fingerprints other than the victim's and the maid's were found. The only thing that was perhaps out of the ordinary was that his cell phone was switched off, which would be unusual during the daytime for an investment banker, even on the weekend. Perhaps the killer had turned it off, so as not to attract the attention of the neighbors with the ring tone, should anyone repeatedly try to get ahold of van Deen?

At first glance, there was nothing that might readily explain why the banker had been slain that Sunday morning.

A note was made of his employer, Global Securities Asia, in the Two IFC tower, as was shown on his business cards. They were promptly informed. The human resources department would have details of the next of kin and might perhaps be able to provide more clues. One of the inspectors headed over there.

As the case was processed, however, no one paid much attention at first to the fact that van Deen's access cards for the skyscraper were missing. There were, it seemed, far more important issues to focus on at this stage.

Chapter 55

Central, Hong Kong, June 2016

IT WAS TEN in the morning in Hong Kong, and Erwan Tanguy was surprised to recognize the voice of The Bear at the other end of the phone. The line wasn't very good, but there was no mistaking the husky, grumpy speech of the former paratrooper. At the crack of dawn, he was already huffing and puffing like a rhinoceros trapped by a team of poachers in the African savannah.

"Mon Colonel," said Tanguy. "Where are you? It must be four a.m. in Paris."

"Tanguy! It is! And you don't need to remind me. I'm at home in my PJs, if you really want to know. And I feel like shit, as I usually do at this time of day. Never was a morning person."

"Strange words from an army officer! I assume it's important. What's up?"

"It's important, all right. Listen carefully. We finally got something on Musafir. Phone call. It may be nothing, but I don't believe in coincidences. I'm not paid to gobble up fairy tales. And if I'm right, the shit's about to hit the fan in Asia—big time."

"Tell me all about it."

"Goes like this. Our friends at the NSA picked up a call a few hours ago. The bastards just woke me up. Didn't want to wait to pass the buck on to you. But, bear with me, it's a bit complicated. The caller's location was Hong Kong, although the number he dialed from was Indian. It was a pre-paid SIM card. Never been used before and neither was the phone. The number he dialed was Pakistani. Same drill at that end—new phone and new SIM card. And the fellow who answered was located in Dubai. Are you still with me? The call was very short—they couldn't be more precise than that on the two parties' whereabouts. Let me read the translation of the recording for you. It was all in Urdu."

"*Al-Musafir.*"
"*I'm afraid you've got the wrong number. And it's very late.*"
"*I'm so sorry. Let me try again.*"

"That doesn't seem to amount to much."

"Taken on its own, I agree. Could be anything, although the Hong Kong location's interesting in the circumstances. But it's the second time we've now heard that conversation, word for word. And the voices were exactly the same. The Yanks are adamant they fully matched. You know their technology. God knows I don't like them much at times, but you can't fault their efficiency when it comes to IT. They're right up there with the Chinese and North Koreans, while we're still in kindergarten. Must be our arrogance and our alleged world-class band of engineers. But I'm digressing. Anyway, the last time a similar call was made was in April. The SIM and phone of the caller, as well as those of the receiver, were different then—but in both cases they were used for the first time, too. Looks like they're being very cautious, which in itself is a red flag. At that time, the call was picked up in Pakistan. Islamabad. Now, you and I know you just don't call there casually. And it was all in Urdu, again. But what really caught my eye, more than anything else, was that it originated from Spain. Madrid, to be precise."

"Shit."

"As you said, it looks to me like our friend Musafir may be communicating with his masters and conveying key stages in their plan to spread the disease."

"What makes you think that?"

"You know me: I'm a simple man. I like drawings, charts and tables. If I plot something like a timeline, the first call would have been made around the time those two women became infected. You know the ones, the Gupta family, who were found dead in that garage just outside Madrid. It looks to me like Musafir wanted to make sure his friend—the father, Vicar, or whatever his name was—had smuggled the right vials from the lab. Once he had proof, he called his Paki friends in the badlands, to let them know they were in business."

"Makes sense."

"Of course it does. And, if I'm right, he's now called them again, to convey he's just about to go live. We know he's in Hong Kong already. And also that he's got the vials. Why else would he call?"

"So, that means maybe we only have a few hours before he strikes! For all we know, although I pray for it not to be the case, he may have started already."

"I'm afraid so. I assume you haven't found him yet, or I would've heard."

"Correct. He's disappeared. We're still actively looking, but he's gone to ground."

"Any views on a possible target?"

"No luck there either, I'm afraid. We're focusing on the transport infrastructure, airport, metro and especially the shopping malls. That's where he's most likely to do maximum damage. It's already hot and humid here. These places are crowded right now, as the aircon's on full blast. The major shopping arcades are all under surveillance. But there are hundreds of them. You know what Asia's like: people gather to socialize in these places, and the Chinese tourists load up on stuff to take across the border. They like it when they can find everything under one roof."

"I get the picture. Saigon's Bến Thành market, with a marble floor and chandeliers hanging from the ceiling. I bet the restrooms are so clean they blind you. It looks like you've all got it well covered, though."

"Hong Kong's on high alert anyway, but for another reason. The Number Three guy is visiting from Beijing this week. The police are everywhere. Constables are posted every few yards in the business district and around the convention center, including on all bridges under which the motorcade will pass. Divers have even been sent into the harbor to search for mines and explosives. The bad news is that they're focusing first and foremost on the state visit."

"Well, you know we'd do the same if we were in their shoes. Public interest takes a different meaning when you're at the top. Just look at the Obama circus when he's attending a G7 meeting! I can already see public servants in Hong Kong shitting their pants if their little emperor gets hit. Anyway, let's pray I'm wrong. Will you please relay the intel to the Hong Kong authorities, and especially to the Chinese, *right now*? I don't want to be on the hook for not warning them in a timely fashion. They should monitor any unusual activity, track any lead, however small. This is real, Tanguy. We have to take it very, very seriously. Eavesdropping is all about identifying patterns. You know that. And that one looks as good as they come. Madrid, Hong Kong, U.A.E., Pakistan and even the name Musafir, it's no coincidence."

"I agree. Thanks for the call."

"You're welcome. I guess I'll head out to the office. Maybe grab a couple of croissants on the way. Might as well see if I can do something useful from there. Looks like you may have a hell of a day ahead of you. Good luck. I hope you can catch him in time. Over and out."

Chapter 56

TEMUR KHAN WAS almost ready to spring into action. He had now transferred the contents of the test tubes in the apartment's refrigerator to a single glass container, encased in a metal outer vial. It was sealed with a screw top and looked very much like an oversized thermos. He had placed it in his backpack, along with two extra-large bottles of double-distilled water.

He had also changed into a suit and tie, ready to impersonate an investment banker or a fund manager on his way back to the office, returning from lunch in the IFC mall. His plan was simple: the area around the Two IFC office tower would be particularly busy around one-thirty in the afternoon, as people returned to work after a short lunch break. He would join the crowd and use van Deen's access card to enter the building. There would be long queues to catch one of the elevators at that time, and he reckoned the security guards wouldn't pay much attention to him.

He would then return to the sixty-seventh-floor men's room and retrieve the mist-maker and water containers he had hidden during the weekend. He would subsequently make his way to the rooftop, where the air intakes for the building's network of air conditioning pipes were located. Access to that area was restricted to security guards and maintenance personnel, but he had another plan for dealing with them.

Once on the roof, he had already identified one of the air intakes, located in a blind spot away from the CCTV cameras. He would empty the contents of the sealed glass container into the tank of the mist-maker, dilute the mixture with distilled water, power up the unit (he knew there were a number of sockets nearby, fit for that purpose) and, finally, send the deadly droplets into the aircon system, where they would ultimately make their way throughout the building's floors, podiums and even underground levels.

Set on high, the entire tank would empty in the span of a few hours; no more. He didn't plan to stay for longer than was absolutely necessary, so he would leave the tower once the mist-maker had started to operate.

He had debated at some length on what to do next. He had thought about conducting random killings within the mall, following which he would probably end up being shot dead by the security forces. But, under such a scenario, the building would likely be evacuated, and far fewer people would then be exposed to the virus. They would also easily track where he had come from, thanks to the mall's network of spy cameras. Part of the terror brought about by a biological attack, as with many a terrorist strike, was not knowing where it had come from, and also how exactly it had been carried out. He could not afford having the authorities immediately find out what had happened. Of course, ultimately it would be revealed, but he needed a safety net to first ensure things went exactly as planned.

Once the first signs of the disease appeared, within a few days, there would be a claim, of course. Al Qaeda would issue a statement, taking responsibility, blaming China and the West. Ismail Khan would see to that, before reaping the rewards of the ensuing collapse in stock market prices.

Meanwhile, Temur Khan would remain hidden. When he felt the first signs of infection, he would contribute to further spreading the disease, visiting cinemas, malls and supermarkets, attending a professional exhibition at the Convention Centre in Wan Chai or the Hong Kong Expo facilities and traveling extensively throughout the MTR network. He then planned to end his life at Chek Lap Kok airport, taking the lives of a number of travelers and further contaminating others.

All this would no doubt dominate global media's attention and send the world a clear message that no one was safe, least of all in the arrogant Middle Kingdom and its satellites, which had become so essential to the world's economic prosperity. China would no longer be a haven. And this, in turn, would so impact the rest of the world that people would remember it for many years to come. He would make the sheikh's vision a reality and die a glorious death in the process.

But for now, he still had to complete the first part of his plan. He left the Shek Tong Tsui rental apartment and walked to the HKU MTR station on Queen's Road West. Its underground platforms were among the deepest in Hong Kong and held a maze of passages that took students to the university campus, on the other side of a steep hill, every day. He rode down a very long escalator and walked to the station's main podium, purchasing a single ticket at one of the vending machines. He did not want to use van Deen's Octopus card. It would make his journey more easily traceable, and he would still have use for the apartment for a few more days, maybe even up to a week. He needed it to remain hidden. For that reason, he had also chosen to wear a facemask to further avoid being recognized, should the police scan CCTV footage. A baseball cap would have looked odd with a suit and tie, as would sunglasses within a building or train.

He swiped the ticket on the reader and took another elevator down to the platform, catching an eastbound train on the Island Line to Central, where he alighted. He decided to walk to the Two IFC tower through the network of underground passages that led directly to the mall.

It was almost the hottest time of the day and, with a coat and tie, he knew he would unnecessarily sweat outside in the high temperature and humidity. He also knew that on this day, police constables would be heavily patrolling the overhead walkway, which also led to the skyscraper. The motorcade of the visiting dignitary, whose name he had already forgotten, was due to pass underneath as he returned from delivering a speech at the Convention Centre in Wan Chai. The authorities didn't want to take any chances of pro-democracy protesters unfolding an insulting banner, or even hurling a brick or other projectiles at the passing car, let alone attempting to shoot bullets at the Beijing luminary or his bodyguards. Paving stones in some of the streets had even been glued down, in an attempt to prevent riots from taking place. Taking the subterranean route would be much safer and also more discreet.

He followed the many corridors and finally emerged in the mall, ending the short journey by riding up an impressively long series of escalators. It was now just after one o'clock.

The shopping arcades were at their busiest. Thousands of executives were heading to or returning from lunch, taking the opportunity to also relax or do a bit of window-shopping along the eight hundred thousand square feet of the IFC mall, distributed across four floors. There were a number of restaurants, most of them full, with people queuing outside for tables. IFC was one of the largest, if not the largest, mall in Hong Kong, and visitor traffic there was unparalleled. With access from the Airport Express, Central MTR station, Hong Kong-Macau ferry pier and Star Ferry pier, in addition to many buses and taxi stations, it also occupied a strategic location for locals as well as shoppers from the mainland and international tourists.

Chances were that if you visited Hong Kong, you'd end up there at some point. And of course, there was also the daily patronage of the fifteen thousand people or so who worked in the Number Two office tower, not to mention its smaller sibling at the other end of the arcade, next to the Four Seasons Hotel.

Temur walked confidently toward the entrance. Unlike on the weekend, all the sliding doors were now open, with a constant flow of people entering and leaving the building. Until the evening, there would be no checking of access cards at the reception desk. But you still had to swipe your pass at the turnstiles that led to the various elevator lobbies, usually under the eyes of a security guard. However, at lunchtime, they would be too absorbed in creating a semblance of order by channeling the stream of executives to the various elevators to pay too much attention to any one of them in particular.

Temur Khan passed the first elevator lobby on the left. But instead of riding the escalator to the lower-floor reception, as he had done on the weekend, he went straight for the elevators that descended to the various parking levels. Access to them was unrestricted, except outside of office hours. He pressed the button labeled B3, which would take him to the third basement, reserved for parking by tenants. He knew exactly where to go.

Chapter 57

Central, Hong Kong, June 2016

THE CAR WAS still there, in one of the parking lot's corners—an inconspicuous Toyota, which he had bought secondhand and left there some seven months before. The monthly rent, HK$5,000, was paid regularly, without fail, from a bank account in the Middle East. It was an extortionate amount at any rate, but the financiers who worked in the building above couldn't have cared less. Driving to work was a privilege, one among many others they enjoyed. Buses and the MTR weren't for them. They didn't mind taking taxis, but queuing for one at rush hour was a waste of time. And so, they didn't.

He had even paid cash in advance, for a full nine months, to the young Chinese man who provided a car-wash service by hand to the tenants, so the vehicle wouldn't gather dust. No questions had been asked and, so long as everyone was paid in good time, none would be. He was unsure if the engine would start. The battery's wires weren't connected and it had been a long time, but that was unimportant. What really mattered was that there was plenty of space in the trunk, and also that this particular corner of the lot was in a blind spot, rather than under the surveillance of the overhead CCTV network.

As with every prospective tenant, the management company had sent him a floor plan of the parking lot when he had inquired about renting a space there. Temur Khan had crosschecked the location of those that were available with the blueprints he possessed, to make sure he couldn't be watched remotely. The management company had then painted the car's license plate code on the concrete floor to indicate the place was now his, and his alone.

The cheap Toyota definitely stood out amid the makes favored by other tenants. There were a number of Ferraris, many of the latest model, as well as Maseratis, Aston Martins and even a few rare McLarens thrown in for good measure. The stock invariably grew in the first quarter of the year, after bonuses were paid in the finance industry, as bankers and traders rewarded themselves for a year's hard work, even though discretionary remuneration had been trimmed in comparison to the pre-financial crisis years.

The Japanese sedan didn't have any impressive spoilers, and its body wasn't shaped like that of a muscular African big cat, but it was a trusty car all the same, and the key thing was that it was still there, even after a number of months.

What Temur now needed was an access card for the service levels, at the very top of the building. The only people allowed access to them were the security guards and maintenance workers. He already knew the former regularly patrolled each level of the parking lot. It was just a question of time before one of them turned up. Since the car's remote wouldn't work, he opened the doors with a key and patiently sat at the wheel, waiting for a guard to arrive.

After only about fifteen minutes, a uniformed man showed up in the distance, walking in his direction. He wore gray fatigue trousers with side pockets over ankle-high black leather boots, as well as a blue shirt with epaulettes and a red beret.

Dorjee Namdak was now in his fifties. For a number of years, he had served with distinction in the Brigade of Gurkhas in the British army, specifically in the Royal Gurkha Rifles, which had a jungle role battalion permanently based in Brunei as well as a light role battalion in the United Kingdom.

He had first passed selection at HQ British Gurkhas in Nepal. It had not been easy. The camp in Pokhara was still the focal point for all recruiting activities there and, in December of each year, the culmination of the process saw just over three hundred young men between the ages of seventeen-and-a-half and twenty-one being selected. Of them, about three-quarters went to the British army, and the balance to a contingent of the Singapore Police Force.

Invariably, the large number of interested individuals always created considerable competition for the relatively few places on offer. The standards imposed by the recruiting staff were extremely high, and the process was quite demanding. The selection itself was purely merit-based. Final recruitment was determined through a number of physical and mental assessments, including papers in English and mathematics, as well as executing a minimum of twelve heaves; seventy sit-ups, to be completed within two minutes; and a timed eight-hundred-and-seventy-five-yard sprint. A medical exam and a thorough interview also ensured that only the fittest and most motivated were admitted.

Next, the men began an eight-month stint at the Infantry Training Centre in Catterick, which trained the recruits who had passed selection, after they had sworn an oath of allegiance to the Queen. Only then would they be able to make the Nepali phrase *kaathar hunnu bhanda marnu ramro* ("better to die than to be a coward") their motto, and proudly receive their beloved *kukri* knife at their passing-out parade.

But that had been years ago and, as far as Dorjee Namdak was concerned, his days of patrolling the jungles of Borneo were truly over. While he still wore with pride impeccably pressed clothes that could almost pass for some sort of military uniform, he was no longer in the peak physical condition his previous job had demanded. All that was required of him nowadays was to keep an eye out for anything unusual and report any such anomalies to the building's security center.

He had of course kept his kukri, which was displayed, along with the medals he had won, in his small apartment in Mong Kok but, as a guard patrolling the skyscraper, he was unarmed. He only had a small portable radio transmitter to communicate with the control room, not that he used it very often. Over the years, he had gone soft, not having uncovered anything remotely untoward. His senses were not as sharp as they once had been, and he had gradually fallen into a comfortable routine.

And so, when the Asian man with the curious clear eyes called out to him through the open window of his Toyota, he had no reason to believe he only had a few seconds left to live. Unsuspecting, he approached the vehicle. The guard was roughly the same height as Temur.

This is perfect, the Uyghur thought.

"Namaste," said the guard, as he drew closer.

"Good afternoon," said the man. "Would you possibly be able to help me?"

"What's the problem?"

"There seems to be an issue with my car, see."

"I'm not sure."

That was all the guard ever said. As he came within a few inches of the open window, the man thrust a blade into the side of his throat. As part of his military training, Dorjee had been taught to fight to the death with a naked blade. All the Gurkhas had, and he instantly knew he had been mortally wounded. The man then swiftly slit sideways to severe one of the arteries and, within two seconds, Dorjee collapsed on the floor, his open wound spurting blood forcefully.

Temur had felt absolutely nothing. Killing the Nepali was just a means to an end. There was no doubt the man was a Hindu—in other words, a kafir—no one of importance. He opened the door of the car on the driver's side, pushing the body aside in the process. He then quickly searched the man's pockets for his access pass and also took the radio transmitter, which would enable him to monitor communications with the security center. He only knew a little Nepali, assuming they spoke in their own language, but probably enough to know what constituted a warning that he had been detected.

He then dragged the dead guard's body toward the trunk. He undressed him and swapped his own clothes for the Nepali's. The man's shirt was now soaked with blood, but Temur had planned for this eventuality and had a spare one in the car. He affixed the guard's Velcro badges and tabs to the new garment. In the trunk were large bottles of Coca Cola, which he used to dissolve traces of the pool of blood that had formed on the concrete floor (as highway patrol agents did with road kill), after locking the dead man in the trunk. He finally wiped all traces of blood from the car's body and wheels. The liquid ran into a nearby drain. Unless someone looked very carefully, there was almost no sign left of what had just taken place.

Temur Khan put the red beret on his head and checked his appearance in the windscreen of the car, grabbed his backpack and walked in the direction of the elevator lobby. It was unlikely he had been spotted but, all the same, he now needed to act quickly. Within an hour at most, he would have started to spread the virus.

He rode the elevator back to the ground floor and walked, surefooted, to the elevator lobby that served the higher levels of the tower. He nodded curtly as he passed, unchallenged, another security guard stationed there. A number of them were on duty throughout the building, on a twenty-four seven basis, and it was unlikely that they all knew each other, he reckoned.

He swiped van Deen's card on the reader and caught a rather crowded elevator car bound for the transfer lobby. On the way up, bankers, brokers and asset managers discussed their activities of the past weekend, mentioning details of outings on launches, wine tastings and after-hours parties, all completely oblivious to the fact that one of their fellow passengers might soon send them to their own deaths.

Chapter 58

Admiralty, Hong Kong, June 2016

ERWAN TANGUY HAD finished briefing Superintendent Ip Wai-ping from the Security Wing, as well as Xie Wei, on the information The Bear had just conveyed. The call intercepted by the Americans couldn't be taken lightly, even if the exact exchange of words didn't amount to much at first glance.

"So, you really believe this is a signal from our man?" asked Ip.

"The call was made from Hong Kong. We know *Musafir* is a code the terrorists use. And the man who was called had a Pakistani number. Moreover, the same people had the exact same conversation a couple of months ago; only that time, the call originated in Madrid. I find the coincidence rather troubling. We can't ignore this and, I believe, we have to take it very seriously," answered Tanguy.

"Sir, he's right. It has to mean something," added Xie.

"But it still doesn't tell us much, even if Peter Tremblay, or whatever his real name is, is now about to strike, as you suggest. We still have no idea where the attack is actually going to happen."

"Granted. But we can always up the alert level by one

notch. Increase coverage. Put more boots on the ground, so to speak."

"I'm not sure there's enough information to justify doing that right now. And the timing is far from ideal. This is the most important day of Zhang Dejiang's visit. Many constables and officers are on duty for this—it has to take precedence. And on top of that, I've just been informed that a high-profile murder was committed during the weekend."

"Is that right? Could it be related to our case?" asked Tanguy.

"Oh, I very much doubt it. An investment banker was found dead at his home this morning. British expat. His throat was slit, most likely on Sunday morning. Probably killed by a mainlander, paid for by a jealous girlfriend—or maybe some drug deal gone bad. It happens, from time to time. Those expat finance types lead rather dissolute lives in our part of the world, you know."

"Yes, I've heard similar stories before. But, from what you're saying, the manner of death actually sounds suspiciously similar to that of Gupta's, the Indian man who was killed at sea by Tremblay. Are you sure this is something we can just ignore?"

"Hmmm, now that you mention it, it certainly calls for more scrutiny. I hadn't thought of it in that way. We still know little about that banker, one Derek van Deen. Maybe there's more to it than it appears. Will you please excuse me? I need to make a few calls, see where matters stand on that one."

"Of course! At this juncture, we probably have to pursue any lead that looks out of the ordinary."

Ip fished out his mobile and made a call on speed dial. For the next minute or so, he conducted an active exchange in Cantonese. He was loud and insistent, and it was clear to Tanguy—even though he couldn't understand a single word of what was being said—who was boss. He then made another, although much shorter, call. Once he had finished, the sense of urgency was palpable.

"I'm afraid you might have been right! Please follow me! I'll explain on the way. Wong," he added to a nearby constable, "call downstairs, now! We need three vans for an immediate intervention. The objective is Two IFC. And get the SDU there as well, chop-chop, with full CBRN gear!"

"What's up?" asked Tanguy, as they joined him, running through the corridor to catch an elevator to the ground floor of the Arsenal House police headquarters.

"An inspector visited the offices of Global Securities Asia, the dead banker's employer, about an hour ago—it's a routine procedure, after a murder case. But, just as he was about to leave, someone from the firm's HR department came into the meeting. She'd just liaised with the tower's security office to cancel the entry pass of the deceased. It's what they do as a matter of course when someone leaves their employment. Granted, van Deen left in unusual circumstances, but the procedure's the same. Thank God they didn't wait much longer to do this! Our man's well and truly dead, but someone's just used his pass to enter the tower, twenty minutes ago."

"What's the building? Could it be a suitable target?" asked Tanguy.

"You bet!" answered Ip, as they rushed outside and

leaped into police vehicles. "I should have thought of it before! Two IFC, one of the tallest office towers in Hong Kong. Eighty-eight floors. It's connected to one of our busiest and largest malls—and it's also just above the in-town check-in for the airport. The Airport Express link leaves from an underground station about four times per hour. A biological attack on the building would contaminate up to fifteen thousand people, perhaps even more. Most of them get to their offices through the mall, and many business travelers go to Chek Lap Kok directly by train from there too. It's clever and it makes perfect sense. IFC's the mother of all targets, as far as Hong Kong's concerned, and I'm kicking myself for not having seen it before."

"Can you liaise with the building's security? Ask them where the fresh water tanks and aircon intake units are located. That's probably where he's headed," said Tanguy, as he donned a bulletproof vest, checking the QSW pistol that Xie had previously given him.

"And they should clear all access routes for us, right now!" Xie added. "There's not a minute to waste! If he arrived more than twenty minutes ago, then it can't be that long before he spreads the germs. He might even already have started."

"It's probably best if they don't try to catch him themselves. That man is extremely dangerous. The death toll could pile up before we know it!" added the Frenchman.

Three police Mercedes-Benz Sprinter vans were now rushing through traffic across Central, all sirens blazing, the IFC building now almost within spitting distance.

"There!" said Ip, pointing out the skyscraper to Tanguy,

his cell phone glued to his ear. "We'll go through the ground-floor taxi ramp. I'm told all the access points for utilities are on the roof. They've blocked an elevator car for us, but we'll need to change at the transfer lobby on the thirty-fifth floor."

Next, he turned to Tanguy and Xie.

"I also just got a message from the CP. This is now officially a shoot-to-kill operation. We can't take the risk of Tremblay escaping. Especially not with a high-profile state visit happening at the same time. I need to ask you, though: the Special Duties Unit won't be there for another five to seven minutes. We don't have CBRN protection with us. Do you still want to go in?"

"What kind of a question is that?" answered Tanguy. "Let's go!"

Two police motorbikes were riding ahead of them and, within a few seconds, they arrived at the bottom of the tower. Ip and his men rushed inside, flashing their warrant cards, not that there was any doubt about who they were. They ran through the clear glass turnstiles, which had all been left open for them, and crowded into the elevator car that would take them to the transfer lobby.

Chapter 59

Central, Hong Kong, June 2016

TEMUR KHAN HAD now reached the rooftop. He had retrieved the mist-maker and containers of double-distilled water from their hiding place, behind the false-ceiling panels in the men's room on the sixty-seventh floor. He had worked quickly and no one had seen him, let alone attempted to stop him. He had then caught an elevator car to the very top of the skyscraper and, using the access card taken from Dorjee Namdak, the Nepali security guard, had finally arrived at the open-air service area through a staircase.

He was now more than 1,300 feet above sea level, where it was noticeably cooler and windier. Framing the entire perimeter of the roof were metal beams, shaped to resemble giant claws or some sort of crown that reached inward and upward. It was a fitting finishing touch to a decidedly impressive tower, covered in lightly reflective glass panels and pearl-colored mullions.

The Two IFC tower stood on eight huge concrete columns, reinforced by three outriggers connected to the core. All had been erected by hydraulic self-climbing formwork. Advanced construction techniques had allowed the floors to be completed at the rate of one every three days. The entire edifice had been built over a 200-foot-wide, 125-foot-deep cofferdam that served as its foundation. The latter, as well as the six-floor basement, had at the time been the largest projects of their kind in the world.

At the center of the rooftop were the top ends of four concrete pillars, whose structures plunged deep within the upper floor plates. Dotted around the roof were also a number of square concrete structures, housing electrical and other utility areas, and which they protected from the elements. Typhoons were a regular occurrence during the summer months, and the deluge of water and strong winds that battered the territory had clearly been taken into account. Also on the roof were massive searchlights and lasers that, every evening at eight o'clock, synchronized with those of nearby buildings along the Central waterfront to create a "symphony of lights," a light show that was a popular tourist attraction. At night, the entire building itself was floodlit, as was its giant sibling, the ICC tower, on the opposite side of Victoria Harbor.

Temur quickly oriented himself and found the air in-takes for the building's air conditioning system. There were six of them, shaped like huge wind tunnels, not unlike ship ventilators from the 1930s. At the base of each of them, he knew, was a wide steel plate that could be unscrewed, almost at ground level. He immediately went to work to dismantle one of them, which took him about two minutes.

Next, he powered on the mist-maker by plugging it in, thanks to a cluster of nearby sockets that workers probably used for maintenance. He finally adjusted the position of the mist-maker so it would blow the lethal water droplets directly into the opening he had just uncovered, at the bottom of an air intake column.

Now came the moment he had waited for over many years. Carefully, he unscrewed the top of the metal container, framing the glass inner vial, and slowly emptied the liquid into the tank of the mist-maker. Once this was done, he did the same with the bottles of distilled water, diluting the mixture and creating almost 2.6 gallons of a deadly germ solution, which within seconds he would unleash into the structure of the building.

Before he did so, however, he closed his eyes for a short prayer, giving thanks for what he was about to accomplish and all the steps he had gone through to reach that very moment.

"*Allahu Akbar!*" he whispered.

That's when he heard the footsteps. Clearly, several people were now also on their way to the top of the tower. And he could tell they were in a hurry, scrambling through the short and relatively narrow service staircase that led to the outdoor podium. Within moments, they would be there. He wasn't sure what exactly had happened. Maybe a surveillance camera had spotted him after all, as he murdered the security guard in the underground garage? Or perhaps using the guard's access card to the roof had triggered an additional security protocol, of which he was unaware? He had not heard anything on the radio but, clearly, the building's control room had identified a security breach and sent people to deal with it.

He decided to address that threat first. If they stopped him now, he wouldn't have time to complete his mission. He was so close he could not allow it to fail, not after everything he had gone through. He walked away from the mist-maker, and toward the access door, ready to confront the intruders.

To his surprise, the first through the door was a Chinese woman, with her hair cut short. She had high cheekbones and clear eyes, almost like his. She didn't wear any uniform but had a bulletproof vest and was carrying an automatic pistol. Whoever she was, she did not appear to be part of the building's security. Maybe this was more serious than it had appeared at first.

As she arrived on the rooftop, she could not see him, as he stood partly hidden by the metal door. He reached out to restrain her and grabbed her around the neck from behind with his left arm. In his right hand was the P226, its barrel aimed directly at Xie Wei's temple. It was only a harmless BB gun, but he needed the other assailants to retreat. Using only his knife would have put him at a disadvantage. A gun could spray bullets in a fraction of a second and, in the hands of a well-trained shooter, take down several people, even at distances of several dozen feet or more. It was enough that they believed he was a skilled shooter, and that the sidearm was real.

"Drop the gun!" he ordered her. "Right now, or I swear I'll shoot you in the head!"

There wasn't much she could do. Pinned as she was, there was no way she could tell whether the gun was a fake. Why would it be, anyway? The man was a terrorist and a seasoned killer.

"Do it!" he repeated.

Xie Wei debated for a fraction of a second whether she

would have time to shoot him before he could squeeze the trigger, but decided the odds were against her. Not with the man restraining her from behind and the barrel pointed directly at her head. She concluded she didn't have much of a choice and quickly loosened her fingers from the polymer butt. Her gun dropped to the concrete floor with a dull sound.

More intruders had now arrived. Walking backward in the direction of the mist-maker, Temur Khan retreated, still holding Xie Wei as a human shield. Facing him, their automatic pistols now pointed directly at them both, were a Westerner, also wearing a bulletproof vest with the word "Police" written across the chest in both English and Chinese, as well as half a dozen Chinese men, no doubt also from the territory's security forces.

"You're outnumbered! It's over, Tremblay! There's no way you can escape. More people are coming, right now. Let her go!"

He had called him by the name on his fake passport, the one he had used at Immigration after disembarking from the container ship. Somehow they'd found out about him. They had connected the dots. There was no point, right now, in trying to analyze where he had failed. But, if he could keep them at bay, there was still a slight chance he could accomplish his mission.

"Back off!" he said. "Or I'll kill her! Retreat to the stairwell and shut the door, and she might live."

"You know we can't do that," said the European man, "not with the vials of SARS you're carrying."

How could they possibly know that? Not only had they

found out who he was; they also knew about his plan. Somehow, somewhere, things had gone horribly wrong, and they were now clearly taking a course for the worse.

As they were talking, he had slowly dragged Xie closer to the air conditioning system's air intakes. He was now only a few feet away from the location of the mist-maker. There was no way he could empty the contents of the whole tank. Not now. But there might still be a chance for him to release some of the virus soup into the building.

Erwan Tanguy had now spotted the apparatus. It looked deceptively simple, but at the same time it was abundantly clear what the man was attempting to do. The target was definitely the air conditioning system. With his gun still trained on the terrorist, he whispered to Ip.

"*Contact the building's security and tell them to shut down the aircon—all of it, throughout the building. Right now.*"

Ip retreated to call the control room on the ground floor. Then, Tanguy addressed Khan again.

"The aircon's been shut. There's no way you'll be able to send droplets into the pipes now. Let her go, Musafir. It's over. You've lost."

Khan was increasingly nervous. A bead of sweat appeared on his forehead.

"You're bluffing!" he replied. "Shutting down the entire system takes at least ten minutes. Now, step back—or she dies."

Khan was now dangerously close to the device. If he managed to flick the switch on, even for a short while, a number of people might still contract the disease.

Suddenly, a helicopter appeared overhead, almost out of

nowhere. On its side painted the word "Police". Inside was a team of officers from the Special Duties Unit, Hong Kong's counterterrorism squad.

For a fraction of a second, Khan became distracted. Xie Wei sensed he was no longer as focused as he'd been up to now.

"Erwan! Shoot him! Shoot him, now!" she shouted.

Erwan Tanguy brought the terrorist's forehead in line with the three dots on the iron sights of the QSW-06 firearm. He grasped the polymer frame tightly and shot two DCV05 5.8x21-mm subsonic rounds in rapid succession. The impact of the double-tap sent Temur Khan backward, as his head exploded in a shower of bone chips, blood and brain matter, some of it splattering over Xie's upper body. She felt the grip around her neck loosen. The shots had been taken at close range, and the noise had been deafening. Stunned, she slowly recovered her senses and firmly pushed with her elbow, sending Khan's body to the ground.

"Are you all right?" asked Tanguy.

"I'm fine," she said. "Nice shot! Looks like giving you that QSW was definitely a good idea."

"Indeed. I'm glad you're okay."

Tanguy bent toward Khan's body and retrieved the P226. He was startled by how light it was.

"You know what? That gun's a fake. I just can't believe he used a replica!"

Above them, the men from the Special Duties Unit (SDU), otherwise known as the Flying Tigers, had started rappelling down from the helicopter, soon joining them on the roof. All were clad in CBRN suits and equipped with

H&K automatic weapons. Tanguy unplugged the mist-maker to neutralize it. He then pointed out the tank of the device to the armed officers.

"What's in there is probably full of dangerous pathogens. You should follow CBRN protocols and destroy it all. And, Wei, we should take you to a hospital. If he was infected, he may have passed on some of the germs to you. You're also covered in his blood."

"Right," she said. "I wonder who he really was," she added, looking at the body one last time.

"Maybe we'll find out, one day. Let's go."

Chapter 60

South China Sea, off Hong Kong Island, June 2016

AFTER SEVERAL DAYS, Xie Wei had finally received the "all clear" from Hong Kong's health authorities. It had been a close call, but she had not contracted the SARS virus. The deadly device—and its contents—used by the terrorist had been destroyed. Where he had purchased the mist-maker had also soon been discovered. After all, it was a piece of equipment seldom used in the territory, on account of the high ambient humidity.

From there on, it had been a matter of simple police work to find the man's hiding place, an apartment that had been rented months earlier through an online sharing platform. The police had turned up at the premises, which had been thoroughly decontaminated. It was clear from the materials they found there that he had used the flat to prepare the vials he had first smuggled from the Madrid BSL-4 facility.

Zhang Dejiang's visit had, in the end, been a success, at least as far as the governments of Hong Kong and the mainland were concerned. Popular acclaim for the Chinese politician had, unsurprisingly, proven harder to achieve, but that had largely been expected. It would probably take one, or even several generations, for China to fully dissolve Cantonese culture into the great matrix of the motherland. Not that it mattered. Not when you boasted a history that spanned five thousand years. Beijing could afford to wait. Even beyond 2047, when Hong Kong's special status ended, if necessary.

Xie Wei finished her glass of wine and replenished that of Erwan Tanguy, who, in turn, topped her own, as local manners dictated. The sailing boat they were on was anchored just off the Shek O Peninsula, to the south of Hong Kong Island.

The hull gently bobbed on the water. On shore, they could see the lush greens and fairways of the Hong Kong golf club, as well as some of the impressively large mansions that belonged to tycoons or were assigned to top executives of the city's conglomerates.

Sailing had been Tanguy's idea. He had honed his skills in Brittany, as a student at the naval academy. It was the perfect environment to catch up with Xie Wei in a relaxed manner. They worked for competing intelligence agencies but, to his surprise, he had discovered they had much in common, in spite of the cultural barrier.

"Thank you for saving my life," she said, toasting him as they both reclined on cushions in the cockpit, which was paneled in teak wood throughout.

"And thank you for not dying," he replied. "There's much I'd have missed otherwise."

"Isn't that so?" she said.

After a few moments, she stood up and walked toward one of the cabins.

"Bear with me for a moment," she said, as she closed the louvered varnished doors behind her.

Tanguy took another sip of white Burgundy. After a minute or so, he called to her.

"Say, how do you spell 'bare'?" he asked.

The doors suddenly open, framing Wei's naked figure. She was smiling. Her body was well toned, with a flat stomach, and she was surprisingly feminine when not wearing her trademark combat uniform. Her breasts were small but firm, inviting and perky. She was decidedly very attractive.

"Take a guess," she said. "What are you waiting for?"

Tanguy smiled back at her, slowly unbuttoned his shirt and followed her back into the front cabin.

It was almost dawn when he was awoken by the sound of his cell phone. He had only slept for a couple of hours. The night had been sweet. For all her aggressiveness, Xie had been a surprisingly tender and passionate lover. He would not forget her in a hurry.

He climbed the few steps of the small ladder that led to the deck, just as the sun rose above the South China Sea. The red, pink and orange light was almost magical.

"Tanguy, old boy, what's up?" asked The Bear in the receiver.

"You know how it is. Just trying to enjoy the moment. Until someone spoils it all by choosing to ignore time zones."

"I just wanted to congratulate you. The Chinese are ecstatic. Looks like you really saved the day over there. There's even talk of a medal, and all that shit. Anyway, well done. You know I don't say this lightly. By the way, did we ever find out who he was?"

"No such chance! We found a garment, a fabric belt typical of the kind found in Central Asia, that may indicate he had spent some time there, but otherwise, he left no clues whatsoever. Musafir will remain a mystery, I'm afraid. Now, why are you *really* calling me?"

"I need your ass back in Paris. Be there by Monday morning. Something's come up. I can't say more on an open line."

"All right."

"Meanwhile, enjoy your *nuits de Chine, nuits câlines…*"

Those were the words of a popular song from the 1950s, when France was just about to lose what remained of its colonial empire in the Far East. It talked about lovers in an exotic Asian location. The allusion was unmistakable.

"What? How could you possibly…"

"We've got eyes everywhere. You know that."

Chapter 61

ISMAIL KHAN HAD just closed the window that led to the terrace of his suite, at the Mena House Hotel in Giza. He had always liked the atmosphere of the old colonial palace that was located in the shadow of the pyramids. Of course, it was also a symbol of the times when the British had occupied Egypt, something that went against everything he believed in, but strangely, he felt at peace amid the verdant gardens and the almost magical charm of the building that belonged to a bygone era. It almost felt like al-Andalus, the Muslim empire in southern Spain that the Moors had ruled for eight hundred years.

The whole Musafir affair had gone spectacularly wrong, and he was still trying to understand where Temur had slipped, ultimately catching the attention of the world's intelligence agencies. The whole scheme had taken years to prepare, and both men had devoted much of their lives to making it happen. Their failure was almost beyond belief.

Of course, it had never been officially revealed that the authorities had foiled a biological attack in a high tower in Hong Kong's business district. They had only mentioned the suicide of a desperate man on the top floor of the skyscraper. But Ismail Khan knew better. Allah be praised, they had not discovered who Temur really was and probably never would. Still, the whole thing had been an unmitigated disaster.

To cap it all, the Federal Reserve in Washington D.C. had decided yet again not to increase U.S. interest rates, which had triggered a sharp rally across most of the world's equity markets, especially in Asia where a number of currencies, including Hong Kong's, were linked to the U.S. dollar. He had lost a fortune for his backers from the Gulf, after shorting a good portion of the US$2 billion they had entrusted to him. And then, after he had finally bought back most of the shares, had come Brexit, triggering a new set of heavy losses from which he would probably never recover. After that, he had felt unsafe in Dubai and had sought refuge in the Egyptian capital.

The heat was almost unbearable there in August, but he had many contacts in the city, especially within Muslim Brotherhood circles. The el-Sisi government had cracked down on fundamentalists, but Egypt was still a hotbed for all manner of Muslim extremists, and he felt right at home there.

It was almost the end of the day, and he would finally escape the harsh, blistering sun. At nightfall, he would take a taxi and start a journey that would ultimately take him to Bangladesh. He planned to stay there for a while, until things quieted down.

In Dhaka, he would also meet up again with a fellow exile—now an old man—Ehmet Beg, Temur's uncle. The

Uyghur had had a close call with the Chinese police, but had not in fact died in Urumqi back in 1989. Once Temur had turned nine years old, Beg had successfully engineered his own disappearance and entrusted the boy to Ismail Khan, to groom him as a formidable weapon for jihad. It had taken twenty-seven years, and the young man had almost succeeded, only to end up being shot dead atop one of Hong Kong's tallest buildings. Theirs and bin Laden's grandiose plan had backfired spectacularly.

The man they called Shiryō slowly climbed the carpeted stairs. He much preferred walking to riding elevators. Besides, he had already noticed that the lifts had CCTV surveillance, whereas the monumental and ornate staircase did not.

Shiryō's trade was unusual. He killed people for money and was very good at it. Whether you wanted to have someone executed, or to make it look like an accident, he was just the man. After a career as an operative in a naval Special Forces squadron in Japan, he had worked for much of Tokyo's underworld, helping to settle disputes among *yakuza* gangs. More recently, he had been responsible for the murders of several high-profile financiers in Hong Kong.[1] But the man who had contracted him there, one of the city's best-known tycoons, had also tried to cross him. He had not lived to tell the tale. Shiryō had shot him dead, before burning down his mansion on the Peak and escaping by boat to the Philippines.

---

[1] See *Hard Underwriting* by the same author.

His mission today was to terminate a man called Ismail Khan. The name he had checked in with at the Mena House was different, but that was unimportant. It had taken him a while to track him down, but he now knew Khan was in his suite on the third floor.

There had been no special requirements for a discreet kill. The people who had paid him, although he had only met one of them, and just briefly, wanted to send a clear message, and that suited him fine.

He finally made his way through the corridor leading to Khan's suite and knocked on the door twice. He heard a noise inside. The knob turned and the door opened partly, revealing a rather tall man, of medium build, in his mid to late fifties, who was Indian or perhaps Pakistani.

"M. Farooq?" he asked.

"Yes."

"My name's Seiji Tanaka. I'm in charge of hotel security. May I please come in? Our housekeepers found something when they cleaned your room earlier. It looks like someone might be wishing to do you harm."

Ismail Khan did not carry and did not have any weapons in his luggage. This man's assertion could only mean that his backers had tracked him down and planned an attempt on his life.

"Let me show you. May I come in?" insisted the Japanese man.

Khan had no reason to be wary. The man was obviously an employee of the hotel, as he could tell from his blue suit and name badge. He opened the door wide and let the man in.

"What is it you wish to show me?"

Tanaka closed the door. He faced the Pakistani and flashed a wide smile.

"M. Farooq," he said. "Or, rather, M. Khan…"

The Pakistani was now on high alert.

"Not that it really matters," continued the Japanese man. "Anyway, I'm here to convey a message."

"What's the message?" asked Khan harshly.

"It's a message from Sheikh Mansour."

Ismail Khan gulped when he heard the name. He immediately tried to hit the Japanese man, but was no longer in his prime and wasn't fast enough. Shiryō blocked his strike with one hand and, with the other, reached behind his back.

He swiftly unsheathed a blade from a scabbard made of magnolia wood that was wedged in the small of his back. He brought his right hand forward. In it was a *wakizashi*, a short Japanese sword made of high-carbon tempered steel. On the blade was a wavy pattern that spanned its entire curvature. In a fraction of a second, he'd adjusted the cutting angle and struck Khan once, diagonally from his left shoulder down to his right side, severing arteries, soft tissue, muscle and internal organs.

In an instant, he had stopped the Pakistani's momentum. Within a fraction of a second, the latter had dropped to the floor. In less than two minutes, he knew he would die, as his vital functions collapsed one after the other.

Shiryō swiftly flipped the blade to its side, to shake off the blood, and slowly placed it back into the scabbard he had since retrieved from his back. He secured it by tying the braided silk cord, or *sageo*, that extended from the wooden *saya* several times both above and below the hand guard, before securing it in place with a simple loop.

Finally, he took a last look at the body and left the room, carefully closing the door behind him.

Acknowledgements

While this is a work of fiction, I spent a significant amount of time conducting research and looking up documentation to ensure that the story remained as realistic as possible (within reason: it's still a novel!).

I've either traveled or lived (in the case of Paris, Madrid and Hong Kong, in particular) in most of the places that are described in the book, from India, Singapore and Malaysia to Uzbekistan, mainland China, the United Arab Emirates, Oman and Egypt. And while I'm yet to visit Djibouti, I've also been to nearby Ethiopia.

In Madrid, I've lived on the very street in which I situated scientist Vikas Gupta's apartment, and I've also worked as an investment banker in the Two IFC office tower in Hong Kong (even visiting the skyscraper's rooftop). Similarly, hotels such as the Ritz-Carlton in Singapore, Oberoi in Mumbai and Mena House in Cairo, and even the Thistle in Johor Bahru, are all familiar haunts.

I've also had the opportunity to tour some of the French army's special warfare training centers and obstacle courses (although my own efforts at tackling some of the latter were rather pathetic, I'm sorry to admit).

Following the publication of my first novel, *Hard Underwriting*, I received many requests from readers for a sequel featuring the Japanese contract killer Shiryō. He only makes a brief appearance in *The Traveler*, but I couldn't resist making him part of the story, allowing him to execute one of the characters with one of his trusty, trademark traditional Japanese swords. I also continue to practice *iaido*, sometimes, every now and then, at a dojo just outside Tokyo, under the guidance of Mitsuo Hataya *sensei*, 9th dan and chairman of the Toyama Ryu Iaido Federation. My diminutive 1st dan rank really pales in comparison to his lifetime achievement!

At the time of writing, there was no BSL-4 laboratory in Alcobendas (or in Spain, for that matter), but much of what I describe in the book was inspired by an almost hour-long video on Boston University Medical Campus' National Emerging Infectious Diseases Laboratories (NEIDL) that was filmed (for security reasons) while the facility wasn't yet operational. The webcast is available on the website BU Today.

There is still no cure for SARS, and isolation and quarantine remain the best ways to prevent the spread of the disease. I traveled in Asia at the time of the 2002–03 outbreak and vividly recall the paranoia and peculiar atmosphere at the time. Coughing on an airplane or in public transport brought uninvited stares, and everyone was walking around with surgical masks, although as Hongkongers are often known to show off, many of those carried luxury brand logos! On a more serious note, the pandemic negatively impacted many pillars of the economy throughout the region, including property prices, financial institutions, tourism businesses and, obviously, transportation networks.

The disappearance of ampoules of SARS virus from a prestigious French laboratory is a true story. In 2014, it was revealed that 26 boxes containing 2,349 vials of the disease had gone missing at the Institut Pasteur. They were probably destroyed by mistake although, to date, they remain unaccounted for.

A lot of information is available online on freeze-drying and reviving microorganisms as well as, rather frightfully, on weapons, not to mention the most gruesome details of autopsies. D.P. Lyle's *Howdunit Forensics* and Lee Lofland's *Howdunit Book of Police Procedure and Investigation: A Guide for Writers* were essential reads to describe crime scenes in as plausible a manner as possible.

A big thank you, too, to fellow thriller writer and former editor at the *Wall Street Journal* Peter Boczar for his help on anything from character development and firearms to fighting styles and techniques (Peter once even had a cameo role in a Bruce Lee movie). This book is a better one because of you.

Dr. Muriel Holder from London kindly agreed to check anything medical, and in particular, related to laboratories—your review and comments were invaluable, although any mistakes that remain are obviously my own.

Thanks also to Michael and Melanie from Edit24-7 in Los Angeles and to Frank in Hong Kong for their timely review, sharp editing and eagle eye proofreading.

And, last but not least, this new book wouldn't have seen the light of day without the support of my wife Christelle, who assiduously read chapter after chapter without fail, not hesitating to let me know when the story or characters went astray. Thank you for putting up with a grumpy creative type, and also for providing pep talks in times of need.

Glossary

Agal: a headwear accessory (originally a camel tether) used by Arab men to keep in place the *guthra* or *shemagh* (see below).

Ashoka Chakra: the twenty-four-spoke wheel featured on the Indian national flag.

Bhelpuri: a savory Indian snack made of puffed rice, potatoes and tamarind chutney.

Bikaneri bhuja: a crispy snack prepared with moth bean, flour and spices, originally from the town of Bikaner in the western state of Rajahstan in India.

Chaat: a generic term to describe savory snacks in India.

Dhow: a lateen-rigged ship with one or two masts, principally found around the Arabian Peninsula.

Dishdasha: a loose, ankle-length robe made from fine white cotton and worn by Arab men.

Feng shui: a Chinese philosophical system that examines how the placement of things and objects affect the energy flow in a living environment.

Guanxi: the system of social networks and influential relationships that facilitate business (and other dealings) in China.

Ghutra: a light, all-white cotton headdress worn by Arab men.

Karambit: a small, curved knife that resembles a claw, found in Malaysia and Indonesia.

Kukri: a Nepalese knife with an inwardly curved blade, used both as a tool and a weapon in Nepal and other countries in South Asia.

Hadith: records of the traditions or sayings of the Prophet Muhammad, and a major source of religious law and moral guidance in Islam.

HEPA: high-efficiency particulate air purifier, or filter.

Ikat: a fabric, the yarns of which have been tie-dyed before weaving, found in Central Asia and Indonesia, among other countries.

Kafir (plural: kuffar): a (generally derogatory) term used by some Muslims for non-Muslims.

KL: the abbreviation for Kuala Lumpur, the capital of Malaysia.

Kris: an asymmetrical dagger, usually with a wavy blade and distinctive patterning, found in Central Java in Indonesia, but also in Brunei, Malaysia, Singapore, Thailand and parts of the Philippines.

Kurta: a (generally) loose-fitting pajama-like garment found throughout South Asia.

La Santé: a prison located on rue de la Santé, in the fourteenth *arrondissement* of Paris.

Lathi: a heavy fighting stick or pole, often used by the police in South Asia.

Maghrib: the prayer performed just after sunset by practicing Muslims.

Masala chai: a flavored beverage made by brewing black tea with a mixture of aromatic Indian spices and herbs.

Mawlānā: a title of honor and respect used across the Muslim world.

Mishaba: a string of ninety-nine prayer beads, each corresponding to one of the names of Allah.

Mujahideen: the term for a person engaged in *jihad*.

Poppadum: a wafer-thin, disk-shaped, spicy Indian cracker or flatbread.

Pagri: the term for "turban" in the Indian subcontinent and Central Asia.

Pakol: a soft, round-topped cap worn by Afghani men.

Phirni: a Punjabi-style, milk-and-rice-based, creamy dessert.

Puri: an unleavened, deep-fried Indian bread, eaten for breakfast or as a snack.

Qibla: the direction of Mecca that should be faced when a Muslim prays.

Sageo: a silk or cotton braided cord affixed to the scabbard of a Japanese sword.

Salat: the five formal daily prayers performed by practicing Muslims.

Salwar kameez: a (usually) loose outfit worn by both men and women across South Asia.

Saya: the scabbard of a Japanese sword, usually made of magnolia wood.

Shemagh: similar to a *ghutra* (see above), but with a checkered pattern.

Shukran: the Arabic word for "thank you."

Silat: a martial art practiced in Malaysia and Indonesia.

Takbir: an Arabic phrase usually translated as "God is great" and recited by Muslims in prayer.

Thobe: see *dishdasha* above.

Tike: a Hindi word for "clear?" or "understood?"

Ummah: the community of Muslims.

Yakuza: the Japanese equivalent of the Italian mafia.

Zuhr: the second prayer of the day for practicing Muslims.

www.ingramcontent.com/pod-product-compliance
Lightning Source LLC
Chambersburg PA
CBHW020825180626
46814CB00001B/107